Fore...
& Always
You

Forever & Always You

ESTELLE MASKAME

Black&White

Black&White

First published in the UK in 2025 by Black & White Publishing
An imprint of Bonnier Books UK
5th Floor, HYLO, 105 Bunhill Row,
London, EC1Y 8LZ

A CIP catalogue record for this book is available from the British Library.

ISBN: 978 1 78530 810 9

1 3 5 7 9 10 8 6 4 2

Typeset by IDSUK (Data Connection) Ltd
Printed and bound in Great Britain by Clays Ltd, Elcograf S.p.A.

MIX
Paper | Supporting
responsible forestry
FSC
www.fsc.org
FSC® C018072

The authorised representative in the EEA is Bonnier Books
UK (Ireland) Limited.
Registered office address: Floor 3, Block 3, Miesian Plaza,
Dublin 2, D02 Y754, Ireland
compliance@bonnierbooks.ie
www.blackandwhitepublishing.com

To Sherilyn.
You don't get to pick your sister,
but I'd choose you every time.

1

He did *not* just mouth what I think he just mouthed.
Oh, boy.

"Fired?" I repeat across the bar, slamming down
a glass. "*Fired*, Buck? Please confirm I'm a terrible
lip reader, because there is no fucking way you just
fired me."

Buck fiercely sets his eyes on me as he storms closer,
pressing his hands to the sticky bar top, the wood
infused with decades of vodka. "You cannot say to a
customer, and I *quote*, 'Touch me again and you'll never
be fertile again after I kick you in the balls.' What the
hell, Gabby?"

I whip a towel over my shoulder and press my hands
to the other side of the bar to mirror Buck, doubling
down on my indignation. "Oh. So, you think it's okay
for your patrons to touch your staff? That creep has
been leering at me all night! He touched my leg."

"Maybe it was an accident."

"Don't be complacent, Buck, or I'll take you down with him." I smile sweetly, but I'm not kidding about that. I'm just scared he means it when he says I'm fired.

"If anyone is being inappropriate with you, you tell me, and I'll deal with it," Buck says with about as much conviction as a golden retriever puppy. He should be enjoying his retirement, golfing with his buddies and taking senior cruises around the Bahamas, but instead he's still running this dive bar for the ten customers a day it gets, and probably will until he drops dead of a heart attack in the back room one day. His hands shake when he pours a drink, goddamn it. In what world would this senior citizen survive some rough and tumble with handsy, drunk boozers half his age?

"Fine," I huff, then grab the towel from my shoulder and start wiping down the bar, silently seething. When did self-defense go out of fashion? Can't a woman protect herself without repercussions?

Buck clears his throat. "You're still fired."

"Buck, c'mon!" I spin back around, pointing the towel at him. "You need me here. Carly takes twenty seconds to pour one drink. I do it in five."

"Maybe," he agrees, "but Carly also shows up on time, doesn't give me attitude, and treats customers like more than just dirt on her shoe." He cocks an eyebrow, daring me to argue.

And okay, fine, whatever. Maybe my timekeeping isn't the best, and maybe my attitude is rather pessimistic, and maybe I do think the drifters who frequent this bar are exactly that—drifters—but I do my work well.

My shoulders sink when I register the determination in Buck's eyes. His mind is made up, and something tells me it has been for a while—he's just been waiting for one last slip-up.

I glance around the dim bar. It's late, just after midnight on a Thursday, so it's quiet. The guy who can't keep his hands to himself and his buddy drink at a high-top by the door. Carly plays personal bartender to the lone woman at the end of the bar who's been sipping wine and texting aggressively all night. There is no atmosphere, just the quiet musing of the six people in here and the musical notes of the slot machine in the corner. It's always smelled so stale in here, like the windows have never once been cracked open to allow fresh air in, and honestly? They probably haven't. I've grown accustomed to the stink of cigarettes that seems to cling to the walls, but that doesn't mean I worry any less about the effects on my physical wellbeing and if one day I'll die young from lung cancer. If I never stepped foot in this place again, it'd be too soon.

But shit, where else am I supposed to go? I'm a college dropout in a small town with zero career prospects. I need something that pays the rent with no frills. I don't want to beg for my old waitressing job back, because I used to internally shrivel up and gag every time I carried dirty plates back to the kitchen. One time, my thumb slipped into a pile of half-eaten mashed potatoes on someone's plate and I instantly threw up in the bathroom. Don't even get me started on *washing* the dishes. I required rubber gloves up to my elbows just to get my hands anywhere near the sink water. Pouring whiskey is the easier gig.

3

"Buck, I need this job. Please."

Buck frowns and, for a fraction of a second, he almost seems sad to be forcing me out the door. "I know, honey, but unfortunately I no longer need you."

I stand numbly behind the bar as Buck joins me, pulling open the register and shuffling through dollar bills. He gathers a small stack and slips the cash into my hand to pay me what I'm owed this week, and I don't even bother counting to check it's correct. I untie my apron from my waist and throw it onto the bar.

"Good luck out there, Gabby," says Buck.

Yeah, I'll need it.

As I shuffle past Carly, she asks, "You're getting off early?"

"No, permanently. Bye, Carly." But I also think: *Damn you, Carly. If only you weren't a model employee, then maybe I wouldn't have looked so terrible in comparison.*

In the back room, I grab my phone and keys from the shelf Buck considers a secure locker and then shuffle back through the bar with my head hanging low in shame.

"What's wrong, honey?" the predator calls over to me, mockingly pouting his lips to mirror my sullen expression. It's like waving a red flag in front of a bull.

Instantly, I pivot on the spot and stride toward him with fists clenched. "I just got fired, so now there's nothing stopping me from—"

"You got fired from *this* dump?" he sneers, exchanging a cruel chuckle with his buddy next to him. Realistically, I am absolutely not going to fight this balding middle-aged man, but I so, so badly want to smack him.

"What kind of loser can't hold down a minimum-wage job in a place this like? That's pathetic."

"You know nothing about me," I spit.

"Oh, but I do," he says, resting his elbows on the table and hunching forward toward me with a nasty smirk. "We see you in here all the time. Rolling your eyes behind the bar, thinking you're all that. But look at you crawling out the door. You're nothing." He waves me off with a dismissive laugh. "So go on, sweetheart. Get out of here."

Those two words make me flinch from the sting of recognition.

You're nothing.

I've heard those words before. The only difference being they came from *my* mouth that time, and I have waited far too many years for this exact moment—for the karma of having my own words thrown back at me. It's what I deserve.

I lower my shoulders in quiet defeat and simply respond, "Thank you."

As the man screws his face up in confusion, I turn my back on him and walk away, straight out of the door. Even after midnight, the air is still warm and humid outside, so I hop into my car parked in the alley out back and crank up the AC. At this hour, the streets are quiet around the rough edges of Durham, North Carolina. While still enrolled at Duke University, I lived in the cutest dorm on campus, surrounded by gorgeous forestry and with downtown just a stone's throw away. Now my current apartment complex has questionable characters as neighbors and a couple of stray cats that someone keeps

5

leaving cans of tuna out for in this July heat. As I drive in silence, my mind spins with a thousand thoughts, like what the hell I'm supposed to do now and how much I'll miss the free tequila slammers, but there is one thought that takes priority over the others—a memory that has tortured me for years, stored deep in the crevices of my brain with a tendency to rear its ugly head more often than I can handle.

*

Austin Pierce collapses into the passenger seat of my car with a groan, and I quit lining my lips with a second coat of gloss in the rearview mirror and fire him a sideways glance.

"What's up, grumpy?"

"Coach is killing me this week," he says, slowly stretching out his legs in front of him. "My quads are destroyed after those one-hundred-meter intervals he had us running yesterday, and he'll probably put me through hell again later."

I roll my eyes at him and say, "That's the price you pay for a full-ride college scholarship. Stretch off those legs and you'll be good to go again." My hair dances in the breeze as I accelerate out of our street, because now that it's April and the weather is warming up, I enjoy having the roof down on the drive to school.

"I can't wait to get the hell out of here," Austin mumbles. "Crunching both numbers and miles at Alabama State, baby. It's going to be amazing."

I sense his gaze on me as I drive, and after a moment's pause, his voice softens. "The only thing that will be missing is you."

"But we'll keep in touch," I remind him, "and I'm sure we'll bump into each other when we both come home for the holidays. I'll tell you all about the Duke frat parties I attend, and you can tell me how spongy the track at Alabama is."

"You make me sound so lame."

"You are lame, Austin," I tease, pouting my lips at him.

"You may suck half the time—most of the time, actually—but I really will miss you," he says, and my playful expression instantly falters into a somber, guilty frown.

I'm a terrible, terrible friend to Austin and I absolutely don't deserve to be missed when we go our separate ways after graduation. I'd love for us to stay in touch, but deep down, something tells me he'll head off to Alabama State, meet nice, genuine friends, and then never associate with me again. And it'd all be my own doing.

"I'll miss you, too," I manage to force out.

As we near our high school campus, I contemplate leaving the car roof down for the first time ever, but the second we approach the parking lot, I just can't do it. I need the privacy when dropping Austin off, and before I even realize it, I've already pressed the button and the roof seals shut above us.

"Here ya go," I say as I pull up in the usual discreet spot before we get too deep into the parking lot or anywhere near the school's entrance. My eyes wildly scan

the handful of our peers walking by, praying as always that none of them are my closest friends.

Austin knows the drill—I pretend to drop him off here as a favor to him so as not to put him through my impatience when it comes to finding a parking spot, and not because I can't bear the thought of anyone spotting him get out of my car—yet he doesn't immediately grab his bag and jump out like he usually does. He lingers, which scares the absolute crap out of me.

"What is it?" I prompt, my nerves spiking as the risk of being seen with him heightens.

"Um," he mumbles, toying with his hands in his lap and chewing his lower lip. "I know this is crazy, and I know you'll say no, but we'll be graduating soon and I'll kick myself forever if I don't at least ask. But with prom coming up . . ."

"Austin . . ." I say warily, nearly threatening.

Please don't do it, Austin. Don't you dare ask me to prom.

"I was just wondering if maybe you'd like to go?" he asks nervously, the words so very nearly caught in his throat, and he forces his blue eyes to latch on to mine. "With me, obviously. Would you like to go to prom with me, Gabby?"

I blink at him in shock, because what the hell is he thinking? I can't even talk to him in the school hallways. What makes him think for even a second that I could ever be his date to senior freakin' prom? Besides, Mark Lowitz already asked me at the weekend, and I should just tell Austin that. It's a genuine reason, and Austin

8

could go on blissfully unaware that I'd have said no to him regardless, but those hopeful blue eyes . . .

God, he always looks at me so sweetly, with such kindness. He has been such an amazing friend to me when I've never done a single thing to earn it, and for the first time in my life, I just can't hurt him. Not this time.

"Okay," I say in a quiet voice, and Austin is almost knocked for six.

"Seriously? The world wouldn't end if we went together?" he splutters as his face lights up in delight, and I feel my car shrink around us, sucking all of the oxygen out of the air.

"C'mon, get out, Austin," I encourage with a weak, feeble laugh as I gesture to the door.

"Okay, okay!" He hastily grabs his bag and swings it over his shoulder as he steps out of the car. As always, he pokes his head back in and says, "Goodbye, loser."

"Bye, loser."

My heart is in my throat as I watch him cross the parking lot and head into school for what will most likely be another long day of hell for him, yet he has a smile on his face because he now thinks we're going to prom together . . . And I feel like the worst human being in the world, because there is no way in hell I'll ever be caught dead attending senior prom with Austin Pierce.

*

Suddenly, I snap back to reality and find myself already parked up outside my apartment building with the

9

terrifying realization that I completely zoned out for most of the drive. I give my eyes a quick rub and then tilt my head with a sigh when I notice one of the exterior lights has blown its fuse. When I first signed the lease agreement for this place two years ago, my mother called and very seriously, and very straightforwardly, asked me if I was a drug addict.

"Is it cocaine, Gabrielle?" she whispered across the line, and then seemed rather disappointed when I laughed and told her: *Absolutely no way!* Deep down, I think she was praying it *was* drugs. That would at least go some way to explaining my extreme fall from grace.

I head up the dim stairs to my apartment and step inside, throwing my keys down on the kitchen counter before immediately pausing. I sniff the air.

Huh.

Something smells . . . like sewage.

And I know damn well fine I do not maintain an apartment that smells like sewage. The number of candles I go through in one week can attest to that. Why doesn't my apartment smell like its usual orange vanilla?

My nose wrinkles as I sniff my way around like a scent hound on a drug bust. I follow the stench toward my storage closet. With the source located, I take a deep breath and reach for the door. *Please, please don't be a dead rodent or something.*

I gasp and recoil from the closet.

God, why couldn't it have been a dead rodent?

Water flows from a hole in the closet ceiling. It floods down over all of my belongings, soaking through cardboard boxes. I poke the tip of my shoe into the carpet and it squelches *loudly*.

I scramble to the kitchen, throw open the cabinet beneath the sink and tighten the shut-off valve until I hear the dripping water slow to a stop in the closet. I sit on the tiled floor, mouth agape.

"No. Nope. *No way*," I say out loud, shaking my head in disbelief. I did not just get fired *and* have a flood all the same night. What could I possibly have done recently to deserve such bad karma? Was it because I told Carly her roots were long overdue a touch-up?

I call the property manager, and he's so grumpy from being woken from his sleep that he is utterly useless. He can't guarantee that he'll get a plumber out in the morning. He can't even guarantee that he'll get one out by the weekend.

"But how can I stay here with no plumbing?"

"Don't shower, don't flush the toilet, don't turn on any faucets," he says.

"Yes, I know what plumbing involves," I snark back. "I mean how can I stay here without doing any of that?"

"Get a hotel for a few days, or stay with someone you know."

I want to ask if he'll be footing the bill for this mandatory hotel stay, but I'm beyond the point of arguing. I demand he gets me a plumber as soon as he can, then hang up and stare hopelessly at my waterlogged storage closet.

I don't have the money for a hotel and I don't do motels, because I do have some degree of standards. The last thing I need at this time of night is a two-hour drive to my hometown of Wilmington, but this is a dire situation and, unfortunately, I don't have much of a choice but to crawl home to my mother. I'll slip in the back door without waking her, then deal with her shock when she finds me camped out in my childhood bedroom in the morning.

Pushing myself up from the kitchen floor, I head into my bedroom and start to gather my stuff. The only saving grace is that the pipes didn't burst above my bedroom closet, so my clothes are dry and intact. I'm in a daze as I fill up a small suitcase, then switch off the electrics at the main breaker. These burst pipes are now a fire hazard, and I could really do with not burning my entire building down. That would make getting fired truly the tip of the iceberg tonight.

I head back outside to my car, start up the engine, and then let laughter rip through me when a warning message flashes across the dash. I now have dangerously low tire pressure. Of course. Of course! Why *wouldn't* there be something else to add to my nightmare of a night?

I kick open my door and walk around my car, using my phone's flashlight to examine each wheel. Somewhere between Buck's Tavern and here, I've picked up a nail. I know this, because it's now wedged into my deflated rear tire.

2

Mom shrieks in such dramatic fashion, the perfectly polished glass of the French doors shake.

"*Gabrielle!*" she hisses with accusation, like I've nearly sent her to an early grave by appearing in her kitchen first thing in the morning when I haven't seen her in seven months. She tightens her white cotton robe around her, mouth still parted in shock. "What are you doing here?"

"Hi, Mom. Funny story," I say, floating into the kitchen with a sheepish smile.

I forgot to pack pajamas in my haste to escape my apartment last night, so I am currently squeezed into an old matching set I found in the closet of my childhood bedroom, and it was a revolutionary discovery at three-thirty this morning to finally accept that my twenty-four-year-old body is no longer the same as it was at sixteen. I was freakishly slim and athletic back then, but I haven't lost *all* of my flexibility. I wriggled through a tiny window last night.

"First of all—and don't be angry—I broke the garage window."

Mom's brows rise with disbelief before her expression quickly settles back into a defeated, blank stare. I reckon she's at the point now where none of my decisions should come as a surprise to her, and the cogs of her mind will be jumping to that drugs conclusion once again. "Why exactly did you break the garage window?"

I laugh, not necessarily to lighten the atmosphere, but because it *is* funny. Only now, in hindsight. In the middle of the night? Not so much.

Mom purses her lips and fixes me with a stern look. "Please don't laugh, Gabrielle."

"Okay, so." I clear my throat. "Some pipes burst in my apartment last night when I got off work, so I can't stay there right now. And then I had a flat which I fixed all by myself after watching a tutorial online. I finally got here around three, but I didn't want to wake you, so I threw a rock at the garage window and got inside that way. As I say: funny story."

Mom's gaze flickers outside the French doors. "I'll need to have our alarm system checked. It's clearly not working. And burst pipes? That's what happens when you rent apartments in awful neighborhoods."

I sigh, because this is exactly why I never come home. Mom's high standards and resulting lectures when they aren't met nearly always send me spiraling. And I haven't even mentioned the whole getting-fired-from-my-shitty-job thing. But I need a place to stay, so I'll suck up the disapproving way she cocks her head at me.

"Can I stay here for a couple days? Just until my plumbing is fixed."

It shouldn't be a question I need to worry about receiving "no" as an answer to. She's my mom and this is the home I grew up in—I should be welcome any time—but our relationship is strained these days. Visits require permission.

"Yes, Gabrielle. You can stay," Mom says after a painfully long moment of deliberation. She turns her back to me and resumes frothing her oat milk at her espresso machine, which my footsteps had interrupted. She flicks her blond hair over her shoulder and says, "Maybe while you're here it'll remind you of the kind of life you *should* be living. Maybe you'll find some inspiration. Some motivation, maybe?" She casts a look back at me, and I wonder if sleeping in my car wouldn't be that bad after all.

"Gabs?" a voice says from behind me, and now it's my turn to jolt in surprise. "What the hell are you doing here?"

"What the hell are *you* doing here?" I fire back, gaping at my brother in the doorway.

"Language, please," Mum scolds as she pours out her coffee calmly and with disinterest. Most mothers would be thrilled to have their two adult children back home at the same time, but no, not Priscilla McKinley.

My brother, Zach, steps forward to throw an arm around me half-heartedly. We met up a month ago in Durham for a drink, but our catchups are few and far between, much like mine and Mom's. "Had a big fight with Claire, so we're giving each other some space for a bit until things cool down," he explains.

"And yet he's here while that freeloader is sitting pretty in the house he pays for," Mom mumbles under her breath, spinning around with her coffee mug hugged to her chest and shaking her head pityingly, like Zach is being taken for a fool. "If you're adamant on going ahead with marrying this woman, can you please reconsider my suggestion?"

"Mom, for the last time, no. I'm not asking her to sign a prenup, and if you mention it again, we'll cut you from the guest list," Zach warns, and he flashes me a frustrated, knowing look that says: *Yep, Mom's still a piece of work. Welcome home to hell.*

"You see?" Mom snaps, clinking her coffee cup down on the pristine marble counter she pays a maid to polish three times a week. "You see the way you both treat me? I only have your best interests at heart, and you roll your eyes and scoff at my advice. It's extremely hurtful."

"I just came down to grab a bagel," Zach says with a shrug of defeat. He plucks a bagel from one of the many kitchen cabinets, shoves it half into his mouth, and then salutes me in solidarity as he disappears upstairs to his own childhood bedroom that he's been forced to return to.

I turn my gaze back to my pouting mother. "Look, I won't get in your way. I'll be gone as soon as my apartment is livable again."

"Back to your admirable life?" Disdain flashes across her features, and she should know better than to let the words leave her mouth, but she just can't help herself. "It's embarrassing, Gabrielle. The women at the country club are always asking about you, and I have to lie! They think you're a fledging businesswoman and have a beautiful home in Charlotte with a lovely partner. Why couldn't that be true? Your father would be so disappointed in you, letting your life go down the drain like this."

My jaw slackens and for a second, I contemplate grabbing that coffee straight out of her hands and throwing it over her.

"Why did I throw my life away?" I repeat, my words like sandpaper in my throat. "Because Dad died, Mom. He *died*." I pause to let the reminder settle in the air, just in case Mom forgot. Sometimes I think she has. "I'm sorry that my grief wasn't perfectly contained like yours. I'm sorry that manicuring my perfect life hasn't been my priority these past few years. You know what? You don't have to worry about me intruding. I'll figure something else out."

As always, my mother looks thoroughly put out by my words. Always the victim, never the villain. Her lower lip trembles and she squeezes her eyes shut, willing tears to form in an attempt to guilt me into admitting that of course, she is right and I am wrong.

When I was a child, Mom was my icon. The designer shoes, the fancy parties, the vacations in the Maldives. She wasn't even a housewife—we had a nanny and maids. Mom lived the high life, fully funded by my father's CFO title within an international organization that pulled in mind-blowing figures each quarter, and my friends and I were obsessed with how cool she was. She may have been a high-maintenance snob, but she was happy back then. When Dad passed, it was like a switch was flicked. She is now deeply repressed and unhappily stoic, and I haven't seen a genuine emotion out of her in years. She didn't shed a single tear over his death. Shushed me at the funeral as my chest heaved with sobs. Gave empty, cold hugs.

It's very clear now she was spiraling into a lingering depression that she's yet to pull herself out of, but so was I, and she was my *mother*. She was supposed to navigate the grief *with* me, not against me. We've become so emotionally disconnected that I fear we'll never build a bridge again, especially when she flings my father in my face like this, completely unaware of just how harsh her throwaway remarks are.

Coming home was a terrible mistake, because now I have fury pumping through my veins and I'm worried I'll do something I regret, like smash another window, but this time out of rage rather than necessity.

As I storm out of the kitchen, I find Zach eating his bagel on the top step of the marble staircase and eavesdropping. He's twenty-seven, but do brothers ever really mature? He shakes his head at me.

"You shouldn't bother engaging with her," he says, and I groan because he's right.

We are both old enough now to have learned that when Mom runs her mouth, it's best to shut it down real quick and not let her words rile us. Simply interrupt with a firm closure to the discussion.

"Look at us," I say, sinking down on the step next to him. I steal the remaining bite of bagel from his hand and toss it into my mouth. "Just a man arguing with his fiancée and a bartender with a soggy apartment. Go us!"

"You're a bartender now? I thought you were a waitress."

"I'm neither now. Got fired last night."

Zach scoffs. "Gabs, c'mon. I don't agree with her often, you know that, but I think Mom's right for once. Your life *is* going down the drain."

He stands from the stairs, taking my hand and pulling me up with him. We both hesitate as we listen to Mom release a very dramatic and very fake *wail* from the kitchen, then roll our eyes in unison and head down the hall together toward our rooms. They are next door to one another, and I still shudder at some of the noises I overheard coming from his when we were teenagers. Traumatizing, honestly.

"Don't turn into Mom, please, I beg," I say, my hand lingering on the handle of my door. "I know my life sucks right now, but I *needed* it to suck for a while. I was waiting for something, and last night, I got it. Now . . ." I smile, only slightly. "*Now* it's the right moment to climb back out of this hole. Just give me some time."

Zach's frown deepens and a flicker of regret travels across his eyes. "You aren't yourself, Gabs," he says quietly, "and you can't blame that on losing Dad. You weren't yourself long before that. I miss the Gabby who would beg me to drive her to McDonald's at midnight for milkshakes. The Gabby who tried her best to give me advice on girls even though you were, like, a baby and knew nothing. And then you seemed to grow up overnight, and for as much as you can't stand Mom, you sure did become her perfect daughter."

We don't break eye contact, and there is nothing I can even begin to say because, deep in the pit of my stomach, his words ring true. There is no defense that wouldn't be a bald-faced lie. All I reply is, "I know."

"And then you became a total loser," Zach adds, lightening his tone of voice, "so when you climb out of this hole of yours, can you please be *you* this time? Not this down-in-the-dumps college dropout, not Mom's bitchy reincarnate. Just my reasonably annoying little sister."

I cross my arms with a smirk. "Well, can I do a sister-of-the-groom speech at the wedding so I can tell everyone about your cross-dressing phase when you were ten? There's photo evidence of you squeezing your fat butt into my dresses."

Zach glowers. "That's beyond *reasonably* annoying."

"See, I'm still a work in progress," I say with a shrug, then open my door and disappear inside my room before Zach can utter another word that resonates too deeply.

My bedroom is exactly how I left it at eighteen. Polaroid pictures of my best friends and me are taped around the full-length antique mirror that leans against the wall, and there's even the dregs of some designer bottles of perfume left on my dresser. When I crawled into my California king in the middle of the night, the mattress seamlessly contoured around my body and the sheets basked me in the scent of lavender. Even though Zach

20

and I are long gone, the maid keeps our rooms pristine. Not a single dust mite in sight.

I make up the bed and throw open my curtains. My bay window overlooks the front of the house and I sink down into the bench in the alcove, tucking a pillow beneath my chin and gazing outside. It's a gorgeous July morning here in Wilmington on the North Carolina coast with vibrant blue skies and sunshine dancing through the trees that line our drive, and once upon a time as a small child, my view was of a large reservoir surrounded by sprawling greenery and wildlife . . . Until the city council approved a housing project immediately opposite our gated, private community of red-brick traditional Georgian homes, and Mom went into a meltdown over real estate values. Unsightly apartment blocks were quickly erected on the other side of the street. Although both communities were worlds apart in terms of social class, it never stopped me from wandering over there. Families moved in, and families meant kids. Much to Mom's disapproval, I had a lot of fun scavenging through the nearby fields with all of my new friends.

I was a much nicer person when I was a kid, because Zach's right. Something changed when I started high school, and there have been so many versions of Gabrielle McKinley since then that it feels nigh on impossible to ever truly find myself again.

My gaze settles on one of the apartments across the street. Second floor, balcony painted blue. My best friend lived there once. We used to wave goodnight to one another, and just when I'm wondering if his family still lives there now, a man I've never laid eyes on before walks out onto the balcony and pins up a shirt to dry. No, his family are clearly gone now. I hope wherever he is, whatever he has done in life, he's doing good. He deserved a better best friend than me.

*

"You look absolutely gorgeous, honey," Mom says for the thousandth time as she kneels to the ground to adjust the hem of my dress again, ensuring it sits perfectly in photos. "And you're very handsome in that suit, Mark."

"Yes, you two look great together!" Dad agrees, snapping some more photographs of us in front of the picture-perfect marble staircase with a proud, beaming grin.

I glance at Mark out of the corner of my eye. We're hugged in close, his hand around my waist, his expensive cologne filling the air, and I should feel so lucky—I'm going to senior prom with Mark Lowitz, only one of the hottest guys in school with a stellar reputation, yet my stomach is in knots.

Across the street, Austin Pierce is also getting ready for prom.

I've been lying to him for weeks now. I lied when I told him we couldn't travel to prom together because my dad wants to drive me there in his sports car and the backseat is only good for groceries. I lied when I requested he wear a red tie because my dress is red. I lied when I promised we'd dance together.

There have been many moments where I've wanted to just rip the band-aid off and tell Austin the truth, but he has been so, so excited and I couldn't bear to let him down. I still want him to go to prom—I just don't want it to be with me.

"You do look super hot," Mark whispers into my ear, and a tingle shoots down my spine as he gives my hip a squeeze. His blue tie matches my dress. "I can't wait for the afterparty at Liam's."

I try not to blush too much in front of my parents. They'll most likely kill me tomorrow morning when I'm rotting in bed with a hangover, but it'll be worth it. Everyone knows the afterparties are the best part of prom night.

"Okay, I think those photos look good," Dad says as he holds out the camera to Mom to flick through, and she nods in approval. "You two better get going or else you'll be late. Drive safe now, Mark, alright? You've got precious cargo on board tonight."

I pull away from my posed stance with Mark and waltz over to Dad in the pair of heels that will no doubt blister my feet by the end of the evening. He gives me a big old hug and a kiss on my forehead, and then Mom pulls me into her embrace, too. They both wish me a wonderful night, and my chest tightens with the guilt of my cruelty once again.

Mark leads the way outside to where his car is parked on our drive, and I suddenly panic that perhaps Austin has already looked across the street and spotted it. I carefully gather up my dress and ease myself into the *passenger seat, urging Mark to get going. My parents wave us goodbye from the porch, and the moment we pull out of my neighborhood, I breathe a sigh of relief that I've managed to leave my house with Mark without bumping into Austin.*

But that relief doesn't last for long, because as we pull up at the venue, I realize this is where things get complicated. How the hell do I avoid my best friend all night?

*

I suck in a sharp breath. The memory is so vivid that it makes me instantly recoil from the window. I race to my walk-in closet and hastily scan the shelves above the clothes that are still here after all this time. There's one thing I'm looking for, something that's been tucked away safe and sound for twelve years, yet I still remember exactly where I stored it back then.

It's inside an old jewelry box my late grandmother gave me. One with ballerinas that twirl and sing when you open the lid, and I spot the pink velvet box wedged between old designer handbags I used to sport going to the mall. I stretch up on my tiptoes and grab the jewelry box.

When I open it, the ballerinas attempt to spin, but they only judder and sing a robotic, freaky tune instead. Quite frankly, I'm surprised they even move at all after so long. Inside, however, there is no jewelry. Just a perfectly folded piece of paper.

I almost can't bear to open it.

It's an agreement we signed at the age of twelve, because we were goofy kids who wanted nothing more than to be so cool and grown up with a binding contract. My heart ricochets in my chest.

Written on the paper, it reads:

We will be best friends forever.

My name sits underneath, written in my very serious attempt at cute calligraphy, and his name is scrawled right next to it in typical boy fashion.

It's like a knife to the heart, reading his name.

Austin Pierce.

There are many things I regret in my life, but I'm not sure any of them can ever come close to the remorse I feel for the way I treated Austin Pierce. The things I did to him, the cruel words I spoke . . . By the time my guilt caught up to me, the damage was done. Our paths had already gone in different directions, and it wasn't until the sudden and abrupt death of my father three years ago that I finally looked in the mirror and knew things had to change. It was the start of my bad karma. As I wallowed in the grief of my loss, I also *embraced* it, because I deserved it. My downfall was long overdue, and in order to truly understand just how miserable I'd made others feel when I was younger, I needed to suffer too. So, I dropped out of college, restricted my finances, cut off my social circles, rented a crappy apartment and applied for bottom-of-the-barrel jobs. It's been a tough few years, living this sad little life of mine, and I wasn't sure I'd punished myself enough for my wrongdoings until last night, when finally someone said it: *you're nothing.*

Now it's time. Time to piece my life back together again, time to make things right, time to find Austin Pierce. He needs an apology, and I need his forgiveness.

It's the very first step in my redemption arc.

3

Austin Pierce is surprisingly easy to find, but anyone is easy to find on the internet. No one can hide the traces of their existence, but I thought I'd at least have to do some detective work and digging. *Nope.* I simply searched for his name paired with North Carolina, and the very first result was a company named *Pierce Wealth Management*. I immediately dismissed it as impossible to be *my* Austin Pierce, because the Austin Pierce I knew grew up clipping food coupons, scraping pennies together to buy candy, and wearing the same clothes every semester even though he'd sprouted in height. It didn't register in my mind that there was even a remote chance of Pierce Wealth Management being connected to him, until I checked out the website. There was a picture.

And fuck, it took me so much by surprise, I dropped my phone down the center console of my car and nearly fractured my wrist trying to retrieve it.

It *was* my Austin. But it was also nothing like my Austin at all.

I stared at the professional headshot for longer than I care to admit, allowing a range of emotions to work their way through me. Surprise at how different he looks since the last time I saw him seven years ago; pride for his clearly very successful career when the odds were stacked against him as a kid; shame for how terribly I treated a boy who was never anything but sweet to me.

Ugh.

Even more surprisingly, the offices of Pierce Wealth Management are right here in Wilmington, our hometown. Austin won a D1 track scholarship to Alabama State, yet seems to have kept his roots here on the coast and moved back home after graduating. In one way, I was relieved I don't have to trek across the country to find him. In another, I realized I had no excuse not to go and find him *today*.

So, I drove downtown, right to the door of Pierce Wealth Management's office, and have now been anxiously nibbling at my cuticles for the past thirty minutes as I stare at the building.

Of all of my terrible decisions, this may have to be the worst one.

What the hell am I thinking? I've had seven years to apologize, and that surely has to be seven years too late. If Austin even remembers me at all, it'll be only with contempt. High school was rough for him, and I'm sure the last thing he wants is the person who made it a thousand times worse showing up at his workplace.

I start my engine back up, then shake my head.

"Just do it, Gabby," I tell myself, then kill the ignition again.

As I step out of my car, I forge a plan. Step one of the plan: think of a goddamn plan. But by the time I reach the automatic doors, they slide open and I step inside with no other option but to wing it and hope for the best.

The building's decor is minimalistic and monochrome with tiled, marble-effect flooring. It smells overpoweringly of jasmine and the woman behind the giant reception desk stands to greet me, revealing her formal attire.

"Good morning! Is there anything I can help you with today?"

"Um." I glance around one more time, noticing framed photos on the walls of the same headshots I found on the website. Several financial advisors work here, but there's only one I want. "Is Austin Pierce available?"

"Are you an existing client?"

"No, but I'd like to discuss the possibility of becoming one," I lie, stepping closer to the desk and smiling politely, fully aware that it must be obvious I have no business being here. I'm wearing jean shorts and a tank, for God's sake. I'm clearly not their typical clientele wishing to invest in index funds.

I pathetically lean my wrist on the desk, flashing the Rolex my parents gifted me when I graduated high school. Maybe that'll convince her I have money. And in one way, I do. Lots of money. Too much money. But it's also money I don't touch, so on the surface I'm just a loser with no job and a flooded apartment and a mother who expects me to spend my Sundays at the country club.

The receptionist clicks away at her computer. "Alison is available right now for a free consultation. Let me grab her for you."

"No," I abruptly interject. I whip a perfect smile back onto my face. "I mean, I'd really prefer to work with Austin. He comes highly recommended to me. If he's busy, I'll wait."

"He's with a client right now, but he'll be available in fifteen. Take a seat and make yourself comfortable! Can I take a name?"

"Um. Carly . . . Carly Buck." Screw Carly and screw Buck. I hope they have the worst shift of their lives running the bar without me tonight.

I sit down on the black leather couch facing a giant glass table covered in finance magazines. I could have been a normal person and, you know, asked old high-school friends for Austin's number and just *texted* him. But no, of course I'm sitting in an office building pretending to be in need of financial advice. This is a pattern with me. I make everything ten times more difficult than it needs to be. Maybe I like to punish myself. Maybe I lack forward-thinking skills. Most likely, I'm just an idiot.

I help myself to some free bottled water after five minutes when my throat turns painfully dry from nerves, and I begin to space out as my mind tortures me once again with more vivid flashbacks from the night of senior prom.

*

As I'm making my way to the restrooms to touch up my lipstick, a gentle hand clasps my wrist. "Gabby."

I freeze on the spot, my heart dropping in response to his soft, anxious tone of voice. I take a quick moment to compose myself before spinning around to face him. "Austin. Hi."

Austin stands opposite me. He's wearing a suit that's a little worn and oversized on him, with gel in his hair and an old leather watch on his wrist, most likely borrowed from his father. He scans me quickly and his cheeks taint with a rosy hue as he offers me a shy, crooked smile. "You look . . . Um, well, you look really nice. But I thought you said your dress was red?" He subconsciously fumbles with the red tie around his neck and my chest heaves.

"Oh, I changed my mind at the very last second," I lie, but I can barely keep my focus on him in between scanning my peripheral vision for any of my friends. If I get caught even mingling with Austin, I'll never hear the end of it. "I've never seen you in a suit before."

"Oh, yeah. It's not a perfect fit, but it was the best we could find at the thrift store," Austin explains sheepishly. For as long as I've known him, he has never shied away from being completely honest with me about how tough things are for his family, and the thought of his parents scrimping together some cash to find him even a second-hand suit for prom makes me feel wildly nauseous.

Bile churns in my stomach and a lump forms in my throat, because I know, deep down, this may just be the cruelest thing I've ever done. I should have just hurt his feelings and let him down gently when he asked me to prom in the first place, but no, of course I had to make everything worse. How am I supposed to survive the next few hours, dashing between two different boys?

"Hey, I'm going to go pee real quick. Would you mind grabbing us some drinks and I'll come find you?"

"Sure," Austin says.

I brush past him and disappear into the restrooms, where I manage to fill fifteen minutes chatting with other girls about their dresses, their hair, their makeup, but eventually Sasha and Nicole hunt me down and drag me out of there. We work our way into a prominent spot in the center of the dance floor and begin to dance.

"So, I overheard that Austin Pierce weirdo tell someone he's here as your date," Nicole says over the music, followed up with a duet of laughter with Sasha, and my blood instantly runs cold.

"Oh, c'mon. Don't panic. No one will ever believe that," Sasha reassures me.

A hand trails its way across my hip bone as Mark scoots up behind me, pressing his body close to mine. From over my shoulder, his breath tickles my ear as he asks, "No one will ever believe what?"

"Not only is Austin Pierce actually here, but he's telling people he's here with Gabby," Nicole repeats with another snicker. "Better be careful, Mark. That loser is trying to steal your date."

Mark cackles, because he knows Austin is not a viable threat to him. He sways his hips to the music, guiding my body in sync with his, his chin still resting over my shoulder. "Like he'd ever get a girl like you. What a delusional freak."

I spin around in his arms to face him and plaster on a smile that's so forced it hurts. "Right? He can keep on dreaming. I'm here with you and only you."

"But aren't you going to set the record straight?" Sasha asks, exchanging a perplexed look with Nicole.

My panicked eyes remain locked on only Mark, willing myself to sink into a dance with him and push Austin completely out of my mind. "Don't care enough to set him straight."

"But he's on his way over here."

I stiffen in Mark's embrace and snap my head to my left, praying with everything in me that Sasha is only pulling my leg, but of course she isn't—Austin weaves awkwardly through the packed dance floor, two glasses of fruit punch in his trembling hands.

Not one person at school has ever treated him with kindness and it breaks my heart to see him navigate the crowd of bullies just to reach me. That's how much he cares about our friendship. He'd walk through hell for me, even though I'm the one who sent him there in the first place.

"Hey, I got you some . . ." He glances up from the drinks in his hands and his gaze lands on Mark Lowitz's hands on my waist. The confusion that crosses his face is unmistakable, and he swallows hard. Mark's tie matches my dress. "Um. Gabby?"

Nicole and Sasha smirk as Mark snorts in amusement just as a few of his friends saunter over to join us.

All eyes are on me and I fight back the sting of brewing tears because I know what's expected of me in order to survive not only the rest of prom, but the final few weeks of high school. So, this is it—the ultimate moment where I finally have to decide what I value more: my social status, or my friendship with Austin.

And it is so, so easy for me to choose, and for that, I think I'll hate myself forever.

"That drink's for me? That's hilarious," I sneer, taking a step toward Austin as my peers watch on in sadistic glee. "Why are you telling people we're here together? You're a stalker. A creepy, weird, obsessive stalker. Stop telling everyone I'm your date."

And God, how it kills me, the way Austin's blue eyes well with torment. I betray him all the time, every single day, when I laugh at him in class and ignore him in the cafeteria, but it's different this time. This time, I purposely put him in a situation that had no positive outcome. My moral compass is smashed to pieces.

"Gabby . . ." Austin whispers in a fragile plea. Our eyes are locked, and he is begging me, begging me not to do this to him, to have his back just this once. He has forgiven me so many times for my behavior, for my rejections and cruelty, and yet I still can't do it.

I still can't be the best friend he deserves.

"Take your drinks and get out of here. Maybe try prom again when you actually grow into that old suit," I tell him with a dismissive wave, but my cheeks are blazing with the heat of everyone's attention on me, eager to hear exactly how I'll put Austin Pierce in his place.

"Look around, Austin. It's senior prom, and you're ruining the vibe. You're not like the rest of us and you definitely don't belong on this dance floor. You're nothing."

Austin gapes at me, and I want to throw myself into his arms, hug him tight, and tell him I'm so, so sorry. Laughter fizzes around us, but I just feel so cold and empty inside. Suddenly, Mark steps around me and snatches the drinks out of Austin's hands.

"No, don't!" I cry, but my attempt to grab Mark's arm is futile.

He throws the drinks over Austin and the laughter filling the dance floor now erupts into a roar. Everything begins to spin, because it's just too much. The packed crowd around us, the DJ blasting pop music, the piercing laughter. My ears are ringing.

"Get out of here, Scruffy Austin," Mark sneers, pointing to the door as he settles back by my side, hand snaking its way around my waist once again.

Austin stands there so hopelessly, so defeated, shirt soaked with fruit punch and the tips of his ears red with humiliation. There is only one person he looks at, and it's me. I'm the only one who can fix this for him. I can see it in his eyes, the tiny, tiny glimmer of hope that I'll make this right for him, but I'm not brave enough to sink with him.

So, I turn my back on him, both literally and figuratively.

I pull Mark with me across the dance floor, my throat choked, my eyes burning, laughter echoing in my ears, and if only I knew Austin Pierce would never speak *another word to me ever again, maybe I'd have chosen to sink, after all.*

*

The sound of footsteps echoing down the hallway yanks my focus back to the Pierce Wealth Management office around me. My pulse races so fast from my final memory of Austin that it throbs painfully beneath my skin, and I feel like I'm breaking out in a sweat as two men enter the reception area and shake hands goodbye. One of them is Austin Pierce.

My gaze fastens on him, and I wonder if this is what people mean when they say it feels like seeing a ghost from your past. My chest tightens and I'm pretty certain there's no air in my lungs for a solid minute.

Was he always that tall when we were kids? He towers a few inches over his already tall client, and his light gray suit is crafted perfectly around his body. Custom tailored with a crisp white shirt underneath and a baby-blue tie that matches his eyes. His blond hair fades in length down to the nape of his neck, not a single hair out of line, and the heavier top layers are styled with gel. He's . . . hot. *Fuck.* I don't recall ever thinking of *my* Austin as hot.

As his previous client leaves, he turns toward me and says, "Miss . . . Buck?"

Okay, fine. Carly Buck is a stupid name. But I'll be damned if I allowed him the chance to refuse to even see me when he heard the name Gabrielle McKinley.

Does it send shockwaves through his core the same way his name does mine? Or am I just a blip of his youth, slowly erased over time?

"Yes, that's me. Carly Buck."

Our eyes meet, and no visible shock races across his features like I expect it to. Maybe I think too highly of myself. Maybe I've been long forgotten, just a girl never worth remembering, and now I'm not sure how to progress with this plan. Austin smiles politely, revealing a set of whitened teeth that definitely weren't so red-carpet straight seven years ago.

"How are you doing today?" he asks, stepping forward and offering out a hand.

"Good," I croak. I slip my hand into his and his handshake is firm, confident. My Austin was never confident. But was he ever really *my Austin* to begin with?

"Come on through."

Following Austin to his office is like trying to drag along two cement blocks attached to my legs. What's the point in seeking redemption from a man who doesn't even recognize me? As we pass the fire escape, I contemplate throwing in the towel and dashing out of here, alarms blaring after me. But it also seems entirely selfish to disrupt the office, so I remain committed to the cause.

I know from Pierce Wealth Management's website that this firm was only founded a year ago, starting in a shared office block before recently moving into this new private building, and the faint smell of fresh paint in Austin's personal office proves it. The walls are bright and white, the black decor matches that of the lobby, and a huge window overlooks downtown Wilmington on this gorgeous sunny morning.

There's a model of a dark green Porsche 911 on a shelf, exactly like the *actual* dark green Porsche 911 my father once drove. Grief nips me, but I suppress it as best I can and take a seat in the leather chair in front of the desk, because right now I have business to attend to.

"So, you founded this firm?" I ask, attempting small talk. It would be rather rude and abrupt to immediately throw at him: *"Hey, it's Gabby, remember me? Your best friend who made your life hell and betrayed you? Fancy forgiving me? Pretty please?"*

"Yes, and although we are new in the industry, we are growing at an incredible speed and have a wealth of high-net-worth clients who are very confident in our knowledge and advice," Austin explains, circling around from behind me after closing the door. He unbuttons his suit jacket and sits opposite me across the desk, sinking into an executive recliner. The smile he gives me is not only coy, but really fucking perfect. He definitely had Invisalign or something. "I've brought on two associates so far and, of course, Helen, our receptionist, who keeps things sailing smoothly. Please don't let my limited experience dissuade you from working with me. I'm very good at what I do, Miss Buck."

He's only a month older than me, but he's so . . . *grown*. A mature adult with his shit together. A far cry from whatever sorry state I'm currently in. The confident, refined way he speaks quite frankly makes me question whether my own mental growth has been stunted in some way. My vocabulary extends to curse words and sarcasm and nothing more.

"Oh, um, that's okay. I believe you," I say, because obviously I did not come here for actual financial advice. Nervously, I play with the ends of my hair and wonder if maybe he'd recognize me if my hair was pin-straight and still severely damaged from taking a hot iron through it every day before school. I haven't tamed my natural blond curls in . . . well, too long. My hair is wild and full of too much volume, but I've been rocking the low main-tenance look for a while now. Mascara is about as much makeup as I'll ever wear these days. "I have some money I'm not sure what's best to do with. Can you help?"

"I can talk you through our client agreement and devise a comprehensive financial plan based on both your short- and long-term goals if working with us is something you'd be interested in. Roughly what kind of figures are we dealing with?" Austin questions, sitting forward, hovering a ballpoint pen over a notepad.

I think of my checking account and fight the heat that blazes across my cheeks. "Eight hundred bucks and some change."

Austin's right eyebrow arches. He sets his pen down and sits back in his chair, interlinking his hands together on the desk. "Unfortunately, we only work with clients who have an investment portfolio of at least half a million. I'm not going to be of much use to you, but your bank can help get you started with a simple savings account."

He rises from his chair, buttons his suit jacket again.

Oh, shoot. He's going to ask me to leave. Panic floods through me and I jump to my feet, pressing my hands down on his desk, willing his eyes to meet mine.

"Austin," I say, my voice cracking.

His blue eyes narrow with the weight of a thousand unspoken words as he presses his hands against the other side of the desk to mirror me. Challengingly, he says, "*Gabrielle.*"

My jaw slackens. The sound of my name on his lips is like a punch to the gut.

"What the fuck? You knew all along?"

Austin cocks his head to the side, all the warmth in his features replaced with that darkening sense of contempt I'd been so prepared for. "Carly Buck. Really?" He snorts, and I feel rage bubbling inside of me over the game he's just played. "I don't know why you're here, Gabrielle, and I certainly don't give a fuck, either. Eight hundred bucks to invest? C'mon. You're missing some zeros there. Quit wasting my time."

He moves to the door, swinging it open and standing back. His demeanor has made such a one-eighty, it's giving me whiplash.

"Austin, please, I'm not here to mess with you," I beg, remaining rooted by the desk. He'll have to drag me out of here before I leave willingly. I'm committed now, and I'll be damned if I'm leaving here without forcing my apology down his throat.

Austin sighs with indifference, like I'm merely a minor inconvenience in his day. "Get out, Gabby."

The way he says *Gabby* does painful things to my chest. I was always his Gabby. My full name was only ever used for formalities, like pinky promises and signing that silly little contract.

"Close the door. Give me five minutes," I plead, physically begging with my hands. "*Five minutes,* Austin, and after that, I'll walk out of here and you'll never see me again. I promise."

He can't feign detachment anymore, because now the emotion sets in and the betrayal of the past flashes across his face like a scar. "Your promises mean nothing."

My guilt is so pronounced it may as well be acid burning my insides. "Austin . . ."

Jaw clenched tight, he pushes the door open even wider. "Gabrielle, I mean it. Get out of my office before I really lose it here."

This is a disaster. It's very apparent that after seven years, the dust has settled. I shouldn't have kicked it back up again, because Austin does not want my excuses and he certainly does not want my apologies. He wants me out of his office and out of his face.

"Okay," I say in defeat, holding my hands up in surrender.

His eyes follow me across the office like a sniper locked in on its target, fierce and threatening, daring me to make one wrong move. But I get it. I shouldn't have come.

I lower my head as I pass him and tension pulses in the small gap between us. It was far too optimistic of me to assume he'd ever want to hear another word come out of my mouth, so although I may not have achieved what I set out for, I take solace in knowing he's doing great for himself. I didn't fuck up his entire life and set him down a doomed path, I just ruined his high school experience—though even that is too much.

As I leave Austin behind, I pick up my pace. There's a serious lack of oxygen in this building and I crave a gulp of fresh air. The fire escape is even more tempting this time around, but I propel myself down the hallway, hightailing it away from Austin.

As I sharply round the corner into the lobby, I clatter into something.

More specifically, Helen from the front desk.

We butt heads with a gasp, and in my haste to recoil, I trip over my own feet and promptly topple straight into the coffee table, a cascade of glass shattering around me.

4

I hate hospitals.

The sterile atmosphere, the overpowering smell of disinfectant, the incessant beeping of pagers. It's utterly depressing, and the fluorescent lighting in this treatment room will be enough to trigger one of my migraines.

"This is *so* unnecessary," I say the second the nurse leaves the room, sinking back into my chair, pressing an ice pack to the back of my scalp. It's difficult to even reach the nice big gouge through my mound of curls, the blond now tinged with dried blood.

Austin leans back against some cabinets, his hands gripping the edge of the countertop, his shirt sleeves rolled up to his elbows to reveal muscular, tanned forearms. A rather grand-looking watch sits on his wrist. "Absolutely necessary when you do, in fact, have a concussion," he says, then points to the ice pack I'm holding against my scalp. "That cut? Trust me, you're much better having the nurse stitch you up than me. I get shaky hands when I've had too much caffeine." He cracks a smile, like he wasn't just kicking me out of his office an hour ago.

I sigh and drop the ice pack from my head, toying nervously with it in my hands. "I'm sorry about the table."

"Don't worry about it."

"I can pay to replace it."

"I said don't worry about it."

The nurse returns to the room, tools in hand. She's been very lovely to me, despite chuckling at first when I told her the cause of my injury. Diving headfirst into a glass table is not one of my finest moments, I'll admit.

"This will be easier if you lie down on your front, so hop up on the bed for me please, Gabrielle," the nurse says, and I follow her instructions and awkwardly climb up on the bed.

Face buried in the paper, I suck in a deep breath. It's only some sutures and those don't bother me, but the numbing injection? Yeah, that's a problem. I close my eyes when the nurse scoots a chair up close to the bedside, laying her tools out on a small tray table and snapping on a pair of latex gloves. Maybe if I don't look . . .

"Okay, Gabrielle, I'm just going to move your hair out of the way and apply the anesthetic."

"Great," I mumble into the bed.

"You'll feel a small pinch and then it will sting for a second or two."

"Amazing."

"Ready?"

"Wait," I hear Austin say, and my eyes ping open.

He crosses the room toward me, stands above my head, and reaches for my hand. He interlocks his fingers around mine and I stare up at him in wild confusion. What I don't do is pull my hand away.

"She's scared of needles," Austin tells the nurse.

"Let's do this quick then," she says, and I squeeze my eyes shut tight as my scalp nips with an intense burning, like the sting of a hundred wasps.

"Ah, fuck," I hiss through clenched teeth, and I squeeze Austin's hand harder.

"Can you feel this?" the nurse asks, and I don't know what she's doing, because no, I can't feel anything. "Good. I'm going to begin those sutures now, so stay very still for me, please."

Austin slips his hand free of mine and settles back into his position against the cabinets, but I keep my eyes open now and study him carefully, albeit sideways.

When we were kids, I would have my annual meltdown when it came time to get my flu shot. I wouldn't eat for days beforehand, my stomach too knotted with fear, and I'd become a very reserved version of my usual bubbly self. Every year, Austin tried his best to help me through it. He would sneak up on me, pinch my arm, and say, "See? You can do it." Even when I was in high school and Mom expected me to be over my childhood phobias, Austin never made me feel like I was being unreasonable. One year, he came by my house on the morning of my appointment and left a small gift basket on the doorstep. And for a kid with not much money, that gift basket cost him a lot.

I can't believe he still remembers I'm scared of needles. Shit. He was so fucking nice to me, and I blew it.

I close my eyes again because I can't bear to look at him for another second.

"All done," the nurse announces after a while.

Rather ungracefully, I push myself up from the bed and stagger to my feet like a baby giraffe discovering its legs for the first time.

"Now it's very important that you rest," the nurse reminds me, tossing her gloves into the trash can. "Tylenol for any headaches. Definitely no sports, and maybe take some time off work if possible?"

"That's okay. I don't do sports and I don't have a job."

Austin tries to catch my eye, but I refuse to meet his. I thank the nurse for stitching me up as good as new, then head out the door with my ice pack. My steps are quick as I attempt to navigate my way out of this maze of hallways.

"Wrong way," Austin says.

With a sigh, I pivot on the spot and brush past him, still never meeting his eyes. He trails behind me and I get the sense he finds amusement in my obvious attempts to evade him, but by the time I find my way out of the building, it dawns on me that I can't actually recall how I got here. All I remember is feeling super dizzy as I swept glass off my clothes right up until the nurse gave me some anti-nausea tablets and everything gradually stabilized.

I spin around to look at Austin, only because I have no choice now. "Did you drive me here?"

"You certainly didn't walk," he says. Pulling a set of keys from the pocket of his suit pants, he spins the keyring around his index finger with a nonchalant whistle. "Car's this way. You're concussed and I won't be held responsible if you spin into traffic, though I'd learn to live with it."

"Ha-ha," I say dryly.

I expect Austin to laugh, or even smile just *a little bit*, but his expression is poker straight. At over six feet, his strides are wide and he takes off across the hospital campus without so much as a glance back in my direction. I power walk to keep up with him.

"Didn't the nurse just tell me to avoid sports? I'm breaking a sweat over here," I call out to him.

"Maybe you should work on your fitness then."

I glower at the back of his head. My Austin was shy and stumbled over his words. Now he's back-talking me? Now he's *witty*? I shouldn't expect him to be the same guy he was years ago, but hell, it's jarring. And not only jarring, but kind of intriguing. I love men who can deal with my sarcastic mouth, though I'd love it a lot more if he clearly didn't despise me.

"How'd you get to my office, anyway? Did you drive? I'll take you back to your car," Austin says, then slows to a halt next to a—*of freaking course*—Porsche 911. Dark green, exactly like the toy in his office, exactly like my father's.

"This is *yours*?"

Austin soldiers on with that blank, disinterested stare of his. "God, you really do have a concussion. I drove you here in it. Now get in, Gabrielle."

The headlights of the car stare me down menacingly as I circle around to the passenger side. I am no stranger to luxury cars, and yet when I climb into Austin's, I find myself running my hands over the leather dash in appreciation. Yellow seatbelts, embroidered Porsche crests on the headrests, a panoramic sunroof. As he gets in next to me, I eyeball him suspiciously out of the corner of my eye.

"How much money do you make?"

Austin pushes a button to start the car, and the engine roars to life with a throaty growl, turning heads in the parking lot. "You can't ask me that," he says, then gives me a pointed look. "Seatbelt. Now."

I roll my eyes as I pull the yellow seatbelt over me. "Why not? You clearly have lots of it. Your office building? Bougie. Your car? Bougie. Your *suit*? Don't even get me started. You're *rich* rich."

"And?" He looks at me hard.

"And . . . I don't know. I guess I'm just impressed you made it," I say, but as soon as the words leave my lips, I realize how backhanded the compliment is. Shoot. I'm terrible at this. Maybe I'm the one stumbling over my words these days. "Not that I didn't think you *could* make it. Fuck. I'm sorry. I'm concussed." I bury my head into my hands, rubbing my temples as though to work some sense back into my dumb brain.

"I get it," Austin says, eyes set forward as he drives, the car moving sleekly toward the exit. "It's a lot to expect the broke kid to climb out of his poverty hole, huh? Please just sit there quietly, Gabrielle, and don't say another word. It's better for both of us."

His words are enough to silence me, anyway. The guilt seeps through my veins gradually and painfully as we head

48

back to the office. I don't know where to look when my thoughts are so loud, and it doesn't help that Austin hasn't even turned on the radio. It's just cold silence. I steal a few glimpses at him as he drives, one hand on his knee, the other on the wheel. His shirt sleeves are still rolled up.

I can't bear the silence for one more beat, so I say, "I'm sorry."

Austin fixes me with a look that's borderline threatening. "Didn't I say don't talk?"

The callousness of his tone stings, but I guess I have no right to feel his attitude is unwarranted, because quite frankly, he has every right to treat me like shit. I treated him a lot worse and now I've come barging back into his life and disrupted his workday.

There's a small private parking lot behind Austin's office building that we pull into, and the car is barely shut off before I've released my seatbelt and stepped out. At this point, I've decided to entirely scrap the idea of brandishing our signed agreement in Austin's face. We were twelve. It means nothing over a decade later.

"Okay, well," I say, hands on my hips, staring across the roof of the car at him as he straightens up and unrolls his sleeves. "I'm sorry for ruining your day. I'm sorry for ruining high school for you. I'm sorry for everything, and I wish you good luck in life."

Austin's eyebrows draw together. He doesn't respond, simply shrugs on his suit jacket and secures the front button. Just before I turn to walk away, he finally says, "That's your apology? *I'm sorry for ruining high school?* Jesus, Gabrielle. You're the worst."

"Um, excuse me." I point a finger across the car roof at him. "Wasn't I trying to apologize earlier? Remember that? When you were telling me to get out of your office? I'm the concussed one yet somehow *I* remember."

Austin scoffs and walks away, heading around the building to the front entrance. I follow, not because I have anything more I'm willing to say to him, but because my car is parked out there. When he reaches the door of his office, he hesitates.

"Goodbye, loser," he says. His tone is a touch warmer now, his features softer, and my heart stutters. I can't believe he remembers that too. It's how we always said goodbye when we were kids.

"Goodbye, other loser," I reply, and the corner of his mouth twitches. I'd appreciate it if he didn't do this whole hot and cold thing with me, because just when I feel ready to abandon the idea of fighting for his forgiveness, he pulls me back in again. Not this time. I spin on my heels and take a step in the direction of my car, but my stomach sinks. "*No*," I whisper. "Noooo."

"That's your car?" Austin asks. "Gabrielle McKinley, the girl who got a soft-top BMW for her birthday, now drives—" he mock gasps "—a Prius? What in the parallel universe is this? I thought you were supposed to be wealthy."

"I *am* wealthy. I'm just not materialistic like *you*," I fire back, then groan again as I dash across the street to examine my car.

There's a yellow parking boot on my rear wheel. The same rear wheel I just replaced in the middle of the night.

Now I'm *trapped* outside of Austin's office. Why is the world so cruel to me?

Austin, most likely out of pure joy at my misfortune, joins me by my car. Over my shoulder, he asks, "You didn't realize you parked in the fire lane?"

"Clearly fucking not, Austin."

I snatch the note stuck to my windshield and skim through the legal garble. I have a set time limit to pay this parking fine and have the clamp removed before my whole ass car gets towed to the impound lot. It's yet another headache I really don't need right now.

"Sucks to be you," Austin says, and I could smack the smugness from his face.

"Yes, it does suck to be me," I snap, twisting around at lightning speed and glowering fiercely. Now I'm triggered. "First I get fired from my job, then when I get home, guess what? My shitty apartment's pipes had burst!" I step forward. "When I admit defeat and decide to come home to my mom's, I then had a flat tire to contend with. *That* tire. The one with the clamp." Another step closer, my anger so palpable I'm convinced I have steam coming from my ears. "I put up with my mother's judgment for approximately five minutes before deciding maybe there was a sliver of truth in her words, so I made the very overdue decision to finally try to fix my life, and I decided to start with *you*." I close the remaining gap between us, tilting my chin up. Austin's gaze is challenging, our eyes locked firm. "And then what happens? I come here to apologize for my wrongdoings, and you don't want to hear it, and then I ballerina twirl into your glass table. Now my scalp is stitched together and my car is clamped."

"Hmm."

My eyes are so narrowed, I'm glaring at him through slits. "*Hmm?*"

Austin's lips curve into a smile and he lowers his head, drawing his face even closer to mine. I can almost taste the mint of his breath when he says, "Look how the tables have turned, Gabby."

Ugh. I flatten my hand on his chest and shove him back. "You know what? Maybe I don't *want* you to forgive me, anyway."

Austin nonchalantly shrugs. "Cool. So how are you getting that boot off?"

"Go back to work."

"Do you require help?"

"*Go back to work*," I repeat more forcefully, because now I'm under immense pressure with him watching. I sink down onto the hot sidewalk in defeat and pull out my phone, dialing the number on the ticket.

Austin, annoyingly, doesn't head back to work like I demanded. He stares down at me seated on the curb, his tall frame shielding me from the blazing sun. "Do you really only have eight hundred bucks and some change in your checking account?"

"Yes, and what about it?" I bite, my phone pressed to my ear as the dial tone continues on and on.

"Weren't you a trust fund kid? Did you blow through all of it already?"

How was I ever best friends with this annoying man? I sigh and look away from him, feigning disinterest in his presence and staring across the street at his office building instead. My trust fund is a sensitive topic. "Haven't spent a penny of it, but thanks for being so patronizing."

Austin holds out his hand, palm up. He nods to my phone as it continues to ring in my ear. "Give me that."

"No."

"Gabrielle."

"*No*. I don't need your help."

"I know you don't *need* it, but I *want* to help," he says, then tilts his head to the side with a gentle expression, like he's trying to reassure me he's offering an olive branch and not a smack in the face. "Every time the ice cream truck came around, you bought me those fudge pops I loved so much. Let me pay this fine for you."

He remembers so many of the little details.

Numbly, I drop my phone into his waiting palm. As he presses it to his ear, he murmurs, "I owe you a lot of fudge pops."

I remain on the curb as he paces back and forth in front of me, eventually getting through to the parking enforcement agency and settling my debt to society on my behalf. It's only thirty bucks and a drop in the ocean to him, but I appreciate it regardless. It's abundantly clear he has an everlasting grudge against me, but maybe he doesn't totally despise me to the ends of the earth and back. We first met sixteen years ago, and were best friends for nearly ten of those. Surely that counts for something.

"Boot will be removed within a half-hour," Austin informs me, passing my phone back. "You can't sit outside in this heat. Come wait inside."

"And view the damage I caused in your reception? No thanks. I'd rather deal with the sunburn."

Austin grins. An actual teeth-on-display smile. "Oh, c'mon. It wasn't that bad."

"I. Smashed. A. Table," I remind him, forcing out the words as the visual replays in my head. Then I add, "With my face."

"Helen's already cleared away the evidence. Our lobby's centerpiece is now a cactus."

"*Oooh.* A cactus!" I say brightly, lifting my brows, before immediately rearranging my features back into a blank canvas. "Yeah, still not coming inside."

"What if I said you could name the cactus?"

Okay, he's got me there. I love naming things. Rabid raccoons, storm-damaged trees, the half-eaten cheeseburger on the side of the road. They always receive a name, courtesy of me.

"Fine," I huff.

I push myself up from the curb and head back inside the office building. True to Austin's word, there's not a single shard of glass in sight. The lobby is spotless once again and the leather couches now circle a potted cactus.

Helen on the front desk pokes her head up to check I'm okay.

"Other than mentally unstable like always? Just concussed and mortified," I say, but my joke goes down like a lead balloon. I'm clearly not mature enough to be around professionals, because Helen frowns and disappears back behind the computer.

Austin points to the cactus. "Well?"

And it's way too easy. There is only one possible name for this plant. "Carly Buck the Cactus."

Austin scoffs. "Carly Buck the Cactus," he confirms. And for the avoidance of doubt that I have just named the office plant after myself like a self-obsessed bitch, Austin calls over to the front desk, "Helen, this is Gabrielle McKinley. Unfortunately, she won't be coming on board as a client at this time, and luckily she won't be suing us for her injuries here today."

"I don't recall promising that. I am *absolutely* suing you."

Austin turns to me, a teasing smirk on his lips. "Try it."

"Watch me."

Helen glances between Austin and me with a worried look, but visibly relaxes when Austin lets out a breath of laughter.

"We grew up in the same neighborhood," he tells her, and I expect him to explain further; tell her we were once inseparable best friends for ten whole years, but no. I'm resigned to being just another kid who lived across the street, which I suppose is more than I deserve. He turns to me. "I need to make some calls to the clients I've had to reschedule. Are you good to hang out here until your car's ready?"

"Oh." *He's saying goodbye for real now.* "Yeah. I'm good here. Thanks for taking me to the hospital."

He smiles tightly and gives me a clipped nod before he heads back down the hall to his office, because unlike me, he has a career and that means he has shit to do.

I sit down on the leather couch, accept the water Helen offers me, stare at Carly Buck the Cactus for the twenty-three minutes it takes for my car to be unclamped, then hightail it out of the offices of Pierce Wealth Management with no intention of ever returning.

5

"*Please* stop screaming every time I appear."

The shriek dies in Mom's throat and she flies across the patio, wine glass in hand, oversized sunhat bobbing on her head.

"What happened to you, Gabrielle?"

There's genuine concern in her panicked eyes as she studies me, whipping off her sunglasses for a better look at the dried blood in my hair. I flinch when she brushes her manicured nails over my fresh sutures. She gasps, horrified.

"*Gabrielle!* Are you on a bender? What have you taken?"

She really needs to drop this drugs agenda she keeps pushing. I've never touched a narcotic in my life—unless the two puffs of a joint in my freshman year of college counts—so Mom's constant accusations are way off the mark.

I sigh and dodge her investigative hands. "I'm not high. I'm not drunk. I'm just laughably clumsy," I explain.

"I'm concussed, so don't lecture me, because that'll only delay my recovery. Capisce? Good. I'm going to grab a shower, then I'm heading back to Durham later."

Mom nudges her sunglasses back over her eyes and sips her wine like it's not the middle of a weekday. Oh, to be a lady of leisure, drinking wine on the patio lounger under the sun while reading a steamy romance novel. "And when you go back to Durham, hmm?"

Clearly, she hasn't taken heed of my warning about the no lecturing allowed.

"Yes, Mother?"

She purses her lips and says, "Don't be so sarcastic. It's not ladylike. Have you considered re-enrolling at Duke yet? I think it's time you finished your final year."

The sting of the anesthetic injection hurt less than this. To be fair, my mother's questions are valid. I dropped out of Duke University three years ago when I was twenty-one and Dad passed, and I was a mere twelve months away from graduating with my bachelor's degree in economics. My mental health was in the depths of hell and I needed time to heal before I could resume my studies in a productive, positive way, but my break from school slowly spiraled into something much bigger. Now, after three years of enduring my bad karma, I'm not sure where to even begin with my return to Duke. I absolutely want a career, something to build and become successful at, something fulfilling. A little like Austin.

"I'll work on it," I tell Mom, and I ignore the doubtful arch of her eyebrow behind her sunglasses as I head into the house.

I'm not entirely sure how she fills most of her days without Dad around anymore. She sunbathes in the yard, attends the country club and heads out for power walks to keep fit, but I'm not sure how truly happy she is. With both Zach and me out of the house for years now, I wonder if she's lonely. This is a big house to be so silent all the time.

"Zach?" I call out, but I get no response. He'll be off trying to fix things with his fiancée, I bet. At least I'm not the only one trying to repair damage around here.

I spend far too long in the shower, because it's easy to take advantage when I'm not the one footing the utilities bill. My back pressed to the wall, I stand for an eternity under the heat of the water, and I grit my teeth as I rinse out my hair, the sutures nipping.

By the time I've dragged myself out from my incubator of warmth and calmness, I've replayed this morning's events with Austin a thousand times over in my head. There were fleeting moments where it seemed he still cared about me *a little*. Like holding my hand at the hospital, and paying my parking fine, but I'm not sure if those count when he was cursing at me in the same breath.

I pull on some clothes from the bag I packed last night and call up my property manager again, chasing an answer as to whether or not he's sent a plumber round to my apartment yet. The answer is no, so now I'm left with the same three options I had yesterday: stay here over the weekend, live in my apartment with no water, or get a hotel.

As I'm debating my options while blow-drying my hair, my bedroom door swings open. Like, what ever happened to privacy? I turn off the hairdryer and stare at my mother expectantly.

"Gabrielle, I've been knocking. It's rude to ignore me."

I pointedly glance at the hairdryer in my hand, then back to her, wondering if she'll realize on her own that I clearly can't fucking hear her knocking, but her disapproving frown never falters. She notices my small suitcase on the bed, zipped shut. I've already told her I'm going back to Durham, so she has no idea I'm still considering the option of crashing here all weekend.

"Will you at least stay for dinner before you hit the road? I'm preparing salmon," she says, and I honestly don't know what shocks me more: her asking me a question that isn't related to my disaster of a life, or her preparing dinner herself.

And I do love salmon. Damn it.

"Yes, of course. Thanks, Mom."

"Ready in fifteen," she says, then closes my door on her way out.

Growing up, dinner was always prepared, cooked and delivered. Gourmet recipes that my mother picked out weekly in advance from a whole catalogue of choices, and late every afternoon, our dinner would arrive, with only a quick heat-up required. As I got older, it dawned on me that we didn't have our meals prepared by chefs because we had money—it was because Mom can't cook for shit. Maybe that's how she's filling her time these days. Maybe she's been practicing her cooking skills. She was always very conscious when it came to nutrition, and as a result Zach and I were well-fed, healthy kids. If Mom saw the crap I eat on a daily basis these days, she'd feel aggrieved that all her hard work of counting macros was for nothing. Hell, I even grabbed a cheeseburger from McDonald's on my drive home from downtown. Okay, fine. *Two* cheeseburgers. I'd been through an ordeal.

I blow-dry the rest of my damp hair, work some mousse through my curls so they have at least some degree of texture and style to them, then head downstairs. I decide, just in case I need to ask for her permission to stay here another night, that I'll be nice to my mother.

"Can I help with anything?" I offer as I enter the kitchen.

Classical music fills the room, candles flicker, and Mom sips yet another glass of wine while simultaneously searing salmon steaks in a pan over the stove. Over her shoulder, she says, "No, honey, just take a seat at the table."

I head through to the dining room and find Zach already seated, drinking the same white wine as Mom, while texting at rapid speed. He sets the phone down with a sigh.

"Oh, you're back," I say.

"And you're still here." Zach suggestively lifts the open bottle of Chardonnay, and I hold out my glass for him to fill.

As I sit down, my stomach twists uncomfortably. Dad always sat at the head of the table, and I think this may be the first time the three of us have sat down for dinner together since he passed. An image forms in my mind of Mom sitting at this dining table all alone every single evening. She may not act like she's happy to have both us kids intruding upon her solitude, but deep down, I bet she's glad of the company. My mother has her faults—her many, many faults—but the one thing I can't criticize her for is how deep her love for my father was. She loved him fiercely, as he loved her, and their marriage was perfect despite their differing personalities and morals.

"No luck with Claire yet?" I ask Zach, tasting the wine.

"Getting there. Things are cooling down, so I'll hopefully be back in my own bed tomorrow night. Ain't relationships fun?"

I snort, because my longest relationship since high school lasted approximately four months and was a complete and utter waste of my time. Dating hasn't exactly been at the forefront of my mind. "How the hell would I know?"

Mom breezes up to the dining table with trays of food. She sets down a pan of gorgeous honey garlic salmon steaks topped with lemon wedges, complemented by sides of steamed asparagus and rosemary potatoes. I'm seriously impressed.

"You made this yourself?"

"She cooks now," says Zach.

"Zachary, no phones at the table," Mom scolds, and he rolls his eyes and compliantly stuffs his phone in his pocket, because even at his big old age, he still has to follow his mother's rules. "So, you aren't driving back to Durham tonight, then?" She nods to the glass of wine in my hand.

"Guess not," I say, taking a large gulp.

Having Zach around might make staying here again tonight that tiny bit more bearable. *Especially* if we just get drunk on Mom's expensive bottles of wine. Maybe it'll even be fun, like a very grown-up sleepover.

The three of us begin filling our plates, and just when I'm about to take my first mouthful of salmon (and I'm practically salivating with hunger at this point despite my two sneaky cheeseburgers in the car earlier), the doorbell rings. The house is so huge, the sound reverberates from room to room.

Mom looks at Zach, Zach looks at me, and I look at Mom. Our expressions are equally blank.

None of us are expecting anyone.

"Excuse me, you two," Mom says, scooting her chair back from the table and smoothing out the crease in her pants. "Let me see who that could be."

I take my first bite of salmon and smirk at Zach across the table. "Maybe it's Claire begging for you to come home."

"One can dream," he says.

We eat silently, listening out for any tidbits of conversation, but we hear precisely *zilch* until footsteps make their way back to us. Mom pokes her head into the dining room, toying nervously with her pearl necklace.

"Gabrielle, there is a man at the door asking for you," she says, and of course I get shot down with her infamous look of betrayal. "I didn't know you were involved with anyone right now. Why don't you ever tell me things?"

"Because I'm *not* involved with anyone," I tell her, setting down my wine and pushing back from the table. There's definitely some visible fear in my expression, because the only man who could possibly show up asking for me at this moment in time is Austin, unless Buck has followed me home from Durham to beg me to come back to the bar.

"He says his name is Austin."

Ah, crap. What could he possibly want?

Zach's interest is piqued. "Austin? As in scruffy Austin from the hellholes across the street?"

"Hey. Don't call him that," I warn.

"That's what *you* used to call him."

Humiliation grips me like a vise. I've already looked back at my behavior when I was young, and I agree that yes, I was a raging bitch in high school, and no, I am absolutely not proud of it. The worst part? My friendship with Austin was pure and genuine—I just didn't want anyone else to know.

"Oh, I don't think this is *that* Austin. This man is wearing a very nice suit," Mom murmurs.

She refers to him with such disdain, like *that* Austin was nothing more than dirt on her shoe. And growing up, that's exactly what he and his family were to her. She despised that I dared ever cross the street to begin with, let alone befriend one of "them". Mom has serious deep-rooted issues.

"It *is* that Austin," I say, and her jaw immediately drops. "Austin Pierce. Has his own firm downtown now."

Mom and Zach exchange surprised looks, but I leave him to deal with her snide remarks without me as I head down the hall with my pulse racing at a million miles an hour.

Austin waits patiently on the doorstep, the golden orange of the early evening sun blinding me over his shadowed figure. He must have driven here immediately after work, because he's still in the same suit from earlier, his car parked at the foot of the drive. I don't even want to acknowledge how surprisingly nice and subtle his cologne still is as I draw near. *How* does he still smell so good?

"You are one brave man stepping foot on my mother's property when she never used to let you come beyond the drive."

A smile creeps through Austin's neutral, unreadable expression. "I get the impression she didn't quite register who I was when she opened the door."

"She didn't." I glance over my shoulder, and although I know Mom and Zach can't overhear us from the dining room, I still step outside to join Austin and pull the door closed behind me. "Why are you here? Have you changed your mind and decided you do want me to cover the cost of the damages, after all?"

"I'm not here about the table, Gabrielle."

I screw my eyes together with suspicion, waiting for him to explain his unexpected and unpredictable appearance, because honestly, I have no idea why else he would have come all the way over here. And I really wish he'd stop using my full name so formally.

"So, are you going to tell me why you're here or are we going to stand here in silence forevermore? Because if so, I'd like to get back to eating my salmon."

Austin scoffs. "Of course you're eating salmon. Delivered personally straight out of the sea. Is there an in-house chef these days?"

"Okay, bye bye," I say, reaching for the door.

Austin clasps my wrist. "Gabrielle, wait."

My gaze drops to his hand, his touch light but secure. My heart decides to cut me a break from its hammering and skips a beat or two instead.

"I came here," he says, clearing his throat, "because I found this."

Releasing his grip on my arm, he tucks his hand into the inner pocket of his suit jacket and retrieves a small, folded piece of paper. He holds it up between his index and middle finger, raising an eyebrow. Yeah, fuck.

"It was on the floor beneath my desk," he explains. "Is that why you came to me today? Because of some note we wrote together when we were kids?"

I try to snatch it from him, but his movements are quicker. He steps backward and unfolds the creased paper, running his eyes over the silly little words we wrote together. My cheeks blaze with heat.

He lifts his gaze from the paper, his piercing blue eyes finding mine. "After everything you did, you think this actually means something?"

I swallow hard, and my voice is nothing more than a quiet squeak when I ask, "Doesn't it?"

"Oh, Gabby," he says, my name laced with pity. To my disbelief, right in front of my face, he tears the note crisply down its center. "If only you were someone I actually wanted to be best friends with forever, then maybe it *would* mean something. But the Gabby I wrote this note with? Not the same Gabby I knew in the end."

It shouldn't sting as much as it does, but ouch. My only saving grace is that I'm self-aware enough to agree with his last statement and I won't embarrass myself further by justifying my actions to him, so I simply nod in solemn acceptance.

"I don't blame you for coming here to tear the note up in front of me," I say, "but for complete clarity, I didn't show up at your office expecting you to be my best friend again. I want to fix my mistakes, and the way I treated you? That was my worst."

The front door cracks open, breaking our eye contact.

"Is everything okay out here?" Mom asks, and it is not out of concern, but out of nosiness.

"God, Mom, privacy?"

"We're all good, Mrs. McKinley," Austin says, way more polite than I am. "Just catching up."

Mom does not return the smile he gives her. She looks to me with a disapproving frown instead. "Your dinner is getting cold. Will you please come back inside and join us?"

"I'll come back inside when I'm ready," I say sharply, because for fuck's sake, I am not a child. This is why I never come home.

Mom tuts and shuts the door with a very dignified, gentle slam. Austin can't stifle his laugh.

"Your mother hasn't changed for as long as I've known her. She never did like me."

"The real estate values, Austin," I whine. "Think of the real estate values! How dare you exist in our vicinity!"

"You'd think I'd built those apartment blocks with my own bare hands, the way she hated me."

We exchange laughter, but it quickly fades. There are these brief moments when the conversation feels natural, unstilted. No tension lingering between our words, just the hint of a former friendship finding its way through.

I look beyond Austin, over to the housing project across the street. It looks worse now than it did before, the building succumbing to years of extreme weather and a lack of maintenance. It was apparent this morning when I saw the random man on their balcony that the Pierces no longer live there these days. Good for them.

"What are you doing tonight?" Austin asks.

"I was going to head back to my apartment in Durham, but I've started on the wine, so . . ." I shrug.

"I thought you said your pipes burst."

"They did."

"And are they fixed?"

"No."

"Then you *definitely* aren't going back to Durham yet."

I cock my head to the side. "Excuse me?"

"Let's hit the bar," Austin suggests. "Drinks on me. Sounds like you've been having a rough week, and I don't imagine you want to spend all evening with your mom, do you?"

I stare at him, gauging his motives. Didn't he *just* tear up that note in front of me and tell me I wasn't someone he'd want to be friends with? Quite simply, I tell him, "I'm so confused. You want to go for drinks with me now?"

"I'm not opposed to hearing your attempt at an apology," he says, "but I'm going to need some booze before I listen to it."

"Really?"

He tucks the torn pieces of paper back into the pocket of his suit. "Really."

"Where?"

"Remember that little dive bar around the corner from the rec center? I'm going to head down there right now and get started, because I'd prefer to be semi-wasted before you show up." He smirks, but I refrain from rolling my eyes because I'm just grateful he is willing to hear me out and I don't want to push my luck too much. Austin retreats from me, heading backward down the steps, his eyes never leaving mine. "Go finish your fancy salmon and you'll find me down there."

"Tequila shots on standby?"

"Obviously. You're the most annoying mumbler in the world when you're nervous and I'll need something strong to numb the pain of enduring it."

This time, when his smile stretches further, I do roll my eyes.

6

Zach gives me a ride to the bar, because he has had one single glass of wine, whereas I have gulped down a second in an attempt to calm my nerves. It doesn't help that Mom is having a breakdown at the thought of me socializing with Austin Pierce, because the Pierces were never "our kind of people." And yes, of course she accused Austin of being a drug dealer, and then of being *my* drug dealer, like the only possible reason we could have for hanging out is a nefarious one.

So, Zach and I ditched her as soon as dinner was wrapped up, even though she wailed from the front door as we reversed out of the drive.

We pull up outside the dive bar where I agreed to meet Austin, and my anxiety doubles. My stomach flips and flops so much, I feel like the only way to stop it might be to violently throw up.

Zach scrunches his nose up at the bar's questionable exterior, but I won't dare admit that Buck's Tavern looked even worse. At least this bar has no graffiti on the door. He looks at me and asks, "*Are* you doing drugs? Because . . ."

"*No*," I say firmly. "Never."

"Really? Never? Because I did for a while after Dad died."

"Zach!"

He laughs as I punch his arm. "I took a couple pills; you dropped out of college. Let's leave it at that." It's beginning to grow dark outside, twilight settling over the city, and he flicks on the car's interior lights to get a better look at me, or maybe so I can't lie to his face. "Why are you going for drinks with scruffy Austin, anyway? I didn't know you guys were friends again."

"We're not," I say, then a sigh follows. "What you said this morning? About me being Mom's perfect daughter in high school? You were right. I was awful, and I was especially awful to Austin. I don't like the person I've been the past ten years, and this disaster of a life I'm currently living since Dad passed? It's my karma."

"So this is . . . what?"

I meet my brother's curious eyes and shrug, because at this point, I'm not entirely sure myself what I'm hoping for. "Redemption, maybe?"

"You think some vodka sodas in some crap bar in your hometown is going to fix what you did to Austin?" he says, and the hint of mockery in his question makes me feel stupid, like I'm some naive idiot for believing exactly that.

"Thanks for the ride," I mumble, throwing off my seatbelt with a clang and stepping out of the car.

"Oh, Gabs, c'mon," says Zach, leaning over the center console to catch my eye again before I slam the door shut.

And maybe it's because I'm two glasses of wine deep and my adrenaline is pumping that I lean back into the car. "I'm a loser, okay? A big fat loser, but I've sucked up this life for the past three years and I've served my time, so now I want to clean up the past and start thinking of my future. Fuck, maybe I'll even get around to being nice to Mom one day too. But I can't go back to Durham and live another year like this. It kills me to admit it, but Dad *would* hate how things have turned out for me. So no, I don't think some drinks with Austin are going to redeem my character, but it's a start. And I *have* to start somewhere, Zach, because I'm already at rock bottom and the only way is up."

Zach widens his eyes as I catch my breath, because it's probably the most I've expressed to him in our entire lifetime together. We have a good relationship despite not seeing each other very often, but we don't talk too deeply. We catch up on things, but never discuss the fragility of our mental states.

"You seem determined," he says.

"I am."

"Then go talk to Austin."

I shut the car door and wave goodbye as Zach drives off. The stomach thing becomes unbearable again. It's jarring, being so nervous around Austin, when he was once the person I felt most comfortable with. I'm struggling a little bit with figuring out what's causing the nerves—my guilt, or *him*.

I push down the rising nausea and head inside the bar. It's not the greatest, but it was the bar we walked past weekly on our way home from the recreation center, and we would joke immaturely about getting wasted in here as soon as we turned twenty-one. Except, of course, we both moved away for college. Oh, and also, we weren't friends at twenty-one because I fucked him over. Yeah, mostly that part.

It's Friday, so the bar is a full chorus of boozy voices. I expect to find the clientele exactly like that of Buck's Tavern—mostly old men sporting two-day-old body odor—but there's a surprising mix of ages in here. However, there is only one person that seems to have come straight from their corporate job, and that's Austin. I spot him at the bar, suit jacket folded over the empty stool next to him. It's been over an hour since we spoke at the house, so I wonder just how many drinks he's managed to work through since then.

Warily, I approach from behind. "Hi."

Austin cranes his neck to look at me, his hand gripped tightly around a glass on the bar in front of him. "Hi." He throws back the dregs of his drink, exhales, then moves his suit jacket from the stool next to him. "Join me. Look, tequila."

As I slink onto the stool, I dubiously study the two tequila shots on the bar as Austin slides one toward me. There is no way I'm drinking that, because first of all, I have no idea how long those shots have been sitting there, getting all warm and gross, and two, I never accept drinks that I haven't personally witnessed being poured. It's a hard rule of mine.

I slide the shot glass back toward Austin. "Sorry, but I'd prefer a fresh one. Who knows what you've put in there?"

"Just arsenic," Austin says with a smile, pushing the glass back again.

I bite my lip hard to stop a laugh escaping. He always made me laugh when we were young, not because he was particularly witty with one-liners or perfectly timed jokes, but because of his unintentional goofiness. He never knew just how hilarious he was, but now that he's confident and *knows* he's funny, I refuse to give him the satisfaction of hearing me laugh.

"Can I get another shot of tequila over here, please?" I call out to the bartender, and it feels slightly foreign being on the other side of the bar for a change. I have to refrain from reaching over and grabbing the bottle of tequila myself. When the bartender sets the shot glass down in front of me, I tell her to add it to Austin's tab and then fix him with a sweet smile.

"So?" I prompt.

"So . . .?"

"Are you drunk enough to hear my apology?"

"Not quite," Austin says. He grabs a shot glass. "Bottoms up, McKinley."

I clink my glass against his. "Bottoms up, Pierce."

We suck down our shots in unison, and while I'm screwing my face up and trying to shake away the bitter taste in my mouth, Austin grabs the spare shot and gulps that one too. He licks his lips without so much as a grimace.

"Show off," I mutter. I flag down the bartender again and this time order something I actually *enjoy* that doesn't feel like acid burning my throat—some cheap white wine—and Austin orders a beer.

"How's the head?" he asks, casually resting an elbow up on the bar and swiveling his stool to face me. His legs are so long, mine end up positioned between his knees. His shirt sleeves are rolled up again, and the top button of his shirt is undone to reveal a dusting of chest hair. I can tell he's got a buzz on, because his expression is soft and lacks the hatred I know he feels toward me.

"Wasn't fun washing my hair, but I think I got all the blood out," I say, my hand subconsciously moving to my scalp, brushing over the sutures. Honestly, I forgot about those. "Was I this clumsy when I was younger? Because I fear it's a new development." As the bartender sets down our drinks, I gasp when realization sinks in. "Shit, I shouldn't be drinking with this damn concussion."

"No," says Austin. "You probably shouldn't."

"But when this is my third glass of wine tonight, stopping now won't make much of a difference, huh? Cheers." I hold up my glass, and Austin taps his bottle of beer against it.

As he takes a swig, his gaze stays trained on me over the rim of the bottle. "You know, I think I prefer your hair like this. The curls are nice. Reminds me of sixth-grade Gabby."

I frown into my glass of wine. "Sixth-grade Gabby was a lot nicer to you."

"Yeah, she was," he agrees. "I'd ask what happened to her, but by our sophomore year of high school, I'd already figured it out for myself."

Ah. His tone is so soft, it makes his words cut even deeper. "I can't defend the way I treated you. The only thing I can say is that I was a teenage girl, and teenage girls are really fucking stupid."

"Don't worry. I was an idiot too," he says, then shakes his head. "A real idiot for letting you walk all over me for so long. But I was a kid with not many friends, so I had no choice but to let you treat me the way you did. Having shitty friends seemed better than having none at all."

Maybe it's because I'm semi-drunk that the corners of my eyes nip with tears. I blink hard to keep them at bay. "You were the most genuine friend I ever had, Austin."

"And yet you couldn't bear to be caught even saying hi to me," he says sharply, that soft tone now hardened in self-defense. "You'd walk with me all the way to the bus, then refuse to sit with me. When you got your license, you'd act like you were doing me a favor by dropping me off before you parked up. And if I even dared to look at you in class, you sure as hell had something cruel to spit across the room at me, and you'd smirk when the class snickered at just how *hilarious* you were. Oh, Gabrielle McKinley, you were *so* cool. I can't imagine how humiliating it would have been for you if anyone had discovered we were actually friends. Don't even get me started on prom."

Now I'm fighting for my life trying to hold back the tears. Every single word that leaves his mouth is a punch to the gut, and my body involuntarily curls inwards with a need to protect my vital organs. This is my punishment, and I deserve all of the guilt his words stir up within me. But I absolutely cannot cry, because I'm not the victim. The villain doesn't get to cry.

Austin shifts to the edge of his stool, leaning in closer to me. The power of his stare forces me to look at him, but I'm already crumbling as it is without now seeing the anguish in his eyes. "Answer me this, Gabby: did I do one single thing to deserve it?"

"No," I admit, the word a mere croak.

The muscle in his clenched jaw twitches. "So my only crime was being poorer than you?"

Every inch of my face aches as the tears push harder to break free. My throat burns, pressure builds in my cheeks, and my eyes sting so intensely I'm convinced they must be red raw. But Austin deserves my full attention, so I hold the eye contact despite how much it's killing me.

I lost my way in high school. As we entered our freshman year, Austin and I were joined at the hip, but it became apparent very quickly that there was a social hierarchy in high school, and those from wealthier backgrounds were at the very top of the ladder. When it came to Austin, it was a case of sink or swim. My status and reputation became the most important thing in my life, and Austin was dragging me down. I loved the safety that came with being popular. I got invited to every party, my jokes were never met with stone cold silence, and I was never the target of abuse. I knew I was privileged and I played up to it, and maybe it was my mother's beliefs instilled in me growing up, but I did fall into the trap of believing I was better than others simply because our house was larger, our cars faster, our clothes designer. High school was so easy for me.

Austin's experience was the polar opposite. He became an outcast, a recluse, even though I knew how great a person he was. But he wasn't brought up the same way the rest of us were, and that made him different. He was the best runner on the varsity track team, but even being athletic wasn't enough to save him. At first, I stood by, caught in a moral dilemma as my cooler friends would torment him. He'd catch my eye across the hall, waiting for his best friend to come to his aid, but I never once opened my mouth to protect him. Somewhere along the way, my reputation became more important than our friendship, and I became just like everyone else, making Austin the butt of every joke. Within the confines of our high school walls, we weren't friends. Back at home in the evenings, we'd hang out together while I promised Austin I didn't mean anything I'd said that day. And he forgave me every single time, until senior prom when the damage was irreparable.

It all seems so silly now, throwing a perfect friendship down the drain over the opinions of *teenagers*. It really wasn't that deep and means absolutely nothing now, but at the time, being accepted and valued was the most important thing in my life. And even that is no excuse.

"Austin," I say, swallowing, "I am so, so sorry."

Someone latches onto Austin's shoulder from behind us and we both jolt in surprise, our eye contact severed. For a moment, it felt like we were the only two people in this bar, but now some girl has her arms wrapped around Austin's neck.

"Hey you! What are you doing hanging around here?" she asks cheerfully, then steals a glimpse at me out of the corner of her eye. She does a double take, releasing Austin from what is quite nearly a head lock and gaping at me instead. Her smile stretches all the way to her eyes. "*Gabby!* What the hell?"

Again, maybe it's the wine, because I didn't even recognize her at first. And that's terrible from me, because she was one of my closest friends in high school. "Sasha!"

I set my glass of wine down on the bar and get to my feet, still trapped between Austin's thighs, and lean over to exchange a hug with Sasha Tate. As she pulls back from me, she runs her fingers through the ends of my curls.

"These are gorgeous! Is this your natural style?"

"Yes," I say sheepishly, sinking into my shoulders. I don't think I ever embraced my natural hair for a single day of high school. It was always pencil straight with too many dead ends, but straight hair was cool, and I would do whatever it took to be cool.

Austin nods to the empty stool on the other side of me. "Can I get you a drink, Sash?"

And I really don't mean to pointedly glower at him the way I do when I hear him say "Sash," but what the fuck? Sasha and I were friends in high school, which means she

80

and Austin definitely weren't. Why the hell do they seem like friends *now*? She was as awful to him as I was, but maybe this means there is hope for forgiveness, after all.

"Oh, just a beer is fine, thanks!" Sasha says, settling onto the stool next to me as Austin flags down the bartender. Sasha has a beautiful, broad smile that creates dimples in her cheeks. She flicks her brunette hair behind her and gestures to me in disbelief. "God, I haven't seen you in so long! I can't believe you're back in town. How are things? Where are you living now?"

"Oh, I stayed put in Durham," I tell her with a shaky laugh, sipping awkwardly at my wine rather than expanding further, because it would be beyond embarrassing to admit to the sad state of affairs my life has become. When I was accepted into Duke University, I walked around the halls of our high school with, in hindsight, a sickening degree of smugness. It's not even an Ivy League school, and there were definitely a few kids in my class who got into those, but Duke is still pretty prestigious and I thought I was so special. "How about you?"

"Still here!" Sasha says proudly, like she's one of the rare few who never step foot out of their hometown. "I opened my own salon last year. Beauty, with a specialty in lashes. Business is doing great! If you need those nails done, let me know!" She nods to my hand wrapped around my wine glass, my nails plain and chipped from working the bar. "What do you do in Durham?"

"Here you go, Sash," Austin says, and I'm grateful for his interruption when he leans over me to hand Sasha the beer he ordered for her. He smiles tightly at me, and

I register every single ounce of sarcasm in his expression. "You guys were *so* close in high school. You didn't stay in touch?"

"Oh, you know, people drift apart when they head off to college . . ." I mumble, throwing my head back as I empty my wine glass.

"I *did* text you all the time, Gabby," Sasha points out, biting her lip awkwardly. "You never responded, so I gave up after a while. It's okay, though!" She reaches out for my hand and squeezes it reassuringly when my face drops. "I don't take it personally. You probably made so many new friends at Duke."

Austin rests his elbow up on the bar again and says, "I'm not sure Gabrielle has any friends."

The way he says it, with that snide little undertone, makes my stomach churn.

"I have plenty," I say stiffly, though it's not even true. I *don't* have many friends, but no fucking way is Austin getting to broadcast the fact.

He purses his lips with mock sympathy and leans further onto the bar to peer around me. "Didn't you know, Sash? Gabrielle dropped out of Duke. Never graduated. You don't even have a job anymore, do you, Gabs?" The smirk he gives me is truly wicked. "She got fired. Now who the hell gets fired from their job as a bartender? She drives a busted-up Prius and is only here because her crap apartment has plumbing issues. Isn't that what you said? Your apartment is shitty? But hey, I'm not one to judge." He pats my thigh patronizingly, and I grab his hand and crush his fingers so hard, my own knuckles turn white. Our eyes are fiercely locked. "I know what it's like to have nothing going for you, but who'd have thought, huh? Gabrielle McKinley slumming it through life."

"Fuck you, Austin," I spit.

My rage bubbles over and I ram my knees into his legs as I stand. I don't dare look at Sasha to see her expression, because all I can focus on is Austin and that nasty smirk of his as it deepens. My body feels like it's on fire, and I know I need to leave immediately before I say something I'll regret.

I storm through the bar, the sea of faces nothing but a blur through my angry tears, and burst outside into the evening humidity. I may have treated Austin terribly in the past, but at least I'm trying to be better. Him, however? He's a fucking jerk.

My hands shake as I pull out my phone and text Zach to come pick me up.

"Not fun, is it, Gabrielle?" Austin's voice reverberates down the street, and I twist my body to look at him, feeling even more enraged that he's followed me outside to taunt me further. "Being humiliated."

"Are you happy now?" I snap, stepping forward and poking a finger into his chest. "Congratulations! You made fun of my sad little life, but you know what? Good! At least now you're no better than me. We're both assholes."

"You made it too easy, Gabrielle," he says, dropping his gaze to my finger still jabbed into his shirt. He places his hand over mine, his grip tight.

"Stop calling me Gabrielle!"

Austin drunkenly smiles. "Aw, c'mon, Gabster."

"You *always* called me Gabby."

"That was back when we were friends," he says.

"And we definitely aren't friends now."

"Definitely not friends now."

My eyes dip from his blue eyes to his hand wrapped around mine, and suddenly my voice feels so small and vulnerable. "Then why are we standing out here together?"

All of the oxygen seems to get sucked out of the air around us and the atmosphere becomes so unbearably tense that I become hyperaware of every single pulse in my body. Austin lowers our hands from his chest and releases his hold on mine, but my gaze is so fastened on his face, I don't miss the nervous gulp he takes before parting his lips to speak.

"I was a dick in there, but you *did* deserve it," he says, voice lowered. "For what's it worth, I do feel bad, and I'm sorry for throwing you under the bus in front of Sasha like that."

"How do you even know her?" I demand, and I pretend to ignore the fact there's still only less than a foot of space between us. "She was never nice to you back in high school, either, yet somehow she gets off lightly?"

"Because I only ever cared about you," he murmurs. "It hurt more when it was you, Gabby."

The wine starts to swirl in my stomach, and I know we shouldn't continue this conversation in the middle of the street when we're both drunk, but I just can't tear myself away from him. Maybe it's that same magnetic force that drew us together as kids that's drawing me to him now. Austin may have just embarrassed me inside the bar, yet I'm still standing here in front of him, clutching at straws.

"Can we fix this?" I ask sharply.

Austin furrows his eyebrows. "Fix this?"

"Us. Our friendship," I clarify. "Is the damage irreparable or is there some tiny, slim chance that maybe we don't have to walk away from one another tonight and never see each other again? Because I'd like to be friends. Please?"

"Even after what I just did back in there?"

"I'll forgive you," I say slowly, "if you can forgive me."

"I can't promise that, Gabby," he says with a shake of his head. He closes the gap between us and ducks to match my height, our gazes level. "But I *can* promise to try. It might take a while. But I'll try, okay?"

"*Thank you,*" I breathe, and I honestly feel the weight lift from my shoulders for the briefest of moments before my mind registers just how close Austin is. His slow breaths brush over my skin and as much as I want to step back out of uncertainty, the desire to be this close to him is even stronger. "How about," I whisper in fear of breaking the bubble around us, "we start from a clean slate? No more humiliating each other. We'll be nice."

"I won't humiliate you again," Austin promises.

"And you'll be nice?"

He pouts playfully, eyes dancing over every inch of my face. "But I've enjoyed being mean to you today.

How am I going to keep being mean to you if you go back to Durham?"

I can't bear the tension of this proximity for a second longer, because our mouths being so close is making me feel dizzy, and not in an "ew, why am I this close to my childhood best friend?" kind of way. I retreat a few steps from him and he straightens back up.

"Crap apartment with no plumbing," I say, weighing the options with my hands, "or Priscilla McKinley's scalding judgment?"

Austin presses his hands to his hips, looking extra serious in his suit pants and shirt, despite the rolled-up sleeves and undone top buttons. "Neither," he says. "Why don't you stay with me?"

My laugh echoes down the street, then gradually fades away. "Oh, you're serious."

"I have spare rooms," he says.

"*Rooms?* Like, plural?"

"Houses have rooms."

"*House?* You bought a freaking house?"

The crunch of car tires draws our focus as Zach pulls up outside the bar. He drops his window and leans out.

"Everything okay?" he asks me, casting a cynical glance toward Austin. It's barely been thirty minutes since he dropped me off, so clearly drinks with Austin isn't going well.

"All good. Austin's just boring company," I say, flashing Austin a smirk as I make for Zach's car. If he wants to be mean to me, I'll be equally mean to him. Just no hitting each other where it hurts.

I climb into the passenger seat and then stretch over my brother, much to his irritation, to look out his window at Austin. "Goodnight, corporate loser."

Austin grins. "Goodnight, unemployed loser."

Zach shoves me off him and closes his window in Austin's face without a second of hesitation. As he pulls away from the bar, I look back over my shoulder through the rear window, watching as Austin shrinks away.

"What was that about?" Zach asks.

"When I figure it out, I'll let you know."

7

The throbbing headache I wake up with is deserved. Only an idiot drinks with a concussion, and now I've likely delayed my healing and will be left with permanent brain damage.

As I'm raiding the kitchen cabinets for some Tylenol, I sense Mom's presence.

"It's pain meds, isn't it?" she asks shakily. "You're addicted to prescription pain meds."

"Yes, Mom. I'm a Tylenol addict," I say, closing the cabinet door to reveal her behind it. I sarcastically wave the small container of Tylenol in the air. "I mean, seriously? You don't even *have* prescription pain meds in here."

"That doesn't mean you aren't searching for some," she says stubbornly, so convinced of her delusional assumptions.

"Okay, I'm not having this conversation *again*." I walk straight past her and fill a glass of water at the faucet, tossing back two pills and praying they'll subdue this killer headache. "You'll be glad to know I'm about to head home."

"Your apartment is fixed?"

"Yes," I lie, and before she can launch into further investigation on my plans career-wise, I add, "Thanks so much for letting me stay here. I'll come back again for Thanksgiving."

Mom chews her lip thoughtfully. "But Thanksgiving is four months away."

"I know!" I pass her the Tylenol container with a sardonically sweet smile and hug her with the least amount of physical contact possible. "Bye, Mom."

I dash upstairs to my room, exchange friendly hellos with the maid I bump into in the hall, and throw together the last of my stuff. I didn't bring much in the first place, so I'm on my way back down the stairs with my cute little suitcase in two minutes flat. Zach has already cleared out for the day bright and early, presumably to head back to his own house to see if Claire will let him through the door yet, but I'll text him later to say my goodbye. He always comes home for Thanksgiving, too.

"Drive safe!" Mom calls just as I'm sneaking out the front door.

It's a beautiful Saturday, as the days so often are on the coast in the summertime, so I hop into my car, throw on some sunglasses and hook up a podcast for the two-hour drive home to Durham. Thankfully, I still have half a tank of gas, and all my tires are inflated and unclamped.

The journey should be smooth sailing with no hiccups, so I settle into my podcast and back out of the drive.

Instead of my usual gossipy, mind-numbing podcasts that I like to indulge in, I've chosen something more appropriate—a podcast detailing the specifics on how to manifest your perfect life.

Now, I'm not really a believer in the whole "if you channel manifestations into the world with positive energy, the universe will listen" thing, because quite frankly, that *has* to be bullshit. But a lot can be said for changing your way of thinking. A positive mind creates positive actions, and I could really do with my concussed, sad little brain being more hopeful going forward.

The second I get back to Durham, I'm going to be more demanding with my property manager, and maybe I'll even look into breaking my lease and finding some place a little nicer. Though in order to do *that*, I need more money. So I need a job. Maybe I'll look into being a barista in a coffee shop, because that's slightly more upscale than working in a dive bar, but essentially the same skills, right? And I do really need to speak with the returns office at Duke . . . But I have no idea how soon I'll be able to resume classes, so I may have a few more dire months ahead of me until things start to look up.

I know Austin was drunk last night when he offered, but crashing at his place would seriously help me out. It's too late now, though, because I'm already on the road and I don't even have his number. Which also makes me wonder how we're supposed to try this friends thing when we're going to be two hours apart, and he's running a successful business while I'm fighting with my property manager and learning how to make latte art.

As I'm approaching a set of lights at some crossroads, I squint through my sunglasses and hunch forward over my wheel to try and get a better look, because surely not. I whip off my sunglasses—*no fucking way*.

"Damn, Universe," I say out loud. "You work fast."

I pull up to the line, lights red above me, and stare over at the dark green Porsche 911 holding its intimidating stance in the lane next to me. The windows are tinted, but after a moment of me gaping over in disbelief, the passenger window lowers.

Austin lifts his sunglasses and smirks.

"You have got to be kidding me," I say, rolling down my own window.

"You trying to race?" he teases, gesturing to the road ahead.

"Oh, absolutely." I pump my gas pedal a few times, revving my engine, only for some concerning black smoke to fire out of my exhaust pipe. "Actually, rain check?"

Austin laughs, stealing a glance at the lights. Still red. "You heading home?"

"Unfortunately."

"Plumbing fixed yet?"

"Still no."

Austin sighs, dropping his sunglasses back over his eyes. "Then can I ask why the hell you're going back to that apartment?"

A car horn blares aggressively behind us. The lights are green and we're holding up traffic.

"Ah, shit," I mumble, shooting Austin an apologetic frown as I step on the gas and jolt forward. Some nutcase rides my ass hard—two seconds late moving from the lights and suddenly you have enemies.

Austin is quick to pull alongside me, matching my speed.

"Pull over!" he yells.

"Okay!"

There's a coffee shop on the side of the road up ahead, so I pull into the parking lot and wave my middle finger at the crazy dude who was kissing my bumper as he continues down the street. Austin follows me, parking in the spot next to me.

"Now that we're here," he says with a smile, "how about some coffee?"

"Hmm."

"What's with the skeptical look?"

"Because I agreed to go for drinks with you, only for you to take great pleasure in embarrassing me," I explain, "so forgive me, Austin, for doubting your intentions."

"We called a truce, didn't we? Now c'mon. Get out of the car, Gabby."

At least he's not calling me Gabrielle anymore.

We roll the windows up and step out of our cars, awkwardly meeting between them. After last night, I'm more confused than I was before. Are we still fighting? Are we friends again? Or do I have to admit that we're stuck somewhere in the middle, muddling through a mixture of emotions with no clear definition on where we stand with each other? Because maybe the fighting thing was easier.

"You look like a decaf Americano kind of man," I tell him, looking him up and down with an air of dramatic judgment.

"Close," Austin says. "Decaf espresso."

"Gross."

We head inside the store and join the line, but not without catching each other's eye every half a second. I can't help it, and clearly neither can he. We're trying to suss the other out, but we keep getting caught out. I'm trying to adapt to the sight of him *not* in a suit. Today, he's casual. His washed-out jeans fit perfectly around his hips and the short sleeves of his plain white T-shirt show off the definition in his arms. And Austin went to college on a track scholarship, so I guess he invested in those biceps when he wasn't ticking off his four-hundred-meter intervals. Looks to me like he definitely still goes to the gym. And that makes me uncomfortable, because I definitely *don't*.

"How often do you go to the gym? If it's more than three times a week, then I'm not sure we can be friends," I muse as we're waiting in line. "You'll want to start taking me along with you, and I'm sorry, but I don't do cardio."

Austin laughs. "Only when I have the time, so I make the cut. You really don't work out?"

"Nope," I say, popping my lips on the "p". I won't admit that I haven't stepped foot in a gym since I flew off a treadmill in front of the packed campus gym five years ago. A humbling experience.

"Huh. You look too good for someone who doesn't work out."

I raise a questioning eyebrow. Was that a compliment? From Austin?

He gets a lucky escape from explaining himself, because the barista calls us forward to order our coffee. Decaf espresso for Austin, iced latte for me. I pay for them, since I did smash his office table yesterday *and* stick my drinks on his tab at the bar. Plus I want the reward points.

We grab an empty table outside on the terrace, one with a parasol that offers us shade from the sun. Honestly, I don't even mind the deviation from my plan of heading home to Durham, because what's the rush? As long as I'm out from under my mother's roof, I'm good.

Austin sips from his little baby espresso cup, then shots it. "Decaf lately," he says, "because I developed a bit of a caffeine addiction at work until I could no longer function without it. Heart rate went through the roof, couldn't sleep, jitters. Getting the business off the ground was tough going."

I swirl my cup in a circle, shaking the ice cubes together. "Do people treat you differently now? *Austin Pierce, the financial advisor.* Or do you prefer wealth manager?"

"Wealth manager. And obviously people do," he says, and I glance up at him in surprise. "What? You expected my answer to be more complex than that? It's really simple, Gabby. When you're successful, people respect you, and people who respect you are nice to you. Life is easier now, but I also wouldn't change my childhood, because it gives me perspective."

"And how was college for you?"

Austin narrows his eyes. "What is this, Interrogation 101?"

"I'm just curious—"

"College was a thousand times better than high school," he cuts in. "No one knew my background. It was a fresh start. Why?"

I shrug, finally taking a sip of my coffee. "I guess I just want to know that things turned out okay for you in the end. That you didn't suffer through college too, you know? It makes me feel better."

"You don't really deserve to feel better, though, do you?" Austin says, his tone hard. Maybe I broke him down so many times before that now he automatically defaults to being defensive around me. "My friends in college being nicer people than you doesn't change the fact that you were fucking awful. You know that, right?"

I freeze mid-sip, staring at him over the rim of my cup, then set my coffee down on the table and straighten my shoulders. "Okay, what is this, Austin? You are *so* hot and cold with me. Ten minutes ago you were joking around with me at the lights, now you have that angry look in your eyes and you're calling me awful. You're either giving me the chance to earn your forgiveness or you aren't. Please make up your mind, because you're giving me whiplash here."

Austin scoffs with indignation. He rises from the table, tosses his empty espresso cup into the nearby trashcan and then storms across the parking lot while I blink after him. He would have never walked away from me before, but I guess that was the problem. There were so, so many times he should have walked away yet never did. As much as I hate seeing him turn his back on me, I'm glad he now protects himself.

But this conversation is far from over, so I take off after him, erratically waving my coffee cup.

"*Hello?* Can you answer me, please?"

Austin abruptly stops and spins on his heels, and my body slams straight into his chest. There are so many different emotions in his piercing eyes that I can barely decipher a single one. They are dangerous yet so full of anguish.

"Because I hate you, Gabby," he says, each word twisted with emotion, "but I also miss you."

"Oh."

"The past twenty-four hours, I've been fighting a battle inside my head, because one second I see a glimpse of the girl I used to adore. The girl who was sarcastic and goofy and fun to be around." He swallows hard, squeezing his eyes shut as he lowers his head in defeat. "And then the next second I remember the way that girl made me feel, and fuck, it hurts, Gabrielle. *It hurts.*"

"Oh." My throat tightens until it feels like I'm swallowing knives.

Austin's eyes flash open, his jaw clenched. Through rigid lips, he says, "So no, I can't make up my fucking mind. You messed with it too much."

I hurt him so much more than I thought.

Even just looking at me seems almost unbearable to him. It dawns on me only now, and perhaps twenty-four hours too late, that even just my presence still hurts. And I don't mean to hurt him. I don't *want* to. But some wounds cut too deep, leaving permanent scars.

I grab his arm before he can take another step away from me. "Tell me what I can do to fix this. I'll do anything, Austin."

Austin glances down at my hand on his arm, my fingers trembling against his skin. "Why did you come by my office yesterday?"

I don't miss a beat. "To apologize."

"Apologize to make yourself feel better," he says, "or apologize because you wanted me back in your life?"

"Both," I admit. I let go of his arm, my shoulders sinking as I draw a deep breath. "I wanted to say sorry for my mistakes, because I want a clean slate to use as a springboard to getting my life together. But now? Now I want you to forgive me because I miss you, too."

Austin exhales as the tension visibly leaves his body, and I wonder if he was quite literally holding his breath, praying for an answer that wouldn't hurt him. He leans against the rear of his car and crosses one foot over the other. I hate it when he's furious, but I hate it even more when he's vulnerable.

He contemplates something for a moment, his lower lip between his teeth, and then he asks, "Can I trust you, Gabby?"

"You shouldn't. Not yet," I say. My heart pounds in my chest as I try to say all of the right things, because I never want to say the wrong thing to Austin ever again for the rest of my life. "Let me earn it."

"Then last night's offer still stands," he says. "Don't go back to Durham. Stay with me for the weekend. That gives your property manager a couple more days to fix your plumbing, and it gives *me* a couple more days to hate you less and miss you more."

Big *oh*. That made me feel funny.

Like, butterflies funny.

And Austin Pierce shouldn't give me butterflies.

That's a recent development after seven years apart.

Something feels different. *He* feels different.

And I'd definitely like to spend the weekend with him.

"You're absolutely sure?" I ask.

"I wouldn't offer if I wasn't sure," he says, and like the flick of a switch, his features soften and a smile starts to toy at his lips. "Do you have enough clothes packed? Because if not, you're not driving all the way back to Durham to get some. I'll take care of it."

"You wear a size six, too?"

Austin cracks fully now. He laughs and I swear his cheeks blush pink. "You're funny."

"I thought we already established that when we were kids."

Austin pushes off his car, pulling his keys from his back pocket. "Follow me back to my place, and try to keep up."

"You *know* I can't keep up," I groan, then point to my rusted exhaust. "You saw the smoke, right? I think my engine is on the outs."

"Fine, I'll be a law-abiding citizen and keep below the speed limits," he says with an eye roll, then pauses with a hand on his door before he climbs in behind the wheel. His playful expression eases, and his nod is reassuring. "We'll get your car fixed this weekend, okay? We'll fix a lot things, Gabrielle."

Ahhh.

As I climb into my car and place my coffee into the cup holder in the center console, I'm fighting nausea. I'm spending the weekend with Austin. At his *house*. And he hates me, but he misses me.

And I *will* fix things, because I so badly want to be that girl he once adored.

8

If Austin's successful career wasn't enough to make me feel like I'm ten steps behind in life, then his house certainly is.

I followed him across the city and into the northern suburbs where I gawked in awe at the gorgeous Tudor-style homes, with their flawless brickwork and overlapping gables, like something out of a fairytale. It's the kind of neighborhood my mother would approve of, and as I parked my well-loved Prius on the drive next to Austin's sporty coupé, I had, for the first time in my life, an odd feeling of not belonging.

And maybe that's how Austin felt his entire childhood, growing up in a neighborhood of homes owned by families with long histories of generational wealth.

"I'm sorry, but what the fuck?" I say in disbelief as Austin lets me step inside the house.

"What?"

I don't even have to go on a grand tour of the two-story house to figure out that it's full of gadgets and expensive paintwork. Much like his office, it's clear Austin has a contemporary minimalist taste, because his home has the same monochrome color palette and *even the same fucking coffee table*. The one I reduced to a pile of glass shards.

I spin toward him, almost accusatory. "I'm not doubting your abilities as a businessman, but seriously? How have you achieved so much so young? Three years out from graduating, and you have a successful career and your own house? And not some crappy house, either. *This* house. Aren't you supposed to spend your twenties climbing the corporate ladder before you see any real returns? You skipped a hundred steps ahead—*how?*"

Austin watches me in amusement out of the corner of his eye as he crosses to the kitchen, all black countertops and gloss white cabinets with a center island to match. Clearly, a recent renovation. "Suspicious? So you think there's something unethical about me?"

I join him in the kitchen and rest my elbows on the island, leaning forward and wiggling my brows at him. "I won't judge if there is."

"No, Gabby. All above board," Austin answers. He presses his hands to the other side of the island, furrowing his eyebrows back at me in a stare-off. "Wanna see the guest room? It's yours for the weekend."

"No glass tables?"

Austin grins. "No glass tables."

He leads the way upstairs, pointing out the bathroom and his home office, warning me to stay out of there for confidentiality reasons, and then presents the guest bedroom to me.

"I'm not a huge decorator," he says sheepishly, hovering by the door.

There's a fluffy carpet that seems almost untouched, an inviting king-sized bed with a stack of pillows, and two nightstands either side of the bed. The room has an en suite, too.

"This is perfect," I say, sitting on the edge of the bed and immediately sinking into the foam mattress that contours around my body. "You're doing me a huge favor, Austin. You have no idea how much I appreciate this."

Now he's *extra* sheepish. "You're welcome. Gets a little boring around here on my own anyway, so I'll enjoy you running that sarcastic mouth of yours."

"Sarcastic, but not mean," I say. We made that deal to be nice to each other.

"You'll be kicked out of here *so* fucking fast if you're mean."

I pout. Sarcastically, of course. "But I've already claimed my new bed," I groan, stretching out my arms and falling backward into the stack of luxurious pillows.

"Don't get too comfy," Austin says, reaching for my hands and pulling me upright, "because we have stuff to do today."

"We do?"

"Important stuff."

"Important stuff that you need *me* for?"

"I don't *need* you," he says, "but I want you to come. I'd ask if you're allergic to dogs, but if I remember right, it's only cats."

"You're right," I say, a smile stretching across my face, because he really does remember *everything*. "Remember that stray we found once? We carried it from door to door, asking if it belonged to anyone, and my eyes swelled up so badly I couldn't see. My dad ended up taking me to the emergency room for a rabies shot, and you left me candy in the front yard."

"*And* you named it Hannah the Homeless Cat."

I laugh, because *of course* I named it. "I don't even know if it was female. Didn't your parents end up taking it to the shelter?"

"Funny you mention the shelter," he says, "because that's where we're heading now. Only it's the dog shelter, obviously. I promise, no cats." He holds out his hand, palm up, offering to help me to my feet. Warily, I place my hand in his and let him pull me up from the bed.

"Are you . . . Are you adopting a dog?"

"Would you stick around if there was a resident dog at the office?"

"Yes, because you'll obviously hire me as its primary caretaker, and I'll feed it biscuits and teach it to play dead and it'll love me more than it loves you." I glance down and suddenly don't feel so playful when I realize my hand is still in his. I lift my gaze. "Are you really adopting a dog?"

"I hate to break your heart, Gabby, but no," Austin says.

I snatch my hand back from his with a scowl. "Boring. Why are we going to the shelter, then?"

"Because it's sponsored by none other than Pierce Wealth Management." Austin grins, those perfectly straight teeth catching me off guard again. "Looks good for business, I get to hang out with some dogs every weekend, *and* it's tax deductible."

I press my hands to my hips. "So why are we still here and not there? C'mon! I wanna see the dogs."

We head downstairs and hop into Austin's car together, and I quite enjoy being the passenger princess as we head downtown. I control the music and the AC, and Austin complains that my music taste is disappointing and my AC preference too dramatic, and I simply ignore his whining. We stop by the pet store en route to the shelter and fill a cart with monstrous bags of kibble that Austin somehow manages to stack in his tiny front trunk, and we pick out some toys together, too. Lots of squeaky ones. As we drive to the shelter, I rip off all the tags.

"You do this every weekend?" I ask Austin as the pile of toys accumulates at my feet.

"I try."

"Which dog is your favorite? I'm sensing . . ." I drum my fingertips against my forehead and close my eyes, pretending to think. When I open them again, I say, "Some three-legged mutt with one eye and missing patches of fur. Correct?"

Austin reaches for a toy on my lap, squeaks it, then throws it gently at my face. "I don't pick favorites."

"Liar. Of course you have a favorite."

"I don't."

"I'll figure out which one you have a soft spot for," I say confidently.

"Good luck, because there isn't one."

We pull up outside the shelter, Saving Paws Animal Rescue, and immediately a woman named Fiona races outside to greet us. Austin introduces me as his friend, which is a lot more than he introduced me as to his receptionist at the office yesterday, so I'll take it. I bundle all of the toys back into a carrier bag while Austin and Fiona grab all the kibble from the trunk.

I've never been to a dog shelter before, but by the time we sign in at the front desk and dump the kibble in the storeroom, I've adjusted to the constant barking punctuated by the odd howl. I carry the bag of toys in my arms with nervous excitement, following Austin around like I'm a lost puppy myself, as he catches up with Fiona on which dogs were adopted this week and any new arrivals.

And then finally, *finally* . . . "Ready to hand out those toys?"

"Yes!"

Fiona unlocks a door for us, revealing a long corridor with kennels either side of the walkway, and the barking kicks up a notch as lots of paws and noses poke excitedly through the kennel doors. She tells us to hang out for as long as we want, then leaves us to it.

"Let's just work our way down," Austin suggests, reaching into the bag to pluck out a toy. He crouches in front of the first kennel to our left, waving the fox plushie at the Akita whose tail is wagging so fast, I'm surprised the whole damn dog doesn't propel through the air. "Hi, Nelly. How's it going this week? Look what I've got!"

Austin passes Nelly the toy, and the poor pup may as well collapse in excitement. She circles her kennel, squeaking the toy in her mouth, her entire body wiggling with joy.

"Hi, Nelly," I say gently, holding my hand through the door, but she's too excited to care.

We switch over to the first kennel on the right-hand side now.

"Bruno's a grump," Austin says, slipping a toy through the door while we get glowered at by the German shepherd curled up in the back corner.

We work our way down the corridor, going from side-to-side and showing each dog some attention as we hand out the toys. Some are nervous, some a little growly, some too tongue-friendly. Each has a sign on their door with their name and their story, and as we near the end of the corridor, I feel a lot sadder than I did at the start. Some of these dogs have been here for a long time, some have been abused and neglected, some were found as strays.

"I thought this was going to be fun," I say gravely, "but I was mistaken."

"They'll find their homes eventually," Austin reassures me.

"But what about Teddy over there?" I point to the elderly Lab mix, and I think I may actually cry as he nips gently on the plushie donut we gave him. He doesn't have many teeth left. "His sign says he's been here for nine hundred and thirty-two days. Do the math on that, Austin. That's over two years!"

Austin looks back at me over his shoulder from his crouched position on the floor, the nervous Chihuahua he's been trying to win over still growling fiercely at him. "Are you crying?"

"The more important question is why aren't *you* crying?" I sniff.

Austin stifles a laugh as he straightens up, and to my surprise, he places an arm around my shoulders and pulls me in close. "Would you like to take Teddy outside to play? Would that make you feel better?" he asks softly, the words getting lost in my hair.

I nod against him. "Yes, please."

"Let's finish up and I'll go grab his leash."

We distribute the remaining few toys, and the very last kennel on the row is home to a miniature golden poodle named Lily, who was found as a stray eating chicken wings out of the garbage. She licks every inch of my hand in an overload of excitement.

"Oh, Austin, I love chicken wings too! And she has curly hair just like me. I think she might be my soul dog."

Austin crouches down next to me and pats the mound of curled fur on top of Lily's little head. "Hey, Lils. If only you didn't want to square up to every other dog, I'm sure you'd have been adopted by now."

I give Austin a sidelong look. "Look at her tiny little paws."

"Very cute, I know."

"And she has a goofy underbite. *Aww*. Look at the way her lips are stuck to her teeth!"

"Unfortunately, no braces for you, Lily."

108

"Austin . . ." I purse my lips, blinking slow and pleadingly. "I really think you *should* get an office dog."

"No."

"An office dog that loves chicken wings and has curly fur and an underbite."

"No."

"And then you hire me as the Pierce Wealth Management's pet wrangler."

"Fuck no. You couldn't even look after the decor."

Crouched together on the floor, both our hands stuck through the kennel door to pet Lily, we glower at each other. The intensity builds and builds until we both crack into laughter in perfect synchronization.

"I tried my best, Lily," I tell the poodle, scratching under her chin.

We get permission to take Teddy out into the agility field and I wonder if there's enough hours in the day to take *every* dog outside to play, because I do feel guilty as we walk Teddy down the corridor, passing all the other dogs. They'll each get their turn with the shelter staff, but still. They don't get their turn with *me*, and that's a real shame, because I like to believe I'm fun to run around with.

"Teddy!" I call, slapping my hands against my thighs to lure him into chasing me, but for a supposedly energetic breed, he doesn't seem to like running much. Maybe it's his old age, but he seems happier sniffing the grass and cocking a leg up on the fence. "Oh. Enjoy your pees then."

I look to Austin for back up, but he's occupied by mindlessly weaving around a set of tall agility poles in the grass.

"You should stick to the track," I say when he knocks the last pole. "You're not very good at dog agility courses." There's a wooden balancing seesaw that I can't resist climbing up, and I hold my body steady in the center, the board tipping back and forth.

"Concussed, remember?" Austin calls out across the field. "Get down from there."

"But I'm so good at it!"

Austin runs over and wraps his hand around my wrist, gently guiding me back down the board until I'm safe on solid ground. I'm getting used to the feeling of his skin against mine the more he touches me, and I debate climbing back up onto the seesaw just so I can feel his hand on my wrist as he guides me down all over again.

"This is the kind of shit you'd do back when we were kids."

"I don't remember us ever hanging out in dog shelters."

Austin smiles as he drops to the grass, leaning back on his hands, long legs stretched out in front of him. "You were always so carefree," he says, looking up at me from the ground. "You lost that about yourself as we grew up."

"And you were always reserved and worried about the consequences," I say, joining him on the grass, "and unfortunately, it seems that hasn't changed. Mr. Sensible Businessman Who Won't Let Me Play on the Seesaw. You're such a *grown-up*."

"Hey, one of us had to be the responsible one," Austin says, digging his elbow into my ribs. "That time you jumped into the lake fully clothed? The only reason I followed you in was because someone needed to pull you out. Couldn't let my best friend drown, could I?"

Teddy pads over and settles on the grass with us, wedging his butt in between Austin and me. I run my hand down his back, his coat warm under the sunshine. Austin scratches behind his ears.

"I bet you'd let me drown now," I muse.

"To death? No," Austin says. "Maybe just to the point of requiring CPR."

We turn to look at each other, and I hate that he makes me laugh. It shouldn't be a surprise to me that we get along so well, because we *were* best friends. We may have grown up, we may have changed, but the foundation is still there. It feels so natural being around Austin.

"Teddy, did you hear that?" I ask, bending forward so I can lower my voice and say into his ear, "I think that was Austin being mean to me."

Austin mimics me, drawing his mouth in close to Teddy's other ear, his gaze smoldering back at me over the dog's head. "Teddy, did you hear that? I think that was Gabby realizing she enjoys me being mean to her."

I sit upright, defiantly crossing my arms. "I do not."

"Yes, you do," Austin counters. "You blush."

"What?"

"You blush," he repeats. He lifts his hand and delicately brushes his thumb over my cheek, and my breath hitches in my throat. "Your cheeks turn a shade of pink. Spreads under your freckles. Softens your eyes."

He drops his hand. "So if it's okay with you, I'm going to keep being mean, because I love it when you blush."

The field spins around me and I manually force myself to breathe. Growing up, I don't remember ever feeling like there was even the slightest possibility that Austin saw me in any other way than just his best friend. That's all we were back then, but now it is impossible to ignore just how different things feel. Terrifyingly different. Different enough to make my heart hammer in my chest in a way I'm yet to understand.

"Okay," I finally respond, searching for breath. "Amendment to our agreement of being nice to one another: we get to be mean, but only if it's *playful* mean. Not *nasty* mean. *Fun* mean. Agreed?"

"Perfect," Austin says with a smile so gorgeous it's wicked. "For what's it worth, I didn't enjoy being *nasty* mean to you yesterday. It didn't feel right, because you were always my favorite person, Gabby."

My heart pounds even harder, painful in my chest. "I thought you don't pick favorites."

Austin's gaze holds mine and he allows a beat of silence to fill the air between us before he says quietly, "I don't unless it's you."

9

I don't know if it's the concussion or the way Austin stroked my cheek, but my head is a mess of jumbled thoughts and I have a severe lack of concentration. I can't think straight. Every time Austin opens his mouth, he needs to repeat himself because I'm zoned out and staring off into the distance.

We said goodbye to all of the dogs at the shelter, which made me emotional because I'll probably never see any of them again, and on our way back to Austin's house, we stopped by the mall to pick out some clothes to tide me over for a few days. Nothing expensive, just some basics. When I started browsing for underwear, Austin decided that was the right moment for him to duck off to the running store, giving me some privacy.

And then he found me again at the checkout and swiped his credit card before I could put up a fight. When I promised to pay him back, he laughed. *Laughed.*

But I'm not a charity case. I can stand on my own two feet, even if they may be a little wobbly at times, so the second I find a new job and start bringing in some cash again, I'll pay him back the hundred odd dollars I now owe him. We were best friends when he had nothing, and I don't want him thinking I've come crawling back into his life now that he's loaded. I didn't even *know* he was rich when I decided to find him.

Back at the house, he needed a few hours to himself to work, so he disappeared into his home office while I tried my best to relax in the huge living room. Part of me wanted to steal this chance to sneak around and explore, to find out more about the Austin he is now, but prying doesn't align with my new goals of being a better, more respectful person. So I stayed put in the living room, flicking through streaming services on the monstrous TV screen and looking up Lily's profile on the Saving Paws Animal Rescue's website. No wonder she hasn't been adopted—her photos are terrible.

I also texted my mother, something I rarely, if ever, do. I told her I made it back to Durham safe and sound, because what else can I do but lie? If she knew I was shacking up with Austin Pierce for the weekend, that would send her fully over the edge and into a nervous breakdown.

I'm deep into my second movie, fighting off the nap my body craves after an afternoon of being far too comfortable in the corner of this couch, when Austin emerges from his office. I'm so tired, I don't even sit up. I peek over the edge of the blanket I'm cocooned under and smile.

"You're finished?"

"For today," Austin says, collapsing onto the other end of the couch by my feet. He glances at that expensive watch on his wrist. "I'm sorry that took so long."

"Hey, you're doing me a favor letting me stay here. Don't worry about keeping me company," I reassure him. Whatever Austin's plans are this weekend, I'll fit myself around them and keep out of his way if required. I don't want him to regret his extremely generous offer of hospitality.

My body stiffens when Austin rests his hand on my leg over the blanket. He doesn't seem to notice, because he nods curiously at the TV. "What are you watching?"

"Um," I say, brain scrambling as I reel in my focus. "I've been working my way through all of the Marvel movies recently. This is *Captain Marvel*."

Austin gives me a pensive sidelong look.

"What?"

"I never thought I'd ever see Gabrielle McKinley again," he says, "let alone see her wrapped up in *my* blanket watching Marvel movies on *my* couch. My brain's bugging out here."

I pointedly pull the blanket tighter around me. "Your AC is too high. I'm freezing."

"Hypothermia wasn't exactly the method of death I had in mind for you, but it'll do," he quips, then grins as he moves from the couch to the AC dials on the wall. He turns the temperature up a few notches. "Better?"

"Thanks."

He rejoins me on the couch, but this time his hand doesn't accidentally find its way to my leg, and I feel a little zap of disappointment. "Do you mind if I watch this with you? And then I was thinking maybe we could get takeout for dinner, because I don't cook much."

I scoff and say, "You're such a bachelor."

"Oh, please. Like you're any better."

I roll my eyes, because he's right—I'm not much of a cook, either. I live on microwave meals and fast food, because buying groceries for one ends in so much waste. But mostly I'm just lazy. Mom never cooked, so she had nothing to teach me, and now I'm a lost cause. "Takeout is fine. You pick."

"Chinese?"

"Only if there's egg rolls."

"There will be egg rolls."

"Then Chinese it is."

"Perfect."

We watch the rest of *Captain Marvel* together, but I fall back into my earlier pattern of being so entirely distracted by Austin's existence that I'm barely functioning. He doesn't so much as brush up against me for the remainder of the movie and that has me questioning my sanity. Maybe my ego is just too big. Why the hell would Austin ever like me? We really *were* just friends as kids, and if he didn't like me more than that back then, then there's no way he could ever like me now after everything I put him through.

My head spins, because I don't even know why I *want* him to like me, or why my stomach churns with dissatisfaction at the thought of being *only* friends when I should be grateful to achieve even that. I *want* him to be my friend again, of course I do. But maybe I also want to explore if there could ever be something more.

And that's a real headfuck, because suddenly I see a lot more in Austin than I ever did when I was younger. A different perspective, a new appreciation, a long overdue acknowledgement.

Touch my leg again, goddamn it.

But he never does.

When the movie ends, we immediately call in our order for delivery after fighting over which dishes are best, and ultimately end up ordering a little of everything. Egg rolls, roast duck, kung pao chicken, wonton soup, honey walnut shrimp, fried rice . . . When the mountain of food arrives and we set it down on the kitchen island, we look at one another over the top of the pile and burst into laughter.

"We definitely overshot this," Austin says, scratching his head. "We'll be eating leftovers for breakfast, lunch and dinner tomorrow. Maybe even Monday, too. How the hell have we ended up with four portions of rice?"

"Don't look at me," I say, shrugging as I continue pulling containers out of the bags. "You're the one who placed the order. But fear not—I have a good appetite. Just you wait and see how much of this I can demolish."

Austin seems thoroughly amused. "Oh, I'd love to see you try."

"A plate would be a good place to start."

"I didn't think you'd be that civilized."

I snap my fingers at him and point to the cabinets behind him, but I clearly have no clue where the plates even are, because he crosses the kitchen in the opposite direction to go retrieve some. He brings over some silverware, too, and we throw a mixture of everything onto our plates and sit down at the table.

Half an egg roll in my mouth, I ask, "What do you usually do on the weekend? Other than lock yourself in your office and drop off kibble to the dog shelter."

Austin watches me across the table, pretentiously moving food around his plate with a pair of freaking chopsticks. "Beers with a couple of buddies sometimes. I'm running the Chicago marathon in October, so Sunday mornings I run. I'm trying to get into golf, too."

"Golf?"

He cocks his head in response to my critical tone. "What's wrong with golf?"

"You're twenty-four," I remind him. "You never hit the clubs? How about dating?"

"Gabby," Austin says, laughing out loud. He pushes his plate forward and crosses his arms on the table, fixing me with a challenging look. "Enough of the questions. What do *you* do on weekends?"

I intentionally smolder my eyes at him before replying, "Watch Marvel movies."

God, all we do is laugh. It's so easy to see why we were friends.

"You never hit the clubs? How about dating?" Austin asks, repeating my questions with a teasing smirk.

"Sometimes, but the clubs are full of Duke students who are way too young for me," I say, heaving a nonchalant sigh, "and all of the suitable Duke alumni I'd actually be interested in have already left town, so I'm left with college freshmen trying to grow facial hair or middle-aged Durham locals. It's slim pickings up there. Oh, you wanna hear my latest dating nightmare? It involves a man with a blatant foot fetish." I toss the remainder of my egg roll in my mouth and pause mid-bite when Austin's smile falters. "What?"

"I've realized I'd rather not hear about your dating life."

"But we're trying to be friends again," I say, pouting. "Friends talk about these things."

Austin pulls his plate back and pokes casually at some duck, briefly glancing up at me. "So you'll be perfectly happy to hear me talk about the couple of times I spent the night with Sasha? That wouldn't bother you?"

It takes everything in me to maintain my easy expression, to not even so much as blink in surprise as my stomach plummets. Not only does Sasha get Austin's forgiveness so easily, she also gets him in bed. And that makes me irrationally envious.

"Nope. Doesn't bother me." The words taste metallic on my tongue.

"You're a terrible liar, Gabby."

Quite frankly, keeping my features this aligned hurts, so I immediately give up my carefree act and hunch forward, elbows on the table. "You're right. Let's not talk about our dating lives."

"See, it's too weird."

"Yeah. Too weird," I agree. But it's not weird at all. It's raging fucking jealousy, and it's making me feel sick. I frown at the dent I've barely made in my plate of food, because at this point I've lost my appetite.

"Yeah, you're really demolishing that plate," Austin comments after a while, and I can't even appreciate how sexy his teasing smiles are, because now I'm lost inside the depths of my chaotic mind and wondering why *he* thinks it's weird to share our dating history. Weird because he's known me all my life, or weird because the thought of me with someone else makes him uncomfortably jealous too?

And that's all it takes to send me spiraling again, my thoughts chasing each other in endless circles as I ruminate over Austin and what *his* mind is doing.

If I don't say something now, I won't be able to sleep.

"Okay, listen," I say, clearing my throat. My earnest tone catches Austin off guard, because a flicker of confusion travels across his features before he straightens his shoulders and offers me his full attention. "At the risk of embarrassing myself to the point where I'll probably avoid making eye contact with you for the rest of the weekend, there's something I need to ask. If I don't, I'll overthink myself to death and end up as an anxious wreck, and I'm not on my A-game with my sarcasm when I'm anxious. I'm probably way off the mark, and maybe it's just my ego thinking too highly of myself, but—"

"Christ, Gabby, spit it out."

His interruption is met with a scathing glare. "You *know* I ramble on when I'm nervous."

"Why are you nervous?"

"Will you shut up and listen?" I run my hands down my face and take a deep breath. My eyes find Austin's, curious and waiting, and part of me doesn't even want to ask the question in fear of the answer. "We were best friends . . . but did you ever like me more than that?"

Silence pulses between us while I hold my breath and instantly wish I could cram the words back in my mouth. Austin's lips twitch with the threat of a smile. He's holding back laughter.

The embarrassment scorches my face. "Can I retract the question?"

"It's not really a question when you already know the answer," he finally says.

"But I *don't* know the answer. Hence I asked."

That laughter he's been fighting finally breaks free, filling every crevice of the house until I'm pretty certain it'll haunt me when I'm lying wide awake tonight at 2 a.m. replaying this conversation over and over again. "Gabby, seriously? You didn't know? You think I followed you around obsessively because you were my friend? You think I left gifts on your front step for the hell of it? You think I asked you to prom as your *friend*? I had the biggest fucking crush on you."

My lips part and air gradually seeps back into my lungs. "You did?"

"C'mon, Gabby," Austin says, shaking his head in amused disbelief. "You were always top of the class with your grades, yet you couldn't figure *that* out?"

"I just . . . I didn't see it back then. Only now in hindsight," I explain, then add, "I'm sorry."

"Why? It's not like things would have been different," he says. "I never stood a chance with you anyway, and we were kids, Gabby. All I missed out on was some high school romance that would have lasted approximately two months and then ended with us dramatically breaking up during lunch in front of everyone in the cafeteria. Trust me, I'm over it."

I drop my gaze to my plate, poking at some chicken. The way I hurt Austin seems a thousand times worse now that I know he had deeper feelings for me than just those of a close friend. No wonder my betrayal cut him so deep. But he's also right, because things *wouldn't* have been different had I known. My mother wouldn't let him step one foot in the house and I couldn't bear the thought of anyone thinking we were friends—there's no way I'd have dated him. It makes sense now why he put up with the awful way I treated him for so long.

"What's going through your mind, Gabby?"

I glance up, a lump in my throat. "I feel like the worst person in the world, and I don't know how to fix it."

"Isn't that what we're doing right now? Fixing it?" His gaze is soft, too soft, and I don't deserve it. "I'm here in front of you. I'm letting you eat my egg rolls in my kitchen. I'm giving you a chance, Gabrielle."

"But—"

"But nothing," he cuts in. Sighing, he grabs his plate of food and gets to his feet. He circles the table and repositions himself in the spot right next to me, scooting his chair in close and intently holding eye contact with me. "When I walked out and saw you sitting there in the lobby at the office yesterday, it was like a gunshot straight to the chest. My blood was boiling, because how dare you show up in my life again?"

I turn away because the truth in his words stings, but he immediately grabs my wrist the same way he always seems to when he wants my attention exclusively on him. I muster the strength to find his gaze once more.

"For as much as I've spent the past seven years hating you," he says, hand still wrapped gently around my wrist, "I can't deny that I like having you around again. That comes with a lot of mixed feelings which I'm trying to work through, but you're doing okay so far, so relax. My blood temperature is moderate. I can look you in the eye, exactly like this, without wanting to throw my fist through the wall." We both manage a tiny smile. "If I didn't *want* to find a way to forgive you, you wouldn't be here."

"Is there anything I can do?" I ask, my throat so dry the words stick.

"Just keep being the Gabby I knew before. The goofy one, not the bitchy one," he clarifies, then lets his gaze dip to his hand around my wrist. Before he lets go, he brushes his thumb over my skin. "I've missed her."

My skin feels electrified as I murmur, "I'm trying my best to find her."

"Well, can you find her while we finish this food?" Austin asks with a grin. He picks up his chopsticks and clicks them together. "My duck's getting cold."

10

As predicted, there are enough leftovers to feed half an army. We give it our best shot, but I admit defeat when the sight of the egg rolls starts making me break out into a sweat rather than salivate with craving. We clear away the food and the dishes, then settle back in front of the TV to watch the next Marvel movie on my list, *Avengers: Endgame*.

I didn't admit it to Austin, but my weekends are so often very boring. If I'm not working the bar, I'm alone in my apartment. Sometimes I go an entire day without saying a single word to anyone, so I speak out loud to myself just to ensure I haven't lost my voice. There is nothing for me in Durham, but I know if I leave, I'll never return to Duke to finish my degree. I'm clinging to whatever strings are left connecting me to the life I was supposed to have, but I'm hurtling toward a crossroad at full speed and I know sooner rather than later I will need to make some decisions about my future.

This exact moment in time, however, I'm just relieved not to be on my own for once. I didn't realize how pathetic my life has become until I came home and had a good dose of hard truths. My father would be disappointed, my mother is embarrassed. Austin is the only one giving me a chance at redeeming myself, and I really need someone else to hold out some hope for me, because I've lost all of mine.

We share the blanket during the movie. We don't touch, not really, but Austin's still close enough to interfere with the natural rhythm of my heart. It's almost a relief when the movie finally ends and he gets up to stretch, the hem of his T-shirt lifting to reveal the waistband of his boxers under his jeans. That's when I question how unstable I really am, because I instantly want him to do it again. And again, and again, and again.

"You're not one of those night owls who stays up till three, are you?" Austin asks, shutting off the TV. "Because I'm a Monday-to-Friday corporate man, so I'm very particular about maintaining a solid sleep schedule. If you want to stay up late, you're more than welcome to, but I won't be joining you."

"You're so mature," I muse, unfurling the blanket from around my body. Maybe the fact that I have yet to graduate is why I seem permanently stuck in my youthful college mindset. And with my youthful college mindset comes an erratic sleep schedule. "But don't worry, I also love early nights," I lie.

Austin turns down the house for the night, locking doors, adjusting the thermostat, switching off lights, and then follows me up the stairs. Tension brews in the new silence as the impending *goodnights* dangle over us. Even though I've spent the past two days with Austin, the idea of spending the night at his place seems a step too far, too fast. What if this is a ploy to murder me in my sleep? Lure me in with fake niceties, keeping his rage at bay, only to smother me with a pillow the second I close my eyes?

"You aren't going to murder me during the night, are you?" I ask.

"Considered it," Austin says. He pauses outside the door to the guest room, turning to face me. "No, Gabby, I won't murder you during the night. And no one else will, either. Alarm is all set."

"Okay." I nervously shift my weight back and forth from one foot to the other, my gaze darting everywhere but Austin. "So . . . Goodnight, then?"

"Goodnight, loser," he says, pushing open the door to the guest room.

"Goodnight, loser," I repeat.

"We really should think of a parting phrase that's better than that."

"Goodnight . . ." I tap my finger against my lips as I think, then in one spluttered string of words, suggest, "*Austin-please-forgive-me?*"

Every time he laughs, I want to think of a thousand more ways to make that sound come from him. "Goodnight, *maybe-one-day*."

"I'll take that," I say, then slip past him into the guest room I've so kindly been given to stay in this weekend.

He clicks the door shut for me and it takes four and three quarters of a second for me to realize I wasn't ready to say goodnight yet.

For as much as being around Austin reminds me of the mistakes I've made in the past and a version of myself I like to think I've left behind, being around him also makes me feel . . . optimistic. For the first time since my father passed, it feels almost like things are finally looking up. I want to chase that feeling, to sink into it.

Chewing my lip, I rummage through the shopping bags I dumped on the bed earlier in search of the silk PJs I picked out at the mall and grab my wash bag from my suitcase. In the bathroom, I get changed and sit on the toilet lid, knees bouncing with nervous energy, as I cleanse my face and brush my teeth. I work a comb through my curls, then crawl into the bed that I'm pretty sure has never been slept in.

As predicted, I stare at the ceiling in the dark, wide awake.

And I last all of five minutes.

Five minutes, and I'm climbing back out of bed and creeping over to the door.

It's been fifteen minutes since we said goodnight in the hall, so it's pretty much fifty-fifty whether or not Austin falls asleep that quick. I'm willing to risk it.

As I work my way down the hall, my heart thrashes erratically in my chest and by the time I reach Austin's door, my breaths are shallow. I have no idea why the urge to see him is so strong that I'm about to barge into his room, but I can't suppress it no matter how hard

I try. Something is pulling me to him, that magnetic force again.

Gently, I knock my knuckles against the door as I crack it open an inch. "Austin?"

His voice finds its way back to me in the dark. "Gabby?"

The nerves skyrocket. I push open the door fully now and step into the room, my eyes adjusting to the darkness just as Austin flicks on the light on the side table. A warm glow casts itself over the room and Austin sits up in bed. I didn't come into his bedroom earlier when I was getting the grand tour of the house, but I'm not all that surprised to find it's near identical to the guest room, except maybe his bed is a California king. As I stare back at him, I twist my hands together in front of me.

"I lied," I say. "I *am* one of those night owls who stays up till three."

"Of course you are," Austin says, his knowing smile making it clear he knew I was lying all along. He runs his hand down the back of his neck, his hair tousled from trying to sleep. "What would you like me to do about that, Gabby?"

The suggestive tone woven through his question sends me all the way to hell and the inviting shine in his blue eyes drags me all the way back. Coming to his room was a terrible idea, because now I can't breathe at all.

"Talk to me."

Austin pushes back his sheets, sitting on the edge of his bed, eyes fastened on mine. He's only wearing a pair of black boxers that fits perfectly around his hips. "Talk to you about what?"

"About the way you used to feel," I whisper.

Time stands still. I'm frozen to the spot by the door as Austin doesn't so much as flinch, his gaze remaining perfectly steady. The bedside light casts a shadow over his face, making his features indistinguishable.

He stands up from the bed, and I don't even attempt to hide the way my eyes rake up and down his body. Austin's built like a track athlete—slim but toned, with legs that are defined with more muscles than I even knew existed. The hair on his chest is trimmed short and I follow the trail of fine hair down his stomach all the way to the waistband of his boxers. I swallow hard.

"At eight years old, I wanted to be your friend," Austin says, low voice breaking through the silence as he takes several cautious steps toward me until there's no space left between us at all.

"At ten, I realized your laugh made me happy."

He nudges his body into mine, pushing me back against the wall.

"At twelve, I wanted to kiss you."

Both his hands find mine and he threads our fingers together.

"At fourteen, I was in love with you."

He presses our joined hands against the wall either side of my head, trapping me in place.

"At sixteen, I wanted to feel you."

He draws in close, his breath hot against the corner of my mouth.

"At eighteen, I hated you."

"And at twenty-four?" I whisper.

Austin's eyes trail over my lips before fixing me with a look so threateningly gorgeous, the entire world stands still. "All of the above, all at once."

Hungrily, his mouth captures mine and our hands tighten together as he presses them harder into the wall. I push my body into his chest, desperate to bring us even closer, only now realizing this is exactly what my mind has been crying out for all day. I force the kiss deeper before teasingly breaking it to take his lower lip between my teeth.

Austin groans, releasing his firm grip on my hands so he can slide his own into my hair instead. The kiss is fast and chaotic and almost too perfect. I take his jaw in my hands and with all of my strength, guide him backward. He sinks down on the end of the bed, pulling me down with him without ever tearing his lips from mine. I settle onto his lap, straddling his hips.

A tantalizing chill runs down my spine as Austin's hands travel down my back to my waist, toying with the hem of the silk top of my PJs.

"Can I touch you?" he murmurs against my mouth. "Fuck, please let me touch you, Gabby."

He doesn't need to ask me a third time. Pulling back from him, I whip off my top in one swift maneuver and discard it on the floor. Austin kisses a path from my jaw down my neck to my collarbone, then down to my breasts. His mouth closes around my firm nipple, sucking gently, and I bury my face in his hair because it's too pleasurable to bear.

Austin stands from the bed, his hands beneath my ass as he lifts me with him. He twists us around and lowers

131

me onto the bed, his body following above me. He runs his fingers over the elastic waistband of my PJ shorts. "And these?"

I look him straight in the eye when I say, "Take them off."

Austin hooks his fingers over the waistband and slides my shorts down my legs. He pauses for a moment to study my body under the glow of the bedside light, sucking in a breath. For as much as I want to cross my arms over my chest or shield my body behind a pillow, I fight off the natural instinct to hide and allow myself to be this exposed. If Austin has wanted this since he was sixteen, then I want the eight-year wait to be worth it.

"Gabby . . . You're so—"

I reach up and hook my hand around the nape of his neck, tugging him back to me so I can kiss him again. Every inch of my body is begging for him to touch me, to feel him. One hand of his sinks into my hair, his other drops between my thighs.

I flinch at how sensitive I am when Austin rubs a finger over my clit. His touch is light at first, then builds in intensity as he gauges how much pressure I can handle, and it turns out, not that fucking much. My legs start to tremble and a gasp escapes my lips when he dips a finger into me. One, then two, stretching me.

"That feel good?" he asks, pumping his fingers inside of me at a rhythm that is so in sync with what my body needs. When I catch his eye, his gaze is wild and his smirk seductive because he *knows* he's making me feel good. "What makes you come is the one thing I still need to learn about you."

"I need you too," I puff out, biting my lip hard to keep me from moaning too much.

"What do you need, Gabrielle?" Austin presses. "Tell me."

I'm in a sensual daze when I answer, "Your cock."

Austin pulls away from me, climbing off the bed and stepping out of his boxers.

"Oh," I blurt.

Concern flashes on Austin's flushed cheeks. "Do you want to stop?"

I stare at his cock, hard and intimidating and a challenge, and I crave him even more than I did three seconds ago. "I definitely *don't* want to stop."

Austin moves back onto the bed, trailing his hand down my breastbone, raising goosebumps over every inch of my skin. "Are you on birth control?"

"Yes, but I'd prefer we went double Dutch. Do you have condoms?"

"Of course. Anything you want, Gabby," he says, kissing my temple before he reaches over to the bedside drawer to grab a condom. He tears open the foil packet and slides the condom over himself. "You're sure? This isn't the concussion talking?"

I grab one of his pillows and slide it under the small of my back. "Just don't throw me around too much. I'm not flexible at the best of times, and my bones tend to weirdly crack, and sometimes I —"

"Shh," Austin interrupts, gently pressing his hand over my mouth to smother my nervous rambling. "You're not very good at talking dirty, are you?"

We bubble over into laughter, and I don't know how it's possible such a new and unfamiliar situation can feel this comfortable and natural. It's just how Austin and I work—our personalities blend perfectly together, making us the best of friends. Except right now, this isn't exactly what best friends do. Well, maybe sometimes.

Austin positions his body over mine, hooking his arms under my shoulders and losing his hands in my hair. As he guides himself inside of me, I gasp at the pressure. It takes a few strokes for my body to adjust enough to let him in all the way, and Austin's breaths are hot against my skin as he presses his face into my neck.

"Oh, Gabby," he murmurs, lips crashing into mine.

My arms loop around his neck for support as Austin picks up the pace, kissing me hungrily, and the fullness inside of me is so pleasurable I never want it to end. My nails tear across the skin of his back, fighting for a grip on reality.

"Turn around," Austin orders, pulling out. He runs his hand back through his damp hair and catches his breath as I flip over onto my stomach. He grabs my hips and drags them upward, forcing my spine to arch. "Don't you dare move. This is now my favorite view of all time."

He plunges back deep inside of me and I bite into the pillow to smother my groan. I try to push myself up onto my hands, but Austin is fucking me so hard from behind that I immediately collapse facedown back into the pillow.

"I've dreamed of this," he hisses. "You taking all of me."

"Austin," I gasp, my moans escaping through clenched teeth as he hits deep inside my core. It feels so good. *He* feels so good.

"It's okay, Gabby. You can handle it," he says, then stretches one hand around me to reach for my clit. "Both?"

I nod into the pillow, my entire body twitching with an overload of pleasure as he maintains a steady speed with both his cock and his hand. It's exactly what I need to come, and I fight through the sensitivity and the over-whelming urge to push his hand away, until suddenly the stars are aligning.

"Almost," I mumble, closing my eyes in concentration.

If he moves his hand a single millimeter out of place in this exact moment, I will fucking murder him. My body is hurling forward up this mountain at full speed, climbing, climbing, climbing . . . I nearly scream. Release bursts through my core and my entire body almost crum-bles into pieces. My hips collapse in defeat, but Austin grabs hold again and pulls me back into position.

"You're so cute when you come, Gabby," he says, pounding harder. "Now I'm right there with you."

I'm utterly breathless, my heart throbbing so hard I feel it in my ears. Austin gradually slows and his groans are heavenly as he rides out his own high, his cock pulsat-ing inside of me. The sound of our heavy panting settles over the room and an orgasmic daze ensues.

Austin slides out of me and I roll over to face him, push-ing my hair out of my eyes. There's something incredibly spellbinding about the sight of a man who's just fucked you; hair damp with sweat, cheeks flushed with color, eyes glazed over.

I'm about to become infatuated with Austin Pierce, and this is *not* what I had planned when I set out to find him.

"Stay right there," he says, holding out an arm to prevent me from sitting up. "You relax. I'll grab you a towel."

He disappears into the bathroom for a few minutes while I lie in bed, my head a buzz of thoughts and my pulses slowing to a rate that's *not* at risk of throwing me into cardiac arrest, and then he returns with a towel over his shoulder and two glasses of water in hand. He's wearing boxers again, sadly.

"Do you need anything else?" he asks, handing me both the towel and a glass, but I shake my head. He finds my discarded PJs on the floor and lays them next to me as he collapses back onto the bed by my side, staring up at the ceiling alongside me. "You feel incredible, Gabby. Better than I could have ever imagined."

"I'm not sure I want your friendship anymore," I say.

"I'm not sure I want your friendship either."

I turn my head to look at him and he turns his to look at me. Our grins stretch until we both break out into laughter.

"There's no way you're going back to the guest room," he says, flicking off the bedside light. He rolls onto his side facing me and plants a quick row of kisses along my bare shoulder. "Goodnight, Gabby."

I brush my fingers through his hair and say through the darkness, "Goodnight, Austin."

11

Austin isn't there when I wake up.

He's not in bed, in the shower, or making pancakes in the kitchen like I secretly hoped because I love nothing more than pancakes for breakfast on Sundays. I stick my head out into the backyard, but he's not out there either, and when I check out front, his car is still on the drive. I even knock on his office door, but no reply ever comes.

I won't deny that for a few seconds before I braved opening my eyes, there was an element of fear. What if I looked at Austin and immediately felt a shift in our dynamic? When I found that note we signed as kids in my jewelry box, my one and only goal was to find my best friend and earn his forgiveness, not find my way into his bed. Things are so easy with Austin, but what if they aren't anymore?

It worries me that he's not here. What if last night was a mistake and he's halfway to Virginia by now just to escape me? It wouldn't be the worst thing in the world.

He's left me his house and his car, and I think I could deal with that.

I raid through the kitchen cabinets for some flour, then grab some milk and eggs from the refrigerator. There's no way I'm missing out on my pancakes just because Austin has decided to go AWOL. I turn on the TV for some background noise and get a hot pan going, but just as I'm about to hit my stride, my phone vibrates on the countertop.

My immediate thought is that it's Austin trying to reach me, but as I grab my phone, I realize we don't even have each other's numbers, which is probably something that needs rectified. The text message displayed on my home screen is actually from my property manager.

The plumbing in my apartment is fixed.

And I should celebrate this information, but instead my stomach sinks.

Two days ago, I wanted nothing more than my property manager to get his ass in gear and send a plumber round to fix my ruined pipework, but now . . . I don't want to go back to my apartment. To Marvel movies on my own, to resounding silence, to reality. I want to stay here and have Austin take care of me.

As I set my phone back down and pour my pancake mixture into the pan, I chew the inside of my cheek, deep in thought. Austin was kind enough to let me stay here until my apartment was fixed as a favor. He would never have asked in the first place if I didn't *need* a place to stay, so I know, morally, I should head home to Durham by tonight. But selfishly, I want to stay here even just for *one* more day. Austin doesn't need to know yet that my apartment has running water again.

I'm a pro at flipping pancakes, yet I still feel insanely smug as I plate up the perfectly fluffy stack. I search the cabinets again for maple syrup, *and there is none.* Who the hell doesn't have maple syrup as a permanent staple in their cabinets? I resign myself to chocolate sauce and some strawberries as toppings, and just as I sit down on a bar stool at the center island and take my first bite, the front door swings open.

Austin steps inside the house, bedraggled and sweaty in gym shorts, and I release an "*Ohhhh.*"

He runs on Sunday mornings, *duh.* He literally told me that last night. Clearly, he was not hightailing it to Virginia, and I laugh at myself for being so worried for absolutely no reason.

Austin's breathing is labored as he shakes out his wet hair. He's also shirtless, his T-shirt tucked over the waistband of his shorts, and his tanned skin is so damp with sweat that I'd be happy to abandon my pancakes and have him take me right here, right now. He seems surprised to see me eating breakfast in his kitchen, because I don't quite get a smile out of him.

"Pancakes?" he asks, approaching.

I slide my plate down the center island to show off my expert pancake-making skills. "I can make you some if you'd like? I make a damn good pancake."

"No, thanks."

"And you have no maple syrup," I point out. "Are you okay? Mentally?"

Austin shrugs. "Too sticky."

Still no smile out of him. He disappears through the house and returns with a small towel, wiping down his face and drying off his hair. He won't make eye contact with me, either, and I realize very, very quickly that something is wrong. The atmosphere between us feels sour, and perhaps I was right after all. The dynamic has changed, but I will myself to fight through the tension.

"How far did you run?" I ask casually, biting into another forkful of pancake.

"Twelve."

"Miles?" I repeat in surprise. I can barely run down the block. "*Twelve miles?*"

Austin throws open the refrigerator. "That's what I just said."

Yeah, this is a problem. This isn't the usual morning-after awkwardness. Austin is being exceptionally cold toward me, and I have no idea why. I thought we were past this. After last night, we definitely should be.

"Are we really doing this?" I ask, setting my fork down with a *clink* and crossing my arms. Austin peers around the refrigerator door with a blank expression, like he has no clue what I'm talking about. "You're really going to fuck me then ignore me the next morning?"

Austin shuts the refrigerator, a bottle of Gatorade in hand. "I'm not ignoring you, Gabrielle."

And now he's calling me by my full name again! I angrily roll my eyes. "Let's not play this game. What's the problem, Austin?"

140

He pulls out the stool on the opposite side of the center island and sits down across from me, finally meeting my eyes. Very flatly, he says, "Last night is clouding my judgment."

"Okay. Explain," I demand.

Austin flicks off the cap of the Gatorade and stares down at the bottle in his hand, his jaw visibly clenching as he mulls over his words before he commits to saying them out loud. "I want to forgive you, but not because you give me the things I only ever dreamed about. I want to forgive you because you earned it, and you don't earn it by sneaking into my room."

"Yeah, fuck you." I scoot my chair back from the table and grab my plate.

Austin's eyes widen in surprise. "Excuse me?"

"Fuck you for believing I came to your room as some ploy to win you over."

"Then why did you?"

"*Because I wanted to,*" I hiss through gritted teeth. I don't even want these damn pancakes anymore, so I tip them straight into the trash can and throw my plate into the sink. "You're right. I *didn't* see you as anything more than my best friend when we were kids, but something feels different this time around. I now appreciate everything you ever did for me, and I'm really impressed by you, because you're kind of amazing. I wanted to apologize, and then I wanted my best friend back, and now I think I want even more. I'm as confused as you are, but trust me when I say that last night wasn't some sort of strategy."

Austin presses his hands to his face and smothers a groan. "Why did you have to screw me over when we were younger, Gabby? What if your love language is fucking me over, huh?"

"Well, it's not. It's words of affirmation."

Austin lifts his head. "Stop doing that."

"What?"

"Being cute," he says. "You weaken me so easily."

"That's kind of what I'm trying to achieve." I give him a wry smile and then sigh, releasing the tension from my shoulders.

Things are complex with Austin, and if we are to fix our relationship, then our lines of communication need to be solid. I move around the island and stand in front of him, cupping his jaw in my hand. His skin is warm and flushed.

"Look at me," I say gently, tilting his jaw up. His ocean blue eyes settle on mine. "No more cold shoulders. You're worried about something? Voice it to me and I will reassure you over and over again that I'm here because I want you in my life in whatever capacity is good with you. Friends . . . Friends with benefits . . . Dog co-parents . . ." I smile as Austin's gaze softens. "I care about you. There was never a time I didn't."

Austin places his hand over mine on his jaw and nuzzles his face harder into my palm. "I know you're a good person, Gabrielle," he murmurs. "You just weren't to me."

My heart aches, because there is nothing I can do to change that fact. The only thing I can do now is never make that same mistake again. I lean down and kiss the top of his head.

Against his hair, I mumble, "You sure I can't make you pancakes?"

"*Fine,*" he huffs. "Go fix me a big stack. Twelve miles' worth."

Now *this* is the Austin I was waiting for. I laugh as I pull back from him. I may have to make myself some more, too. In hindsight, throwing mine in the trash was an overreaction.

"Go shower while I get a batch going. You're all gross."

"Hey. It's eighty degrees outside," he points out.

"Felt like eighty degrees in your room last night."

"Felt like a hundred."

"Felt good."

"Felt really good." Austin smolders his eyes at me, his hand playing mindlessly with mine. "Interesting. You blush when I'm mean to you, and you blush when I . . ."

"Get. In. The. Shower," I order, pulling my hand free from his and crossing back to the stove. I get the heat going again, but it pales in comparison to the heat of my cheeks.

12

Austin drives my car across town to the auto repair shop all while complaining about my beloved Prius's pathetic acceleration, useless AC fans, and lack of parking sensors.

"If you can't use your own eyeballs to maneuver a car, then you're the one who has problems," I tell him. And conveniently leave out the fact I reversed into a barrier at the mall last month.

Austin looks over at me, and I don't know why, but the sight of him driving my busted-up car is even sexier than him driving his luxurious one. "Why'd you get rid of the car your parents got you, anyway? Did you need quick cash or something?"

"Yeah," I lie, because it's easier than saying: *I didn't deserve nice things.*

"You really confuse me," Austin says.

"What's confusing, exactly?"

"You. This life you're living," he explains, shaking his head as he drives. "The falling behind at Duke and dropping out after losing your dad? That, I get. The rest, I don't."

"The rest?"

"Working odd jobs. Renting a crap apartment. Driving this pile of rust. You don't seem to have any friends. Or ambitions. You're . . ." He bites his lip and sucks in a breath, letting the words die in his throat. "Forget it."

I'm not even offended. My gaze never leaves his face, not once. "Finish that sentence."

Austin scowls, reluctant to say it. His fingertips dance guiltily over my steering wheel and he at least looks me in the eye when he says, "You're a loser."

"Thanks."

"You're a loser by *choice*," he adds sharply. "You could be in school. You could have started your career by now. You have a trust fund that you claim you haven't spent, so you can absolutely afford to rent an apartment that won't flood and own a car that isn't billowing smoke in the rearview. You have a personality that could win so many friends, yet you only have me."

I ignore every sentence he just spoke except the last.
You only have me.

Up until last night, I wasn't sure I had even that.

"Maybe you're all I need," I say, smiling sweetly at him.

"Cute," Austin says, but it's not enough to distract him from his psychoanalysis of me, because he immediately adds, "Don't ignore everything I just said. What's up, loser? What's the deal?"

"There is no deal," I say with a shrug.

"From one former loser to another," Austin says, "it's not fun."

We pull up on the roadside next to the auto repair shop, and I wait patiently in the car as Austin heads inside to hunt down one of mechanics. I'm useless at these things. My father took care of *everything*, for all of us, all of the time. When it came to signing the lease for my apartment, Zach had to walk me through every step of the process, and he only knew because Dad had walked *him* through every step once. Dad took a lot of pride in taking care of his family. Mom never stressed over a single thing, and any issues Zach and I had growing up were resolved quietly and quickly.

I'm getting better at doing things for myself, though. I changed my flat tire on my own. I'm dealing with my property manager on my own. Fixing my mistakes on my own.

Austin returns, throwing open the passenger door and pressing his hands to the roof of the car as he bends down to look at me. "They're going to check it out, but we need to leave it here for a bit. You up for a walk?"

I stare up at him from the safety of my passenger seat, legs crossed lazily. "A walk?"

"That thing you do with your legs when you cover ground."

"When did you become such a smart-ass?"

"I'm only a smart-ass to you, loser," he says, then extends his hand to me. "We can't wait around for hours. My parents live not too far from here, and I haven't seen them in a couple of weeks, so I was thinking . . ."

147

"You want to take me to meet your parents? So soon?" I bat my eyelashes at him.

"You've already met them," Austin says, forcing his hand into mine and yanking me out of the car. He's so strong, it only takes one swift pull to have me on my feet in front of him. "Granted, it's been a while."

I tilt my chin up to look at him, so close to one another our chests almost touch. "You think they'll remember me?"

Austin's gaze dips to my lips. "You're pretty unforgettable, Gabby."

I have to look away, because I'm blushing *again*. He's right, I do enjoy when he's mean to me, but I think I love when he's sweet even more. And thanks to his conflicting feelings about me, I get both.

"How far is their house from here?"

"Fifteen minutes, maybe, but with your short legs to contend with . . . make it twenty."

"*Ugh*," I whine, stepping around him. It's hot as hell today, and this humidity is going to send my curls haywire. "When I show up at your parents' house looking like a sweaty rat with hair that's doubled in volume, it's on you."

Austin slams my car door shut and says, "But I like helping you work up a sweat."

I glower at him, but I'm smiling at the exact same time. Actually, I love it when he flirts even more than when he's mean and when he's sweet. Maybe I just love everything about him. "How about you don't turn me on when we're en route to your parents'? That'd be really great, thanks. Which way?"

"This way," Austin says, heading left down the street as I fall into step by his side. "And I think . . . Nope. Can't follow that instruction. By the time we get home later, I want you begging for me."

I immediately stop walking. "Oh my God. Who *are* you?"

Austin also stops, turning around to look back at me with an incredibly sexy smirk. "I'm very clear with my words these days. If I want something, I'll make that known. Even plead for it." He cocks his head to one side in amusement at the flash of heat I'm suffering through. "Aw. Are you shy, Gabby?"

"No, I'm just . . ." I splutter, but I don't even know *what* I am right now. Turned on, for starters, but nowhere near confident enough to flirt back. I flirt via suggestive innuendos. Austin flirts very literally.

"Just what?" he presses.

"Just getting used to *this*," I say, gesturing between us. I can't believe this is my Austin saying these things to me. We used to hunt out lizards together as kids, for God's sake.

"And are you complaining?"

"Definitely not complaining."

He grins. "Then shut the fuck up and come here."

I move toward him, closing that gap I created. That smirk is so gorgeous, it makes me feel dizzy, like the ground under my feet is unstable as I bring myself to stand in front of him. I think I'm severely crushing on Austin Pierce in a way I have never crushed on anyone before. There goes my racing heartbeat again, and the goosebumps, and the nervous tremor in my hands . . .

Austin cups my cheeks and tilts my face up. "I'm sorry," he whispers, grazing his lips over mine, "for this morning."

"I'm sorry," I whisper back, "for everything."

"You better be." He presses his lips to mine, sinking us both into a kiss that's so soft and simple, just his mouth and mine for a moment in time I want to memorize forever. Austin draws back, his smile reaching his eyes. "Now be a good girl today, and you'll get more later."

I throw my head back to the sky, Austin's hands still cupped around my jaw. "Lord, please. Take this man away from me."

Austin laughs and angles my head back down again so he can plant one final peck on my lips. "C'mon, loser. Start walking."

And the walk isn't *that* bad. We stick to the shade beneath buildings and trees as the industrial park gradually eases into residential neighborhoods, and the conversation with Austin is just *so* easy that time passes quickly. Around him, I don't need to think before I speak. There are never any unnatural pauses in our chat. We bounce off one another, and I haven't had this much social interaction with another human being in *months*. It's been pretty damaging to my mental health to keep to myself as much as I have been the past few years, and being around Austin is lifting my mood an immeasurable amount. We even exchange our phone numbers, finally.

And as we approach Austin's parents' house, I'm too happy to even be nervous.

It's a lovely neighborhood. Not a private gated community with extravagant homes like Austin's neighborhood, but a very down-to-earth street with cute Colonial homes and kids' bikes left out in front yards. It's a huge step up from the projects they once lived in and I'm so glad they found their way out of there.

"This is really nice," I say as we step up onto the porch. There's even a car on the drive, and Austin grew up without his parents ever owning one. It seems things have really turned around for all of them, and I can't help but wonder if that's thanks to Austin taking care of them. "Did you help them out?"

"No," Austin says. "They moved pretty soon after I left for college. Dad's still a trucker and on the road half the time, but Mom finished her studying and climbed from custodian to nurse to now practitioner. And my grandmother passed, so there was a little inheritance there, too."

"Oh," I say. "I'm sorry about your grandmother, though I'm glad things got better for all of you."

"I won't lie. With their schedules, I had no idea either of them would even be home."

I narrow my eyes. "You made me walk twenty minutes on the off chance they would be?"

"Sun's out, Gabby," he says, smiling. "Appreciate it." He raps his knuckles against the door before pushing it open, calling out, "Mom? Dad? It's me."

I follow him through the door, nervously toying with the ends of my extra curly hair. Thanks, humidity.

Austin's right—I've met his parents before, many times back when we were kids, but I haven't interacted with them at all since my friendship with Austin blew up. Whether or not he ever told them the full extent of how I treated him, I have no clue, but I'm walking in here braced for hostility.

No one calls back to him. No one comes running through the house.

Austin furrows his eyebrows as he advances through the house with me close on his heels, and I note that it feels exactly how their old apartment in the projects used to feel. Honestly, kind of a cluttered mess. Belongings scattered everywhere, photo frames stuck haphazardly on the walls, the kitchen countertops covered in mail and cables. The complete opposite of the perfectly manicured home I grew up in, so spotless it was like no one lived there at all. Austin may have grown up in a cramped apartment, but at least it breathed life.

"Oh, they're out back," he says, pulling open the door to the yard.

Outside, his parents relax in lawn chairs, coffee mugs in hand, and I think of my mom sitting in the yard all by herself, drinking wine and reading her books, when once upon a time she would sit outside laughing with Dad.

"Austin!" Caroline exclaims, sitting upright from the lawn chair in surprise. "I didn't know you were stopping by."

"And by some miracle, you've caught us both for once!" Mike adds, and I'm impressed that I still remember both their names. He dumps his mug on the small glass table—*triggered*—between the lawn chairs and gets to his feet. "How's it going, bud? Who's this?"

Mike looks at me curiously, and I feel myself wishing to shrink away behind the safety of Austin's tall figure, except Austin takes a giant step to the side to fully reveal me, and I'm left exposed with no place to hide.

"You guys remember Gabrielle," Austin says, but there's the slightest hint of nerves in his voice. Maybe he has no idea what to expect, either. "From across the street?"

"Oh," Mike says flatly, and the polite smile on his face immediately rearranges itself into a frown. He exchanges a look with Caroline, who scowls in response before casting a scornful look in my direction.

Yep, they hate me, which is to be expected and is no less than I deserve, but which now makes this very awkward.

"Hi," I say sheepishly, but neither of them even replies. It's absolutely mortifying, being ignored with such contempt. Austin bringing me here was a terrible idea.

Caroline stands from her lawn chair and treads warily toward us. She places a hand on Austin's arm and studies him thoroughly. "Honey, what's going on? Why is she here?"

"We're working some things out," Austin says, checking in on me out of the corner of his eye. Perhaps he's regretting this idea, too. Maybe he's regretting *everything,* but I don't want him to regret giving me a second chance. I don't want his parents putting doubt in his mind, so despite the absolute look of *death* his father is currently giving me, I bravely shuffle closer to him.

"Now why the hell would you be so stupid as to get in contact with her again?" Mike asks, shaking his head in disapproval as though I'm not standing right here in front of him. Mike's a rather intimidating man—tall just like Austin, but built like a wrestler, with broad shoulders and muscular arms covered in decades-old tattoos that have seen better times.

Frustration etches itself into every crevice of Austin's face, and he rubs his hand over his jaw as he heaves a sigh. "I didn't. She came to me."

Caroline scoffs and sets her fierce eyes on me. They're ocean blue, just like Austin's. "Oh, I see. He's good enough to be in your life now, is he? Has enough money to be worthy?"

"*Mom*," Austin warns, and he actually takes a defensive step in front of me, which is really fucking appreciated because I think I might cry. "Gabby, ignore them."

"Ignore us!" Mike repeats with an indignant laugh. "Isn't it convenient she comes crawling back *now*? C'mon, Austin. Don't be a goddamn idiot."

"Listen to your dad," Caroline says, reaching out to touch Austin's arm again, but he immediately shakes her off. "I'm not comfortable having her in this house, Austin. Please, I'd like you to leave, Gabrielle."

"Okay," Austin says angrily. "I'll come see you guys another time then."

"No, not you," Mike says.

"Yes, me too. If you're both going to talk like this *right in front of her*, then we're both leaving," he explains, and Caroline's mouth parts in shock. "You have opinions?

Then you share them with me later. In private. You don't act like this."

Caroline seems to pale as she places her hand over her heart, in a gesture of rejection. "We're only looking out for you."

"I can look out for myself," Austin snaps, and I flinch as the guilt pumps through my veins. I don't want to be the reason he argues with his parents. "She found me to apologize, and it's up to me whether or not I accept it."

"Austin, it's okay," I say, finding my pathetic little voice. "I'll leave."

"Thank you," Mike says sharply, gesturing to the back gate.

As I take a step forward, Austin catches my elbow. "No, Gabby."

"*Austin,*" Caroline pleads, but since she can't seem to get through to him, she turns her focus on me instead. "Gabrielle, you must understand, surely?"

"I do," I say, nodding meekly, "but I regret everything I ever did. If I could change the past, I would. We were just kids, Caroline, and I know what I did was awful, but we're adults now. We can move on, can't we?"

Caroline and Mike look at one another with an incredulous air of astonishment, and something strange settles in the pit of my stomach. Am I just being ignorant? I know I was the worst person in the world to Austin, and of course his parents are going to fiercely have his back no matter what, but we were *teenagers.* I don't expect them to *like* me, but I definitely wasn't prepared for such outright hatred. We're twenty-four now. High school was forever ago, yet it may as well be yesterday with the way they're treating me. Their grudge may even be stronger than Austin's.

"Just kids . . ." Mike mutters, his intense eyes piercing straight through me. "You think that makes it okay, do you? Your father certainly didn't think so, otherwise he wouldn't have—"

"*Dad,*" Austin hisses, abruptly cutting Mike off.

Caroline widens her eyes at Mike, conveying the very clear and concise order not to say another word, and the stifling atmosphere around the four us plunges into something even worse—stone cold silence.

I turn to Austin, but he's squeezing his eyes shut and pinching the bridge of his nose in exasperation. Mike's hardened exterior suddenly seems flushed with guilt, and Caroline is the only one who makes eye contact with me. My entire body feels as though it's turned to ice, and I stand there stiff and vulnerable, my thoughts racing to make *any* kind of sense of Mike's words.

I swallow hard and stare at Mike. My voice so quiet I'm surprised anyone even hears me, I ask, "What do you mean?" But Mike can't look back at me. He scratches his neck and keeps his mouth sealed shut. "Austin," I whisper, twisting to face him instead. I move a step closer and clutch his wrist, staring pleadingly up at him. "What does he mean?"

"Nothing, Gabby," Austin murmurs, but his words are the least convincing thing in the world. His expression is contrite, downcast, as his eyes lock on my hand around his wrist.

"My father wouldn't have *what*?" I prompt, harder now as the blood rushes to my ears. There's a sickening sense of panic and fear, like they all know something I don't, and I can't bear to be the only one left in the dark. "If you don't look at me right now, Austin, and start talking—"

Austin lifts his gaze. "I can't."

"Wow." I recoil from him, because how dare they speak of my father and then not tell me what the fuck they're talking about? They didn't even *know* my dad, and the confusion makes me feel faint. "Caroline?" I try, one last time.

But Caroline only shakes her head slowly, and even *she* looks guilty. "We can't, Gabrielle."

There is no way I can stay here a second longer, not with their refusal to offer me an explanation. Caroline and Mike? Whatever. They hate me and owe me nothing. Austin, however? It hurts that he won't tell me.

I clench my jaw and flash him a seething look of betrayal, right before I turn and walk away. Furiously, I kick open the gate and storm out onto the street.

"Gabby!" Austin yells. He barges through the gate after me, racing down the drive.

"We're supposed to be building trust," I spit at him, pausing only for a second to let him catch up. "You guys are talking about my dad. How can you not be honest with me about that?"

Austin pushes his hands back through his hair and groans in frustration. "I can't tell you," he says, "*because* of your dad."

I scrunch up my face, even more perplexed than I was half a second ago. "What? That makes no sense."

"Can you please forget my dad said anything?"

"*Forget your dad said anything?*" I repeat. Now I'm at the point where I'm that pissed, I could laugh. "I'm walking back to the shop to get my car, and then I'm going home to my apartment because my plumbing is fixed. It's up to you whether or not you tell me the truth between now and then. And if you don't . . ." I release a shaky breath. "Then yeah, I don't think we can be friends again, after all."

Austin's face falls, and I can't bear to look at his sad blue eyes.

I set off down the street and don't look back, not even once.

13

I'm not sure how long I'm prepared to wait it out on Austin's drive outside his house.

Turns out my car wasn't on its deathbed, after all. It just had some dirty-ass air filters that needed replaced, and once I settled my debts with the mechanic, I reclaimed my keys and drove back to Austin's place. I wanted to quickly gather my stuff and head home to my apartment, but my plan was halted by Austin's locked front door.

And I know—I could totally just ditch my stuff, because I don't have *that* much with me in the first place, but I'll be damned if I leave behind my favorite hair mask. It's expensive and just about the only moisturizer that keeps the frizz out of my curls, so no way. I'll face Austin one final time if it means retrieving my hair products.

So I wait in my car outside, my feet up on dash and the AC blasting pitifully. It's a risky game to play, because Austin could be hours at his parents' house while they convince him of a thousand more reasons why I'm a bad idea.

However, my phone vibrates after an hour.

Austin: *Where are you?*

Me: *Outside your house because you're holding my stuff hostage.*

Austin: *I'm at the office. Come here.*

Me: *You have to say please.*

Austin: *Please, Gabrielle.*

Austin: **Gabby.*

With a disgruntled sigh, I swing my legs down from the center console and reverse out of the drive. I'm sick of waiting, so I'll drive downtown to the office even if it's only for the purpose of tackling him to the ground and wrestling his keys out of his pocket myself. When it comes to my hair mask, I take no prisoners.

I head down to the office and this time, I don't make the same mistake of parking in the fire lane. It's Sunday and the office is closed on the weekends, so I park up in the staff parking lot behind the building instead. Only Austin's car is here, and he's inside the office waiting for me, and that makes me really fucking nervous for a reason I can't quite put my finger on.

I make my way around the front and head inside.

The office feels eerie when it's closed. There's no Helen behind the front desk to greet me, no quiet music playing from an invisible speaker. Only a very sad-looking cactus named Carly Buck. I hope Helen will remember to water it.

All of the lights are off, so sunlight streams in through the windows and casts shadows through the dim building as I head down the hall. The door to Austin's office is shut, so I warily open it.

He's staring out of the window, his back to me, arms folded. He doesn't even flinch at my arrival and it takes me only a split second to read the room—the atmosphere is tense; Austin's body tenser.

"Why does this feel so cryptic?" I ask, but my question doesn't lighten the mood.

"I needed space to think," he says quietly, "and I do most of my thinking in here."

"Unless you're going to tell me why my dad became the topic of conversation back at your parents' house, then please just give me your keys," I demand, holding out my hand and expecting him to turn to face me, but he doesn't. "I'm not playing this weird game. We're either friends or we aren't, and if you can't be honest with me, then I'm sorry, but I'm out. So keys, *now*, please. I'll get my stuff and be gone."

"Just sit down, Gabby," Austin says.

"No."

"*Sit. Down*," he instructs more firmly, and I roll my eyes behind his back.

Reluctantly, I pull out the chair opposite his desk and sink down into it, the same way I did two days ago when I naively believed he didn't recognize me. I don't get too comfortable, though. I sit on the very edge of the chair, irritatedly tapping my foot.

Austin finally moves from his frozen stance, but each tiny movement seems to take a lifetime. He walks around his desk, picks up the toy car from the shelves on the wall that I noticed the other day, and sets it down on his desk in front of me.

He asks, very solemnly, "Gabby, does this look familiar?"

I stare at the green Porsche 911, then look up at Austin in confusion as he towers over me, feeling like I'm under scrutiny and this is a test I'm required to pass. "It's a toy model version of your car."

"Yes, but why else does it look familiar?"

"My dad had a car like that, too."

Austin presses his lips together. He sits on the edge of his desk by my side, his expression twisting with a peculiar emotion, and picks up the toy car again. He stares down as he quietly fiddles with it in his lap. Finally, he says, "Your dad is my biggest inspiration and my best influence."

It's just about the last thing I would have ever expected him to say. Austin never even knew my father. "What?"

"Every summer when you and Zach went off to camp, I was lost without you. And so was your dad." Austin glances up and meets my eyes, and I realize that emotion I'm seeing is fear. "He was never like your mom. Always spoke to me in the street from the day we moved in, and those summers when you were gone, I think he was glad to have me around. Took my dad and me fishing. Slipped me what he thought was just spare change, but what felt like a million bucks to me. And that Porsche of his? Exactly like this one?" Austin rolls the toy car along the desk. "He took me for long drives along the coast and gave me exactly the kind of advice and guidance I needed when I was a kid with no hope."

162

A very abrupt wave of grief crashes over me, catching me off guard. I'm beyond the stage of feeling winded every time my dad's memory is brought to life, yet when Austin speaks of him, it rips me open at my core.

Because Austin's words remind me of the one thing I always knew about my father: he was a good man with a pure heart and a lot of love to give, irrespective of how successful he was. He was humble and treated every person he met with the same amount of respect and dignity. He attended charity fundraisers, volunteered in our community, and despite his very successful career in finance, always treated his family as his biggest achievement in life. *Of course* he would have looked out for the kid across the street.

"I didn't know that," I say, my voice so dry it cracks.

"Your dad is the reason I chose to major in accounting. When he talked about his career and how he climbed the ladder, I wanted to be just like him. I wanted to have a house like yours. A Porsche of my own one day. So I keep this around," Austin murmurs, tapping the toy car, "because those conversations out in his car inspired me the most."

"He really was the best," I say, managing a smile.

I can't believe I didn't know my dad and Austin spent time together like that, but I don't even care that I'm only just finding it out. Austin knew my father as more than just some neighbor across the street, and that fills me with a sense of joy that one more person in this world has fond memories of him.

Austin interlocks his hands in his lap. "I was at his funeral."

"You were?"

"I hid way in the back, because I couldn't bear to see you," he explains. "But I just want you to know I was there, because I will never forget all of the things he did for me. All of the things he said." For the first time since I walked into this room, Austin's frown reveals the hint of a smile, the fondness of his memories of my dad breaking through. "Who do you think taught me how the stock market worked when I was sixteen? I used to fall asleep thinking about the Global All Cap."

"This is good, Austin. I love that you knew my dad," I reassure him, scooting my chair closer to him and placing my hand over his in his lap. "Why are you so nervous telling me this? Did you think I'd be angry that you spent time with him? Because I'm not. It makes me really happy, actually."

"Because this isn't what I need to tell you," Austin says, his eyes darkening. "This is only the prelude to the truth."

The comfort that's been building inside of me immediately vanishes, replaced instead by a knot in my stomach. I don't like this anymore. "The . . . The truth?"

Austin pushes off the desk and turns his back on me again. He runs a hand through his hair in exasperation and I can tell he's fighting a battle with himself. "Morally, I can't tell you," he admits, "but you've just walked back into my life after seven years and I don't think we could ever be friends again, not really, unless I tell you this."

My heart hammers. "Austin . . ."

He twists around and somehow his expression is even more tormented than before. "I'm breaking your dad's wishes by saying this, but . . ."

"Please just say it."

Austin briefly squeezes his eyes shut. He takes a deep breath and says, "There was a secret trust left in his will. For me."

I don't respond. This information is so out of left field, I can't even comprehend it at first. Dad left money for Austin? That just doesn't compute with me, because Zach sent me his copy of Dad's will, which I read through, and Austin Pierce's name was absolutely not in there.

"But I've read it, and there wasn't—"

"*Secret* trust, Gabby," Austin repeats. "It went via a trustee with instructions from your dad to be passed on to me. I don't think he wanted you guys or your mom to know, so I was never supposed to say anything. Are you angry?"

I blink at him, still stunned. I feel numbed by these new facts, but definitely not angry. "Why would I be angry?"

Austin furrows his eyebrows, like the answer is obvious. "Because the money left for me should really have been yours and Zach's? And maybe you'd be angry at your dad for that? I don't want you to feel like I stole something from you."

"I don't care about money, Austin," I say, shaking my head. I feel weird and I try to dial in on what exactly it is I'm feeling. I don't feel betrayed by Dad, because I really don't care how he chose to divide his assets, but am more hurt that he felt the need to keep it a secret.

The only explanation I land on is that Mom would have never stood for it. She would have contested it for all she's worth if she knew where that money really went.

"You thought there was something unethical about me, for how quickly I've built this company," Austin says, "but it was all thanks to your father. It would have taken me a decade to reach the point of being able to funnel cash into creating my own firm, but he gave me a head start that I will forever be grateful for." He sits back down on the edge of his desk and drags my chair forward so that I'm positioned between his legs. He reaches for my hand, twisting his fingers around mine and locking our hands tight. "I don't want your dad gifting me that money to taint your memory of him, and I don't want you to resent me for receiving it. But at least when you leave today, you know I've told you the truth. We still have trust, okay?"

I nod, but my mind is spinning at a million miles an hour. "So, this is what your parents were referring to? The money my dad left?"

"My parents think—and, fuck, Gabby, I promise I don't believe this too, but . . ." He bites his lower lip and flinches before confessing, "My parents are convinced he left me that money as an apology."

"An apology . . . because of me?" I whisper.

Austin doesn't even need to confirm it. The flicker of remorse in his eyes is enough.

And oh, how that stings. The world seems to collapse around me, because what if that's true? What if Dad knew how badly I'd treated Austin and was trying to apologize for his daughter's mistakes? If he did know, he certainly never addressed it with me. What if the embarrassment was too much? What if he was quietly disappointed? Dad always fixed things silently in the background, and maybe this was another one of those times.

"Hey," Austin says, squeezing my hand harder to pull my attention back from my ghostly stare at the wall. "I think he just had a soft spot for me. The kid with nothing across the street who he'd mentored for years. He just wanted to make sure things turned around for me, that's all."

I glance up at Austin, tears burning the corners of my eyes. "Do you think he knew how awful I was to you?"

"*No,*" Austin says firmly, leaning forward and cupping my face in both hands, like I need reassurance physically shaken into me. "How could he? I certainly never told him, because I was way too obsessed with you to ever risk losing you." He draws his face level with mine, hands still on my jaw, eyes holding my gaze. "This is why I know you're a good person, Gabrielle, because you were raised by one."

My heart swells and I can't fight the overwhelming mix of emotions for a second longer. I break into an ugly sob as my body heaves, and I fall forward into Austin's chest, smothering my face into his T-shirt.

Gently, he places his hands on my neck and guides my head up to look at him. "I only like it when you cry over shelter dogs," he says, brushing away my tears from my cheeks. "This, I don't like. Why are we crying, Gabby? Everything's okay."

My lips continue to quiver as I blubber, "Because I don't deserve it when you're this nice to me, and I don't know how much my dad left you, but I wish it was more, and I wanted to go home to my apartment, but I don't think I do anymore. I want to stay right here with you."

Austin touches my lower lip with the pad of his thumb, gaze memorizing the curves of my mouth. "Then stay," he whispers.

I stare up into his ocean blue eyes, pulled in by their protective warmth, and it suddenly all clicks why I've felt so drawn to him the past few days. Austin feels like a safety blanket, exactly how my father felt. He held my hand in the hospital, took care of my parking boot, made sure I had enough clothes for the weekend, and helped me get my car fixed. All things I can absolutely do myself, and I've had no choice but to pull myself together the past few years and grow up, but sometimes it feels nice to have someone else looking out for you. I've missed how that feels. I think I may even have forgotten.

Shakily, I stand from the chair. With Austin perched on the edge of his desk, our heights are level, and he clasps my waist and tucks me neatly between his legs. Our gazes never shift, our eyes locked. And I can't wait a single second more.

Slipping my hand around the nape of his neck, I tug him close and press my lips hard against his. My cheeks are still stained with tears, but all I want is his mouth against mine, and that I get. Austin's hands dig wildly into my hair as he kisses me fiercely, the moment fueled by heightened emotions and an overwhelming desire to share them together.

I push my body against Austin's, raking my hands down his chest and undoing the button of his jeans as his cock bulges against the zipper. "I want you," I whisper. "All of you."

Austin groans against my mouth. "You have no idea how much I want *you*, but I don't have—"

"Are you clean?" I cut in, biting the soft skin of his neck as I slip my hand beneath the waistband of his boxers and take him in my hand.

"Ah, fuck, Gabby," Austin mumbles, tilting his head to the side and allowing me better access to his neck. His hands grip the edge of the desk, his eyes closed. "Of course I am."

"Me too."

Austin reaches for my wrist, forcing me to pause as he opens his eyes to look at me. "You're emotional. Think about it first, please. I want you to be comfortable with this."

I trail my lips along his jaw until I come to a stop at the corner of his mouth. "I want to feel *you*."

"Fuck, okay."

In one swift movement, Austin drops his hands to my ass and lifts me straight off my feet. He spins us around and sets me down on the desk now instead as my legs instinctively wrap around his waist. The craving fully creeps in now, all boundaries accounted for, and Austin's kiss deepens as his hands wander more eagerly. He rakes my top up over my head, then his, our bare chests pressed together as he pulls my shorts down my legs so that I'm only left in my underwear, propped up on the edge of this huge desk.

As Austin slips a finger inside of me, I press my face into his shoulder and breathe in his scent, body relaxing in pleasure.

"You're soaking, Gabby," he hisses against my ear, the seductive heat in his voice sending me spiraling. His fingers circle my clit until my legs start to uncontrollably flinch in response, and then he reaches for my hair and gently pulls my head back from his shoulder. "See for yourself."

I part my lips as Austin slides his fingers into my mouth, and I suck on them, tasting myself on him, confidently holding his gaze as his eyes roll back in his head in arousal.

"Now I really do need to fuck you," he snaps, pressing his hand to the soft skin between my breasts and pushing me back until I'm lying flat on the desk. He keeps his hand on my chest, holding me down as he drags me a touch closer to the edge of the desk.

He frees himself from his jeans, but doesn't bother stepping out of them, and it's so irresistible, a man so desperate to take me, he can't even take the time to fully undress. With his free hand, he moves my panties to the side and positions himself between my legs.

"You're so sexy like that," I tell him, trying to sit up for a better view, but he only pushes me back down into the desk.

"Don't move," he instructs.

A shiver of anticipation runs down my spine. Austin runs the head of his cock over my clit, teasing, then eases himself inside of me. I gasp, throwing my head back and arching my spine in response to the raw fullness of his cock. He feels just as incredible as he did last night, and I'm not sure I'll ever get enough of how good he makes me feel.

"Please stay," Austin pleads as his first few strokes are gentle, slow. "Please stay so I can feel you like this every fucking day. You are . . . You're heaven, Gabby."

If I didn't already know my love language was words of affirmation, then I'd definitely know now. I could listen to Austin speak to me like this all day. Not only does his body make me feel good, his words do too.

Austin's hips move faster as his pleasure mounts and he chases after his high. His thrusts become so wild, the computer on the desk rattles and my delicate little moans may as well be the soundtrack. He remembers my instructions from last night, and balances his strokes with working his fingers over my clit, until very quickly I'm squirming out of control on the desk.

"Almost there?" Austin asks, and it's a good job he's still holding me down, otherwise I think I may have rolled off the edge of this desk by now.

"Yes. Don't stop," I beg.

"Good, 'cause I'm barely hanging on," he says breathlessly with the tiniest of laughs. "You make me come so fast, Gabby. I'm fighting for my life over here."

I squeeze my eyes shut and concentrate, dialing in on the pleasure. It's building and building, and it feels so damn good, it's almost unbearable. A gasp rips from my throat as I clench my thighs tight around Austin, shockwaves of euphoria spreading through my body, all the way to my toes.

"I like it when you come around my cock," Austin says, and he grabs my hips and finishes almost perfectly in sync with me. He groans through clenched teeth, sweat dampening his temples, his body twitching. As he pulls out, he exhales a long breath of air and reaches for my hands, helping me to sit upright on the desk. "Jesus. I think I'm more obsessed with you than I was when I was sixteen."

I laugh, even though my legs are still trembling and my breathing is chaotic. I run my hands through Austin's hair, pushing it back off his damp forehead. "This definitely wouldn't have felt this good at sixteen."

Austin's gaze is a hazy smolder. "What? Four seconds wouldn't have been enough?"

I laugh and plant a kiss on his lips, then glance around the office a little helplessly. "I don't suppose you have a towel in here?"

"No, but the washroom is on the other side of the lobby," he tells me. "You can clean up in there."

"I feel like Bambi," I say as I slide off the edge of the desk and onto my feet. You know the orgasm was good when your legs feel this unsteady afterward. "This might be one funny-looking dash across the office building. You don't have cameras in the lobby, do you?"

Austin shakes his head, sporting a sheepish smile as he zips up his jeans. "No cameras yet. I'm too cheap for that."

"Okay, be right back."

In my underwear, I sneak out of Austin's office with my arms tucked protectively around myself and dash down the hall toward the lobby.

And for fuck's sake!

What is it with Helen, the receptionist, cornering me at this junction?

I scream. Helen screams. Austin yells, "Gabby?"

Helen stares at me wide-eyed in shock while I stand frozen in front of her like a semi-naked deer caught in headlights. I know I said I felt like Bambi, but this just takes the cake . . . Austin approaches from behind and immediately steps in front of me, concealing whatever modesty I still have at this point. At least he has his jeans on, though no shirt.

"Helen, what are you doing here?"

And poor Helen looks thoroughly mortified, her cheeks flaring red as she backs away from us with her hands up. "I left my hand cream here on Friday, just wanted to come by and grab it, but you know what? It's all good! Who needs smooth palms, anyway?" She gestures sealing her lips shut like a zipper and as she flails out of the building, she calls back, "I didn't see anything. Promise!"

Austin looks at me, and we both burst into laughter that's so pure and genuine, I decide it's a sound I want to listen to forever.

14

I drive home to Durham that night, even though it's the last thing on earth I want to do.

The past few days with Austin, it's felt like I've been wrapped up in a safe little bubble, but that's not reality. The reality is that I have no job, no degree, no life plan. And as much as I would love to be Austin's houseguest for longer, there's a renewed sense of determination rising through me and I know the right thing to do is go home, just for a little while. I need to get a grip on my life before I even consider bringing Austin into this mess.

Besides, he's a fully functioning adult with a nine-to-five. He has to work and can't just spend his days entertaining me, so I head home with the promise that we will call every day. Austin *wants* me to figure things out, and so does my brother, and of course my mom. The only one stopping me now is myself.

So, I make that decision to return home to my lonely apartment.

And the pipes have indeed been welded back together, and the water is running again, and although it's a relatively crap apartment in an even crapper complex, it always felt like my own little home. But when I'm trying to get some sleep that night, I stare at the ceiling and realize this isn't home at all.

I sit up, flick on a light, and formulate a plan of action.

*

The next afternoon, I push through the door of Buck's Tavern. The usual scent of stale cigarette smoke seems a thousand times worse after being gone for a few days and I wrinkle my nose as I cross through the bar. Even though the customers here tend to be the lost citizens of society, it's too early on a Monday for even them to be here yet. Carly stacks glasses behind the bar and Buck sets his hands on his hips as he stares me down.

"Now what are you doing here, Gabrielle?" he asks as I approach, and I think it's pretty damn obvious why I'm here. Why else, other than to bat my eyelashes and beg for my job back?

"Buck, I want to apologize," I say, and he eyeballs me suspiciously, because not once in my entire life have I apologized to Buck for anything, and I have done a hell of a lot of things in this bar that required apologies. "You were right. I had an attitude and a superiority complex, but I *did* do my job well, and I really would like a second chance. No more sass from me, I promise."

Buck scrutinizes my expression. The sincerity in my eyes must be clear, because he sighs and throws me an apron from behind the bar. "Can you work right now? The girl I hired to replace you was a no-show last night, so I have no hope she'll turn up today."

"See? You can't run this place without me, Buck," I joke with a grin, and he rolls his eyes, but secretly I think he's relieved I've walked back through the door.

I tie the apron around my waist and join Carly behind the bar. She seems happy to see me, which makes me feel guilty for never giving her the time of day. We've worked alongside each other for a while now, yet we've never had a real conversation other than tossing a coin to determine which one of us will be on bathroom duty.

"Hey, Carly."

"I'm glad you're back," she says. "How was your weekend?"

I laugh and reply, "I'm gonna need an hour to fill you in. Would you hate me if I said I named a cactus in a Wilmington office after you?"

*

Later that week, I finally pluck up the courage to meet with the Time Away Office at Duke University.

After withdrawing three years ago, I'm a bundle of nerves as I make my way across the campus, but I have been avoiding this for far too long and the time has come to discuss my return. *One more year.* One more year of studying and I'll have my degree. The bulk of the work is done, and I know I can do this. I can absolutely see this through until the end.

In all honesty, I've felt mentally strong enough to return to school for the past year, if not two, but there is something about resuming my normal life that triggers a strange sense of guilt inside of me, like moving on from losing Dad means forgetting him. The rational part of my brain knows this is not true. Dad would want me to finish school, and although my grief will always be there, I need to live my life around it.

The advisor I speak with is lovely. Reassuring of my worries and comforting of my panic. My transcripts are all in order and my grades when I dropped out were strong enough that there'll be no issues picking up my classes exactly where I left off. The only major setback is that I've missed the deadline for the upcoming fall semester, so the soonest I can now return is next year, which kills my momentum slightly. We file the return request, anyway. I will figure out how to spend the rest of the year later.

As I'm crossing the campus to head back to my car, I make a call.

"Hello, Gabrielle," answers my mother. "Is something wrong?"

And that's a testament to our relationship, that I call her so rarely, she immediately assumes there must be a problem. I should probably put some work in there, too.

"Hi," I say. "I just wanted to call and let you know I've started the return process at Duke."

"Oh, Gabrielle!" Mom exclaims, and I can hear the sheer relief in the way she says my name. "This is great news. Are you starting this semester?"

"I've missed the deadline, so it'll be the spring semester instead now."

"That's okay, honey. What are you going to do until then?"

"I'll keep busy," I say, leaving out the finer details. I'm not sure how much approval my plan of slinging drinks at Buck's for another six months will get from her. There's also the recent development with Austin which I'm sure will keep me busy too, what with driving back and forth to Wilmington to visit him, but it's definitely way too soon to tell her *that*. If my friendship with him was unbearable back in the day, I can only imagine what she'd have to say now.

For the time being, my lips are sealed.

*

As I enter my second week of being back in Durham, I've developed a terrible, terrible habit of obsessively checking on the Saving Paws Animal Rescue's website to see if any of the dogs Austin and I visited have been adopted. Teddy, the Labrador we took outside into the agility field, has now been there for nine hundred and forty-three days. The thought of that number reaching one thousand makes me want to cry.

"Carly," I say, setting my phone down on the bar, "I don't suppose you'd like to adopt a Labrador named Teddy?"

179

Carly flatly answers, "No."

"Buck, you look like a man who could use a companion," I say, smiling sweetly down the bar at Buck, who does not, in fact, look like a man who could use a companion. "Oh, oh, oh! We could have a bar dog!"

"And who will look after this bar dog when the bar is closed, hmm?" Buck challenges.

"Me."

"Your lease agreement allows for dogs?"

My shoulders sink, because my lease strictly states no pets allowed, which is neither here nor there, because there's no way I can adopt a dog, anyway. I'm going back to school soon. It wouldn't work. But Teddy . . .

"I'll be back in five," I say, then grab my phone and disappear into the back.

An idea has been forming in my head for days now, and I can't bear the thought of Teddy never finding a home for a second longer. The shelter's website needs a serious overhaul, because the photos of the dogs are, honestly, awful. The shelter runs entirely on donations, so I know their budget is tiny and they're doing the best they can with such limited resources, but I have a trust fund gathering dust and a charitable legacy I've decided I want to continue.

I sit on the stoop at the back door and press my phone to my ear as the sun beats hot against my face. My knees bounce anxiously as I listen to the dial tone.

"Saving Paws Animal Rescue," a voice eventually answers. "Fiona speaking. How can I help?"

"Hi, Fiona!" I say, relieved it's the exact person I wish to talk to. "My name's Gabrielle. I came by a few weeks ago with Austin Pierce, if you remember me?"

"Oh, yes, hello! How are you doing?"

"Good, thanks." After a deep breath, I explain. "I've been thinking about the dogs, and it'd really make me happy if we found them their forever homes. Especially Teddy. Can I run an idea by you? It'll be worth your time, I promise."

*

Then that weekend, as I'm elbow-deep in the sink washing glasses, Austin Pierce walks into the bar.

15

"Austin!" I gasp in surprise.

It's Saturday night, the only time of the week Buck's Tavern is packed, yet Austin is so distinguishable through the crowd of faces that I'm drawn to him the second I glance up from rinsing shot glasses.

He slides onto an empty stool at the bar, wedging himself between the biker with a raging attitude problem and the wasted divorcee who's been snapping at me all night for not topping up her double vodkas quickly enough. Brave man, Austin Pierce.

"Can I just get a soda from you, please, Gabby?" he asks, waving his car keys.

I shake my head in disbelief at his presence as I immediately default to autopilot, grabbing a glass. "What are you doing here?"

"I know you're taking some time to get things together, but it's been two weeks since you pouted at me and it's becoming unbearable." He smiles, and it's so

183

innocent and simple and really damn gorgeous, I think I might die.

"So, you drove two hours to see me pout?" I ask, the butterflies in my stomach batting their wings.

"I'd drive ten."

How? How does he make me blush so easily with only a handful of words? *That's* what's truly unbearable. Although I've missed Austin the past couple weeks, I haven't missed the feeling of being one smoldering wink away from a heart attack. We call each other every day, but it's not the same as having him sat here in front of me now.

My chest squeezed tight, I set his soda down on the bar between us. "On the house."

"Excuse me!" the divorcee next to him wails, slapping her hand on the bar to steal my attention. "My glass is empty, Abby!"

"It's *Gabby*," I remind her for the third time tonight. "With a G."

Austin stifles a laugh and crosses his arms on the bar as he gets comfortable. Out of the corner of my eye, I notice Buck watching me from across the room, and that's my reminder to keep myself in check and be nice to the customers before I slip into my old habits of losing my temper with them.

"*Bear with me,*" I mouth to Austin, because as much as I'd love to stand around and catch up, I'm in the middle of my busiest shift of the week and I can't be caught slacking. I'm on thin ice already, and I doubt Buck would be keen to give me a third chance if I screw this up again.

The vodka is down to its final dregs, so I make my way down the bar to fetch a new bottle, squeezing past Carly. "That's him," I hiss under my breath. "That's Austin."

Carly looks up from the cash register, instantly spots the gorgeous man whose eyes are trained on me, and swoons. "Yeah, I'd let him throw it down with me on a desk, too."

"Carly!" I whack her arm as I laugh.

"It's quiet down this end of the bar. I've got you covered for five minutes," she says, plucking the bottle of vodka from my hands and cracking open the seal. "Who are you taking care of?"

"Who do you think?"

Carly groans and I follow her back down the bar. She sees to the divorcee demanding her double vodka, and I see to Austin.

"Hi," I say, pressing my hands to the edge of the bar, locking out my elbows and leaning forward. "I can talk for five."

"I like watching you work," Austin says, gaze smoldering so dreamily, my knees buckle. "You look cute with your little apron."

"You're so distracting," I say with a quick roll of my eyes, but I'm blushing and there's no hiding it.

The weekend I spent with Austin felt like such a fever dream, so surreal with a thousand different emotions at play, that I worried with some distance, he'd see clarity and decide he still does, in fact, despise me to the bone. But now he's here in the dive bar where I work, flirting, and it's like one giant sigh of relief.

"Is this weird?" Austin asks. "That I drove here just to see you? Because now I'm thinking maybe it's weird."

"It's not weird," I say.

"Obsessive?"

I smile. "Possibly."

Austin groans and lowers his head onto his folded arms on the bar. "You see what you're doing to me, Gabby? Turning me to fucking mush," he mumbles. "How embarrassing."

"Is this jackass having a mental breakdown?" the biker next to Austin mutters, eyeballing him in concern.

Austin lifts his head. "If I am, you can blame her," he responds, playfully gesturing toward me.

"Come with me," I say with a pointed nod to the end of the bar.

I leave the entire bar full of customers in the semi-capable hands of Carly and meet Austin down by the hatch. I dip underneath and straighten up in front of him. I glance at my watch. It's nearing midnight.

"Last call's at two, so I'll probably be clear around three," I explain. "If you want to hang out and have some drinks until then, you're welcome to stay at my place tonight. There's not much space, but I promise the plumbing is rock-solid." A smile teeters onto my lips, hopeful that he'll accept the invite.

"In that case," Austin says, "can you grab me a beer?"

"My boss is currently watching us, so *of course I'll get you a beer, darling.*"

"*Darling,*" Austin repeats, testing the word on his lips. "I like that."

My cheeks heat up again, so I disappear under the hatch and resume working the bar with Carly. Austin slinks into the stool he left and I slide a beer over to him. He opens a tab and gets comfortable as I try my damn hardest to get back into a working rhythm, but it's seriously difficult with such a gorgeous human watching my every move. Every time I pop open a new beer for him, he tips me ten dollars.

"Can you stop?"

Austin raises an eyebrow as he takes a swig of his beer. "Admiring you?"

"Tipping me so much," I say, throwing his ten-dollar bill back at him. "A buck is fine. It's just a beer. All I do is pop the cap."

"But you do it so attractively," he flirts, pushing the bill back toward me. "You're working hard, and I'm enjoying watching you work hard, so let me tip you to show some appreciation."

"Just take the damn tip, Abby!" Divorcee snaps, and I glare at her despite Buck being within ten feet, because it's really time we ought to call her a cab and send her home.

I grab the bill and stuff it into the pocket of my apron that's already rammed full of tips from tonight's shift, and work my way back and forth along my end of the bar. Ever since I decided to give Carly a chance and get to know her, we've been in much better sync, to the point where I even enjoy working these hectic shifts with her because we do it so perfectly. We have the fine art of bartending as a two-women team down to a tee.

As it nears last call and the bar gradually empties, Austin calls it quits on any more beers, which honestly, I respect. As someone who now spends my life serving the drunk, there is nothing I hate more than dealing with wasted adults. Thank God Austin knows where to draw the line.

At two-thirty, Buck rounds up the final stragglers and sends them out the door. I ask very nicely if Austin can hang out here while we finish cleaning up for the night, and maybe my improved work ethic is winning me some favors with Buck, because he agrees.

And I have never mopped the floor so fast in the six months I've worked here.

Buck empties the cash register, Carly takes care of the dishes, and I wipe down the tables at lightning speed. We have the lights out and the doors locked just fifteen minutes after closing.

"Good work," Buck acknowledges on the way out.

"See you guys tomorrow!" Carly says, and it will forever amaze me how constantly chirpy she is, even at nearly three in the morning after a grueling fifteen-hour shift.

Austin follows me to my car parked in the alley out back, and the very first thing he says once we're inside is, "Now I understand where Carly Buck the Cactus's name came from."

I grin as I start to drive. "Funny, right?"

"You're just . . . so goofy."

As I head home to my apartment, somehow with Austin Pierce in tow, I become increasingly worried that

I left the place a mess this morning. I can't remember if I made the bed, or picked up dirty laundry from the corner of my room, or washed the bowl I ate my Cheerios from. Austin's home was immaculate. Mine is not.

"I'm technically a college student again, and that correlates with being a slob, okay?" I warn him as I park up outside my building, my tone defensive in fear of the judgment I'm about to have cast upon me.

"I seriously don't care," Austin says. "My dorm at school was . . . Well, let's just say my bed was less of a bed and more a mountain of Red Bull cans."

That makes me feel a little better.

We head up the stairs together and it takes me a couple of tries to get my door unlocked, because is there anything in this apartment that *isn't* broken? I flick on some lights and am relieved to see that, actually, I've left my apartment in much worse states than this.

As I watch Austin scope out my place, it feels like I've stepped into a parallel universe. Austin Pierce, my childhood best friend, here in my crappy Durham apartment many years later in our mid-twenties. Something I never for a second thought would ever happen, but alas, here we are.

"This is weird. You being here," I say out loud.

"I know you're coming back to Wilmington next weekend, but I just couldn't wait another week," Austin says, meeting my eyes across the living area. "Besides, now that you're definitely going back to school for another year, I guess I better get used to the drive up here. You couldn't have studied at UNC Wilmington, huh?"

189

"You couldn't have opened your firm in Durham, huh?" I shoot back with a rivaling pout.

"A few weeks ago, I'd have said one hundred and fifty miles wasn't enough distance between you and me," he says. "Now it's one hundred and fifty miles too many."

"How are you single when you're this much of a sweet talker?" I ask, and it's not even hypothetical. I have no idea how Austin, this gorgeous, charming, successful man, is single.

"Maybe I've just been waiting for you."

"*Ooookay.* I think those beers are getting to you now," I say with a laugh. I cross over to him and take his arm, pulling him with me to the bathroom. I raid the cabinet beneath the sink and brandish a pack of spare toothbrushes. "Here. Teeth, then bedtime."

We brush our teeth side-by-side, our gazes locked in the mirror and silly, sleepy smiles on our faces. It's after three, and I'm exhausted.

"I need to wash off the bar," I tell him, shoving him out of the bathroom before he can even make the age-old classic joke about joining me in the shower.

I can never climb into bed after a long shift. It always seems like that cigarette scent clings to my skin and I can't bear it. So even at this hour, I pull back my hair and hop into the shower for a quick refresh. When I walk into my bedroom a few minutes later, wrapped in a towel and on the hunt for a set of pajamas, I find Austin sprawled on his stomach on my bed wearing nothing but his boxers. His clothes are folded in a neat pile on my dresser. He lifts his head from the pillow with a dopey grin.

190

"Hi, Gabby."

"Hi, Austin."

I turn my back to him as I drop my towel to the floor and pull on some gym shorts and a tank. When I face him again, I see the suggestive glint in his eyes and it kills me that I'm this exhausted, because God, I've missed him.

"I see what you're doing," I tell him, "but I'm . . . *so* tired."

"What am I doing?"

"Giving me sex eyes."

"These are not sex eyes," Austin says, pushing himself up from his stomach. "This is just how my eyes look when I'm wondering how it's possible you became even more beautiful than how I remembered you."

"It's three in the morning, please stop flattering me."

Austin groans dramatically and says, "If I must."

I kill the lights and blindly find my way over to my bed, pulling back the comforter. Together we snuggle up underneath, facing one another in the dark.

"We never had sleepovers when we were kids," Austin murmurs in a low voice.

"Probably because you were a boy and my mother hated you."

He's so close to me that his gentle laugh dances over my face. "I know you're tired, so I won't talk."

"You can talk." I shuffle closer to him, molding my body around the contours of his and pressing my face into his warm chest, eyes closed as I focus on the slow beating of his heart. "You can talk until I fall asleep."

Austin wraps an arm around me, his hand resting in my hair. "I hate it," he admits.

"You hate what?"

"How easily I'm forgiving you."

Silence pulses between us in the dark. Everything feels so heightened with our bodies intertwined like this, and I hold my breath, waiting for more.

"I hate that I always dreamed of you apologizing one day," he whispers, "but I hate it even more that I dreamed of *forgiving* you. I hate that this is exactly what I wanted."

"It's okay," I say, pressing even closer into him. "It's okay to forgive me."

"Gabrielle. Can you promise me something?" His whispers send chills down my spine.

"Anything."

His body stiffens around mine as he draws his mouth close to my ear, his breath hot against my skin. There is fear embedded in the request as he says, "Promise me you won't break my heart again."

In the silence, I'm certain he must hear the thundering beat of my heart. I want to grab hold of him and never let go, I want to shake my promises into him, I want to be the best friend he always deserved. So I say, "I promise."

And this time I mean it with every fiber of my being.

16

There aren't many things that can pull me out of a deep sleep, but a single whiff of pancakes is guaranteed to do it. My eyes ping open and I glance to my left, but Austin isn't fast asleep by my side. From somewhere in my kitchen, I hear the clang of a pan.

If there are potentially pancakes up for grabs, I absolutely must investigate.

Throwing back my comforter, I hop out of bed and head through to the kitchen. Even though I suspected it already, it's still a jolt to my system to find Austin freaking Pierce standing in my cramped kitchen wearing last night's clothes, flipping pancakes and humming to himself.

"Good morning," he says over his shoulder, sensing me approach.

"What are you doing?"

"You made me pancakes at my place on a Sunday morning, so I'm returning the favor," he explains. "They probably—okay, definitely—won't be as good as yours, but I've given it a shot, anyway. I was just about to come surprise you."

"Can't sleep through pancakes," I say.

His laugh is delicate as he stacks the pancakes onto plates, and that's when I notice he's even poured out two glasses of juice and looked out my family-sized bottle of maple syrup. I haven't had anyone make me breakfast since I left home for college at eighteen, and my chest pangs with a cruel burst of nostalgia. I can't bear it sometimes, that painful realization that certain chapters of my life are over. I will never be a teenager eating pancakes on a Sunday with my father ever again, and that's such a hard truth to swallow, it makes me feel physically ill.

"What? Do they look terrible?" Austin asks with concern as he spins toward me, plates in hand.

"No . . . No, they look perfect," I reassure him. "I'm sorry I have no kitchen table."

We sit down on my raggedy old couch together and I drown my stack of pancakes in so much maple syrup, I may as well just be eating the maple syrup with a side of pancakes rather than the other way around, and Austin watches on in despair.

"Seriously?"

"Yes, seriously," I say, biting into a forkful. "Your pancakes are pretty good."

"I'm surprised you can taste them," he grumbles, and I retaliate by adding a tiny bit more syrup while looking him dead in the eye.

I will not be judged for my maple syrup consumption.

"You know this means we've started a tradition now, don't you?" I point out. "We now have to eat pancakes every Sunday we're together. And if we're not at my place or yours, we have to hunt down a diner."

"I think I can get on board with that."

"You *think*? No, you *will*."

"Pancakes on Sundays," he agrees, holding up his hands in surrender. His eyes brighten as an idea flashes through his mind, and he sets his plate down on the coffee table and gets to his feet. "Do you have paper anywhere?"

"Top drawer on the right," I say, pointing over to the kitchen. "Why?"

Austin doesn't give me a reason. He grabs a sheet of paper from the drawer and an engraved *Pierce Wealth Management* ballpoint pen from the pocket of his jeans, then sits back down on the couch next to me. I hunch forward to watch over his shoulder as he sets the paper down on the coffee table.

He writes, in pretty damn perfect handwriting: *We'll have pancakes on Sundays.*

Underneath, he signs his name with a very sexy, very professional signature. Nothing like the scrawled *Austin Pierce* he once wrote at the age of twelve.

At one point in time, my taste in men was tradesmen who were a little rough around the edges and covered in dirt after a day's work. I'm realizing very quickly my type is now businessmen in suits with engraved ballpoint pens and sturdy office desks.

"What do you say?" Austin asks, sliding the piece of paper toward me and offering me the pen.

I take the pen from him, but hesitate before signing my name. "Our agreements in the past haven't turned out that well . . ."

"I'm hoping you've learned enough from past mistakes that you won't break this one."

My chest tightens, and I know we're only goofing around and talking about *pancakes,* but it feels like this is about so much more. We're still repairing our friendship, and although there is a romantic layer this time around that is still developing, I know that at the very least, we will be friends.

I made him that promise last night, so I go ahead and sign my name alongside his.

"I think you should be the one to hold on to it," I say, handing back his pen.

Austin folds up the paper several times until it's nothing but a tiny square, then tucks it into the front pocket of his jeans. "I'm sorry I tore up the last one. I wish now we still had it."

I take another bite of my syrup-drenched pancakes and shrug. "It was just a piece of paper. It's okay. And I *did* break that agreement, so . . ."

Austin smiles. "I know, but it also brought you back to me in the end."

Our eyes lock and, for a very long time, neither of us say anything. The butterflies in my stomach are multiplying at such speed, they rise all the way up my throat, rendering me speechless.

I hate myself a little bit for never realizing how sweet Austin was back when we were kids, because his confidence and wit may be a natural result of him growing up, but his pure, kind nature has always been ingrained in him.

"Oh, I can't believe I forgot to tell you," Austin says, breaking our eye contact as he grabs his phone. "The shelter is hosting an adoption event next month. Check this out."

I nod eagerly as Austin shows me the flyer that's started being shared on the Saving Paws Animal Rescue's social media pages—the flyer I roped Zach, my super-duper graphic designer brother, into creating.

"That sounds amazing!" I exclaim, but I study economics, not acting, so I'm not sure how well I pull it off.

Because what Austin doesn't know is that I'm the organizer.

The past few days, in between my daily shift at the bar, I've been making far too many phone calls for a woman who fucking hates making phone calls. I've been in constant back and forth with Fiona from the shelter as together we work through all of the details. I'm in the process of finalizing catering, and I have an incredible pet photographer lined up to take new photos of the dogs for the website, hopefully wearing the adorable party hats I've ordered. I've hired the largest dog park in Wilmington for an entire afternoon, and I'm currently working on nailing down activities for kids, but finding bounce houses to hire during the summer is proving challenging. Hopefully, the event will draw in a good crowd and some of the dogs will find their new homes. Especially Teddy.

"We'll definitely have to be there," Austin says.

I smile. "Oh, for sure."

I *could* tell Austin that I'm the one behind the event, but I'm rather enjoying doing something meaningful for once without seeking any praise. He won't know it, but the conversation we had in his office two weeks ago about my father cast a terrible realization over me.

Twenty years from now, I don't want the first thing anyone thinks when they hear my name to be "oh, that mean girl from high school" or "that bitch from the bar." I want people to think of me the same way they think of my father, with respect and admiration, and I have a long way to go before I reach that point. I have to start somewhere, so I'm taking a page out of my dad's book and starting with charity work.

"I hope lots of the dogs get adopted."

"They will," Austin assures me.

We scoff the remainder of our pancakes and since Austin made them, it's only fair I do the dishes. The morning seems to fly by, not least because I need to be back at the bar for opening at twelve and Austin needs to head home to Wilmington to hit the streets for a sixteen-mile run, so the time to say our goodbyes rolls around much faster than I'd like.

On the drive to the bar, he clears his throat and says, "There's something I'd like to ask you." When I throw him a panicked glance in response to the seriousness of his tone, he laughs and adds, "Don't worry. It's nothing bad."

"What would you like to ask me?"

His hands twitch with a hint of nerves as he toys with them in his lap. "I found out yesterday the firm is short-listed for a business award, and the ceremony is over in Charlotte at the end of next month. Nice dinner. Nice hotel. I was hoping you'd come?"

"Congratulations!" I say, but my enthusiasm travels all the way to my hands and I accidentally swerve into the opposite lane.

"*Gabby*," Austin says, grabbing the wheel. "I'd like to actually attend these awards, please."

"Sorry," I apologize sheepishly, glancing sideways at him. "Of course I'll come, Austin."

He exhales a deep breath of relief just as I pull up in the alley outside of the bar. His car is still parked around here somewhere, wherever he left it last night, and it's time for him to head home after our impromptu sleepover.

"I'm sorry you have to run sixteen miles," I say.

"I'm sorry you have to deal with the drunks," he says.

"Hey, I made a fortune in tips last night thanks to some extremely generous bachelor. He was pretty cute, too."

Austin cracks into laughter and gets out of the car. So do I, and we stare over the roof of the vehicle at one another, not quite willing to say goodbye yet.

"So I'll see you next weekend? And the weekend after that for the adoption event? And the weekend after *that*?" Austin asks.

I pout at him, now hyper aware that he enjoys it when I do. "Are you *sure* we can't help out by adopting Teddy ourselves?"

"You don't give up, do you?"

"Nope." I drum my fingertips over the roof of my car and narrow my eyes challengingly, seductively. "Are you going to kiss me before you go?"

Austin strides around the car, clasps my waist, and kisses the hell out of me.

17

It's becoming apparent that my life has very quickly spiraled into counting down the days until I next see Austin, and I was never one to be obsessed with a man. It's a tiny bit terrifying and a tiny bit thrilling, but spending my weekends with Austin is now the highlight of every week.

As I make my now usual drive to Wilmington, my head spinning with my plans for the shelter's adoption event this afternoon, I experience, for the first time, a moment of crystal-clear awareness. As I sing along to my playlist with the August sunshine warming my face through my windshield, I realize I'm happy. Not fireworks exploding kind of happy, but a calm and content and okay kind of happy.

And that's a hell of a lot more than I've felt in a while.

I may still be working in a dive bar, but I've dropped the ego. Buck is actually a pretty great boss when you work hard for him, and we have settled on the agreement that

I cover all weekday shifts as long as I get the weekends free to spend with Austin here in Wilmington, and Carly may be slow at pouring her drinks, but she's always got my back.

My apartment still sucks, and that won't change no matter how many throw pillows I attempt to decorate with, but it's only temporary until I start school. I've decided I want to apply for on-campus accommodation again, and this time around, I'll make an effort to form genuine friendships that go beyond getting wasted together at frat parties.

It's nice to feel like I'm moving forward again. I've spent far too long treading water and, as it turned out, it was time to sink or swim.

And God, I'm really glad I chose to swim, because otherwise I wouldn't have this goofy smile on my face as I drive. Even when someone cuts me off, I don't lay on my horn for five solid seconds like I usually would. I'm happy, and I'll be even happier if Teddy gets adopted later.

In an effort not to take credit for today's event, I may have told a white lie or two to Austin. He has no idea I'm already on the road, because I need to help with the event set-up first and assist with transporting the dogs over to the park I've hired. Fiona and some of the other staff have managed to rope in a handful of volunteers too, so we have enough hands on deck to ensure the event runs smoothly.

I'd be lying if I said there wasn't a massive knot of nerves in my stomach, and it only tightens further as I navigate through downtown Wilmington. I pull up at the park and take a deep breath. Today is going to be one hell of a busy day, but I'm determined to make it a success.

"Fiona!" I call across the park when I spot her, dashing over. "This all looks great! Thank you so much for overseeing everything."

Fiona pulls me into a brief hug. We've been in nonstop contact the past few weeks. "No problem at all! We really appreciate you funding all of this, and we've had such a great response to the advertising that I think we'll get a great turnout."

"Has the photographer arrived yet?"

"She's in the gazebo!"

I head past the bounce houses currently being inflated and the arcade game stalls being erected and over to the gazebo that is way bigger than I thought it would be. Inside, I find some men assembling individual pens for the dogs. It's too hot to have them outside without the shade, and there are cooling fans on rotation and gallons of water stacked in the corner. I've organized everything from afar while Fiona has been on the ground setting my plans in motion, and between the two of us, I think we have most bases covered.

I find the photographer, run through exactly what I want from her, and then spend an entire hour writing out info cards with cute doodles about each dog and attaching them to the pens. When the catering company shows up, they set up their grills and promise me they'll serve the best cheeseburgers in North Carolina. I don't believe them, of course, but I like their confidence and enthusiasm.

Thirty minutes before the event is due to start, Fiona and I hop into her van and head back to the shelter for the first of many trips back and forth. En route, I call Austin to tell another white lie.

"Hey, I'm running late. Weekend traffic, ugh," I say, casting a grin at Fiona. "Just head over to the park without me and I'll meet you there."

"Are you sure? I don't mind waiting for you."

"I'm sure. Bye!"

At the shelter, Fiona and I load dogs into the crates inside the van, eight at a time, and dart back and forth to the park. We unload them into their pens and by the time we have every dog transported over, I'm sweating and need a five-minute break on the grass under one of the fans in the gazebo to cool down. Just as the public begin to arrive, I whip round all of the dogs and attach adorable little "Adopt Me!" bandanas to their collars.

"Good luck," I whisper into Teddy's ear as I scratch the top of his head.

I head outside the gazebo, and Fiona and I exchange nods of approval. All set and good to go. She carries a clipboard with a stack of application forms, and this is the point where I decide to discreetly blend into the thickening crowd. Just another member of the public . . . Absolutely *not* the mastermind behind this.

"I thought you were running late," a voice says as a pair of hands wraps around my waist from behind. Austin brushes his lips over my shoulder, leaving kisses on my warm skin. "How'd you beat me here?"

"Found a shortcut and broke some speed limits," I lie. I twist in his arms and oh, how lovely it is to see his gorgeous face after another week of dreaming about it. "Hi."

"Hi." He cups my jaw and tilts my head up, and there is something so irresistibly sexy about his manly hands on my face as his designer watch glistens in the sunlight. "Are you excited for the dogs to find homes?"

"Let's go see them," I say, pressing a quick kiss on his lips to satiate my desire for him (nowhere near enough), and slip my hand into his. I pull him into the gazebo and put on my best act. "Oh, wow! How amazing is this?"

"Oh my God," Austin says, dropping to his knees on the grass in front of the pens. His laugh is joyful. "They're wearing bandanas. Don't cry, Gabby."

"Why would I cry?"

"I feel like shelter dogs wearing bandanas is the kind of thing you'd cry over."

I whack his arm as he rises from the ground and we take a stroll through the gazebo, saying hi to all of the dogs we already know. Other people do the exact same. Families with kids looking for a new addition, retirees seeking companions, and . . . my mother.

"Mom!" I exclaim, though I shouldn't be surprised to see her here considering I specifically invited her to come along. I'm just amazed she has shown up, because she is absolutely not in the market for a dog. "You're here!"

And she is easily the most out-of-place woman in this gazebo. You'd think it would be common sense not to wear high heels to the park, but my mother would rather die than wear sneakers, and I won't even start on what a disastrous idea it is to wear a white pant suit . . . But I couldn't host my first charitable event without inviting my family, so I keep my lips sealed, because I'm grateful she's even here in the first place.

"Are you sure these dogs don't have fleas, Gabrielle?" she asks, forehead creased with concern as I approach her hiding timidly in the corner of the gazebo.

"They don't have fleas."

She bites the inside of her cheek, dubiously eyeing the dogs lapping up all of the attention from the public. "And have they had their shots?"

"Yes, they've had their shots."

"And you've seen the paperwork to prove that, have you?"

"Jesus, Mom, they're just dogs," I say, rolling my eyes. "You don't have to go near them, okay? Thank you for coming."

Mom meets my gaze for the first time and I even get a smile out of her. "You're welcome, honey. It's nice to see you again, and I'm glad you're making good use of your time—"

I abruptly clear my throat to interrupt her before she can spill the beans on my little secret. I reach back for Austin, hovering awkwardly a few feet away, and yank him forward. "Mom, I'd like you to meet Austin. Again."

Okay, fine—I invited Mom because I wanted her to meet Austin in a casual setting rather than having to sit through a formal dinner, not because I wanted her to praise me for my event management skills.

"How's it going, Mrs. McKinley?" Austin says politely, digging his elbow not-so-subtly into my ribs. I should have definitely forewarned him about my mother's attendance, but in the midst of organizing a thousand different things, it slipped my mind.

Mom fiddles with her pearl necklace as she looks Austin up and down, and already I want to smack my head into a wall in frustration because she is just so fixed in her ways. "Hello . . . Austin," she says, but it's difficult for her to get his name past her lips without it being delivered with a bow of disapproval. "And you two are here together, because . . .?"

"Because we're friends again," I say without hesitation. "Austin still lives here in Wilmington, so we've been catching up. He works downtown in finance, remember?"

Something peculiar flashes in Mom's eyes and her shoulders relax, just a touch, just enough. A small crack in the walls she has built around her, the ones that keep the grief of losing my father permanently at bay. "Finance? That's a great choice. Gabrielle's father was very successful in finance. He was—"

"Very good at what he did," Austin finishes, and he and I exchange a knowing glance. Mom will never know just how much my father changed Austin's life for the better.

"Austin's really good, too," I tell Mom. "His firm is up for an award."

Mom raises an intrigued eyebrow. "Oh? You seem to have done well for yourself then, given your odds."

My eyes squeeze shut in mortification, because she just can't help herself. It's ironic, talking about odds, considering I was dealt the much stronger hand, and yet Austin is the one with a successful career while I'm yet to even get my degree. Mom really has no right to be so patronizing, considering her own daughter's circumstances.

"Yes, Mrs. McKinley, I had pretty bad odds," Austin agrees, his tone hardening in defense. "But that was all—just bad odds. I was a nice kid who worked hard and treated people with kindness, so I think I deserved to have some luck thrown my way, don't you?"

"Well, yes, of course . . ."

"Great! Then you can stop looking down on me going forward," he says with a tight smile, leaving my mother flummoxed and grappling with her words.

"I do not look down on you!"

"You do, Mom," I cut in gently, scoldingly tilting my head at her. "Austin and I are friends again, and I'd really like it if you respected that this time around. He's a good influence on me."

Mom is not accustomed to being put in her place, but I also didn't invite her here to stir up an argument. Surprisingly, for once, I don't enjoy the quiver in her lower lip. She may be the worst judgmental snob and the most melodramatic person I have ever met in my entire life, but I still love her despite her glaring flaws. I really do want her to accept Austin, even if it *is* too many years overdue.

I'm just about to change the subject when Zach approaches us and I breathe a sigh of relief, thankful for the interruption.

"Hey, sis," Zach says through a mouthful of cheese-burger, throwing an arm over my shoulders. I haven't seen him in a month since we both crashed at the house, but he really came in clutch with designing the flyers for this event. "Wow, Mom. You came to this?"

"Yes," Mom mumbles, her eyes on the ground. I suspect she'll leave soon.

"Where's Claire?" I ask with caution. Last I heard, Zach and his fiancée were patching things up, but I worry they've taken a bad turn again.

Zach points his half-eaten cheeseburger across the gazebo and I spot Claire fussing over one of the dogs. *Phew*. Things must be okay. "Gabby, if she ends up falling in love with some mutt, I'm declaring war on you. I'm here for the free food, not to adopt a dog. Oh, Austin." Zach blinks at Austin in surprise, then tilts his head at me. "Still figuring things out, I see?"

I smile. "Getting there." My stomach rumbles and I realize in my haste to leave Durham this morning, I haven't eaten all day. The sight of Zach's burger suddenly has me ravenous, so I tap Austin's arm. "Let's go grab some food."

Austin is more than happy to escape being cornered in the gazebo with my mom, so we leave her and Zach behind and head outside into the sun to source some burgers for ourselves. I knew the turnout today was expected to be high, but it still amazes me just how bustling the park is. Music blasts from speakers, the delicious scent of burgers fills the air, and kids' laughter echoes from the bounce houses. So far, everything is running smoothly without a hitch.

Maybe I should have studied event management instead of sensible, boring economics. I'm not that bad at this, and if even just half the dogs are adopted, I'll consider today an immense success.

Austin's fingers trace their way down my arm until his hand settles into mine. "I'm sorry for talking to your mom like that."

"Are you kidding? She totally deserved it," I say, giving his hand a squeeze. "I never listened to her when I was eight and wanted to be your friend. What makes you think I'll listen now that I'm an adult? Besides, I think that was actually a step forward with her. She'll grow to like you, but those little remarks of hers are probably something you'll just have to get used to. God knows I get them too. She can't help herself."

Austin looks at me out of the corner of his eye as we walk, smirking in amusement. "We have some work to do when it comes to winning over the parents."

"Hey, at least my mom only judges you. Your parents *despise* me, so I have a hell of a lot more work to do than you do."

"Can't say I blame them too much. You're easy to despise, Gabby," he says, "but equally easy to forgive."

We grab ourselves some cheeseburgers and find a shaded spot beneath a tree. We sprawl out together on the grass, perfectly content with enjoying the atmosphere and looking out at the crowd. I can't help but pay attention to every single person that leaves the gazebo, wondering if they've filled out an application form. Just as Austin and I are debating which dogs are the most likely to get adopted, my brother strides across the park toward us.

"*You*," Zach hisses, pointing an accusatory finger at me. "Oh, the way I'm going to kill you, Gabby."

I look up at him from the ground, sunglasses shielding my eyes from the bright sun. "Excuse me?"

"I'm now going to have a scruffy little dog living in my house!" Zach groans. He places his hands on his hips and rants, "And its teeth are fucked up so it'll probably end up with none at all by the time it's elderly, so I'll be left looking after some gummy little blind poodle one day."

Austin and I exchange a look, as we both realize it at the exact same time.

"You're adopting Lily? The miniature golden poodle?" I ask, because out of all of the dogs, *of course* Zach just has to be talking about the one I thought was my soul dog. Lily, the curly-haired, chicken-wing-loving, antisocial poodle. "Did her sign say she was found eating chicken wings out of the trash?"

Zach grows even more exasperated. "Why are the pair of you laughing? Is there something wrong with that dog? Tell me now, Gabby, because if I take this thing home and it's demonic, I swear to God . . ."

"No! She's perfect," I reassure him. "I just didn't know you were considering a dog."

"Because I wasn't!" Zach snaps. "I told you—I came for the free food, but now Claire is in love with that

211

lump of fur and I've been bullied into filling out an application form."

"Maybe having a dog will make you less grouchy."

Zach graces me with his middle finger before storming back over to the gazebo, and I giggle under my breath as I picture him walking a tiny poodle around his neighborhood. He'll deny it, of course, but he'll love it. It's always the men who don't want the dog who fall in love with them the most. And Claire is incredibly sweet, so I know Lily will be taken great care of.

"That's one dog adopted for sure," Austin says, leaning back on his hands. "And if Lily and her underbite can find a home, then I have high hopes for the rest."

We only have the park for a couple hours, and eventually the crowd begins to thin, the grills get shut off, and the bounce houses begin to deflate. Mom has disappeared without saying goodbye, but I don't blame her for being too caught off guard by Austin's confidence to want to find us again.

"Shall we help get the dogs back to the shelter?" I suggest to Austin, because that's exactly what I need to do, anyway, so I'm relieved when he agrees.

Inside the gazebo, the photographer is popping party hats on the dogs and taking some final snaps for their new headshots on the Saving Paws Animal Rescue's website, because how can anyone *not* want to adopt a dog wearing a party hat and bandana?

"Gabby!" Fiona calls over with a beaming grin spread across her face. She thrusts her clipboard at me, a thick stack of completed application forms piled up high.

"Look at all of these! We've had *so* much interest in most of the dogs!"

With bated breath, I ask, "And Teddy?"

"Unfortunately, no applications for Teddy yet."

The pang of disappointment is straight-up gut-wrenching. It's so heartbreaking to me, thinking of the innocent dogs without a couch to nap on, just because they're too old or not cute enough or a little bit nervous. I may be pretty damn good at organizing an adoption event, but I'm clearly too sensitive to deal with the aftermath.

Fiona immediately notices the glaze of tears in my eyes, and she rubs her hand soothingly up and down my arm. "Hey, hey. It's okay. You did good! I reckon at least twenty dogs will be in new homes next week and that's because of you!" One of the volunteers calls across the gazebo for her and she dashes away before she realizes she's just ruined my little secret. Thanks, Fiona.

Austin immediately turns to me with narrowed, intrigued eyes. "Gabby."

And of course, I completely ignore him. "Let's go see Teddy and give him some belly rubs."

"Gabby."

"His pen is up there somewhere."

"Gabby," he says once more, and I give in and meet his eyes, remaining sheepishly silent. "You did this?"

"Maybe . . ."

"*All* of this?"

I shrug as heat blazes across my face, because the last thing I wanted was any credit. "I want to be more like my father," I admit, my voice quiet. "He was kind and charitable and humble, and I realized after our talk in your office that I wanted to continue that legacy. So I gave Fiona a call last month and we pulled this all together."

Austin is deep in thought, still registering the fact that I was behind all of this. He gestures around the gazebo. "How did you pay for this?"

"Cracked into the trust fund," I answer, managing a smile.

"Why didn't you tell me?" he asks, but his tone is gentle. He's not angry that I left him in the dark, I don't think. Just confused. "I would have chipped in. I'm their sponsor, remember?"

"I wanted to do this on my own," I say, and I hold his gaze as I strengthen my voice. "I wanted to prove to myself that I could do something good for once. Not to impress you, not for attention. Just . . . *good*."

Austin's smile is so slight, it's almost indiscernible. He steps forward and wraps an arm around me, the other hand resting on the small of my back. He kisses the crown of my head, right near the healed cut from my accident a month ago. Right by my ear, he murmurs, "I'm proud of you, Gabby."

And a barrage of tears instantly pricks at my eyes, because I can't remember the last time anyone was proud of me.

18

Austin tosses a pillow at me and says, "We're building a fort."

"A fort?"

"Yes, a fort," he confirms. He disappears through his house and returns moments later with a bundle of bed sheets in his arms. "So that thing I said about us never having sleepovers as kids? It made me realize we have therefore never had the opportunity to make a fort together."

"You're right. We haven't."

"And we need to rectify that immediately."

"We absolutely must."

And I'm not sure what exactly I had in mind for my Saturday evening plans with Austin, but rearranging furniture and draping sheets over chairs definitely wasn't it.

We build a killer fort that takes over the entire living area, using all of the sheets and blankets we can lay our hands on, and then we stack pillows inside for maximum comfort. Austin microwaves some popcorn and grabs his laptop before joining me inside the best fort I've ever made. As we lie together on the pile of pillows of blankets, watching *Black Widow*, because Austin is now involved in my Marvel movies marathon, I can't think of anything else I'd rather be doing.

"Thank you."

My head rests against Austin's chest as the words vibrate through him, and I tilt my chin to look up at him. "Thank you?" I repeat. "Thank you for what? What did I do?"

Austin wraps his arm a little tighter around me, our legs entwined as the movie plays on the laptop sat on a pile of books by our feet. "The past few years I've been so serious," he explains. "Professional mindset at all times. Always thinking about stock fluctuations and 401Ks. Even on weekends, I'll work extra from home. When I hit the bar, I'm thinking of investment strategies in between beers. When I run, I spend each mile mulling over a different client's portfolio."

"Because you're committed," I say, "and really good at what you do."

Austin laughs. "Yes, I am, but my point is . . . I've been a little less serious since you showed up, so thank you."

"That's a good thing?" I ask, raising a brow. If anything, I'd presume that makes me a bad influence. I don't want to be a distraction from his career.

"Yes, Gabby, it's a good thing. I needed your goofy humor back in my life so that I'm not crunching numbers in my head all of the time." He smolders his eyes at

216

me and kisses my temple. "Reminds me of how it felt to be a kid."

I pout my lips at him, only because I know now just how much he loves it. "Am I too childish, Austin?"

"No. You're perfect."

"That's a lie," I say, rolling my eyes.

He grins and says, "You're perfect now that you aren't bullying me."

"Austin!" I jerk up from his chest and support my weight on one hand instead as I stare down at him with a frown. "Don't say things like that."

"Why? Feel guilty?" he teases.

"Obviously."

"Good, then find a way to say sorry."

His gaze is inviting, his smirk challenging, and that's as clear a green light as any.

Grabbing a fistful of his T-shirt, I passionately take his lips with mine. I've been waiting what seems like an entirety to feel his hands on my body again and I'm not waiting a second longer. I'll catch up with the Avengers later.

I swing my leg over Austin's stomach and straddle his hips, flattening my chest against his as his hands securely grasp my waist, but I want to be the one in control. I grab his hands and pin them to the pillows around him as he strains against me, deepening the kiss because his mouth is the only resource he has.

"I can't touch you?" he rasps, and I feel his frustration in the way he locks his wrists beneath my grip, fighting for freedom.

As I kiss my way along his jaw, I very deliberately draw my mouth close to his ear, lower my voice, and simply say, "No, darling."

I release my hold on his wrists and grab his jaw instead, angling it upward to allow me to kiss my way down the stubble on his neck. My other hand trails down his chest, skipping over the waistband of his sweat shorts and brushing my palm over his solid cock bulging against the soft cotton.

"Oh, hi," I say. "That was easy."

"You don't need to work for it, Gabby," Austin says, lifting his hips to press himself harder into my palm. "I have to fight the altitude every time you smile at me."

I shift my body back, settling onto my knees between his legs. Austin sits up a little, resting on his elbows and gazing down at me with hot anticipation, and oh, how I refuse to disappoint. I hook my fingers over the waistbands of both his shorts and his boxers and tug them down in one swift pull.

His cock springs free, slick with anticipation, and I wrap my hand around the base and work my way enthusiastically up his shaft. Austin hums contentedly under his breath and when I steal a glance up at him, his eyes are closed. As I work my hand, I gather spit in my mouth, then lean in close and seal my lips tight around his tip.

Austin flinches at the sensitivity of my wet mouth wrapped around the head of his cock and the groan that reverberates around our little fort is the most gratifying sound in the world. It motivates me to deliver, and I circle my tongue around his tip, light and teasing, before taking all of him to the very back of my throat. Despite my no-touching instruction, Austin can't help but lose his hands in my hair, gathering my curls out of the way. Every time he responds to my movements with a moan, I make a mental note of what it is exactly that he likes so I can memorize it forever. I get into a rhythm, switching my attention back and forth between the shaft and the tip while also working my hand along the base.

I glance innocently up at him from beneath my eyelashes and our eyes lock for only a split second before he throws his head back into the pillow with a tremendous groan. "Stop."

"Stop?"

"Stop," he repeats, "because I'm going to come and I haven't fucked you yet."

"Okay, I'll fix that," I say with a smile.

I undress at lightning speed. Whip off my shirt, unclasp my bra, shuffle out of my shorts and panties. I feel so wet and swollen with my desire for Austin, and I readjust back into position over his lap, my knees either side of his hips.

"You're so fucking pretty," he says, hands tracing the curve of my waist all the way down to my ass where they remain. "Maybe *this* is my favorite view. You're perfect at every angle, Gabby."

My hand wrapped around his cock, I guide myself down onto him and my eyes roll in satisfaction as he fills every inch of me. For a few moments, I remain still, unmoving. Our eyes meet and the lust in his gaze as he admires me is enough to turn me wild.

"Hi, loser," I breathe.

Austin squeezes my ass. "Hi, loser."

"Corporate loser."

"Bartender loser."

"Runner loser."

"Duke loser."

I smile. "How about we're both just losers?"

"Both losers," he confirms, hooking his hand around the back of my neck and pulling my lips down to his.

I press my hands flat to his chest for support and I bounce on my knees, taking his cock over and over again, until my lack of working out becomes apparent and the burn in my thighs is too much to bear. I roll my hips instead, grinding back and forth and achieving the stimulation on my clit I so desperately need. My moans become erratic, uncontrollable, and Austin takes over, locking his arms tight around me and thrusting hard from beneath me.

It's a blur, the way his groans punctuate mine and our movements spiral out of control, until suddenly we both collapse at the exact same moment. I fall forward onto his chest as pleasure rips through me and Austin's body involuntarily twitches and jerks.

Breathlessly, he asks, "Did we just—?"

"We did," I splutter. My heartbeat hammers in my chest and I struggle to catch my breath, my skin scorching hot and damp with sweat from so much exertion.

"Fuck, we're so synchronized. That's incredible."

I remain sprawled over Austin for a few minutes as I recover while he strokes my head and randomly kisses my forehead every now and again, both of us mindlessly watching the movie. I should get cleaned up, but I can't bring myself to move and ruin the moment. Who knew how nice post-sex cuddles could be?

"Gabby," Austin says. He skims his fingers delicately over my bare shoulder, his touch electrifying my skin. When I glance up at him in response to my name, his smile is gentle and his eyes warm. "I forgive you."

My heart stutters, and it's only just recovered. I lift my head from his chest to look at him properly, studying that warmth in his blue eyes to suss out how genuine this declaration is. His face is still flushed with color and I worry he's just in an orgasmic daze.

"I don't want you to forgive me just because I'm a master at giving you head," I say.

Austin laughs. "You *are*," he says, moving his hand to my face as the laughter settles into sincerity, "but I think I forgave you a while ago. Maybe it was that mischievous look in your eyes when you smothered your pancakes in maple syrup. Maybe it was when you cried over the dogs in the shelter. Maybe it was when you promised me you wouldn't break my heart again." He stares silently into my eyes as his smile falters. "But I forgive you, Gabrielle."

"You do?"

"I do," he confirms with a nod. He tilts my jaw up, moving his lips toward mine, but I well up into tears before he even has the chance to kiss me. "Gabby! This is good. You don't need to cry."

I laugh through the tears, because I honestly can't fight them. The relief spreading through my body is too overwhelming. That first day I walked into Austin's office, it seemed like there was no hope at all of forgiveness.

"It means so much to me that you gave me a second chance, Austin."

He swipes away my tears with his thumb. "If I didn't give you a second chance then I'd be missing out on this new tradition of pancakes on Sundays. By the way, I bought maple syrup."

And goddamn, the things I'd do to him *now*.

19

Austin offering me his guest room to stay in was futile, because I have yet to sleep in any bed in this house other than his. His 6 a.m. alarm sends me groaning into the pillows as he quietly slips out to run a mere eighteen miles, but by the time he returns, I'm wide awake and have water, electrolytes and pancakes waiting for him. We are starting to integrate our lives, working around the other, and I'm enjoying that foundation of partnership solidifying around us.

"I'm dying to know how Zach's first night with Lily went," I muse while stacking plates into the dishwasher.

"We should hit the beach today. Invite your brother and his fiancée. Tell them to bring Lily," Austin suggests, and I waste no time at all reaching for my phone and bullying Zach into agreeing to a beach hang-out.

Being on the coast, we are completely spoiled with gorgeous beaches. Once when we were on the cusp of being teenagers, Austin and I stayed out *way* too late down at the beach, still traversing the sandy plains long past sunset, and I remember to this very day the lecture my mother gave me that night when my father eventually found Austin and me. I wasn't in trouble so much for staying out late as I was in trouble for staying out late with *Austin*. I also stupidly applied sunscreen to my entire body except my face, so I sported a killer sunburn on my nose for days after, and Austin took a peculiar reaction to the long grass we prowled through and broke out in hives, but we sure did have fun that day.

As we drive to the beach now, I ask, "Do you remember—?"

"That time we stayed out too late at the beach?" Austin finishes.

"And I got sunburn—"

"On your nose."

"And you were—"

"Seemingly allergic to beachgrass."

We exchange smiles. It will take a lifetime to unpick all of the memories we shared together as kids, but we have forever to do so. We already know each other inside out, and that skips a thousand steps in the dating process. At least I think we're dating. Are we?

"Question," I say.

"Shoot."

"Are we dating?"

Austin looks sideways at me. His voice is soft, gorgeous, addictive. "Do you want us to be dating?"

"I don't really care what we call it, just as long as we're *something* and I haven't deluded myself entirely,"

I babble, feeling the heat blazing over my skin. I have no idea what we are right now.

"I don't think we're dating," Austin says, placing his hand on my bare thigh and sending shockwaves through my body. "Dating is figuring out whether you actually like someone or not, right? But I've *always* liked you, Gabby, so . . . We're *something*."

I nod in a distracted daze. "Okay. *Something*. Good. Also, I'm going to need you to retract your hand from my thigh."

Austin's smile stretches into a devious smirk as he runs his hand higher, his fingertips trailing over my inner thigh and brushing the frayed hem on my jean shorts. "You don't like this?"

I grab his hand, nearly crushing his fingers beneath my tensed grip. "Austin Pierce, stop trying to seduce me."

"Why?"

"Because it's working." I throw my head back into the headrest and groan out loud. I'm really starting to hate how easily the mere *thought* of Austin turns me on, let alone when he touches me. "You think we'll find a sand dune large enough to disappear behind for five minutes?"

"Can't. Allergic to the beachgrass."

"Damn allergies," I mutter.

When we arrive at the beach, Zach and Claire are already there with Lily in tow, gathering lawn chairs out of their car. They were the only application for her, so they were able to take her home last night after Fiona from the shelter did some home checks.

"Lily!" I call, and the miniature poodle's tiny head pops up in response to her name and she pulls hopelessly on her leash to run to me. "Hi, baby!"

"She's stronger than she looks!" Claire says with a giggle as she gets dragged over.

I drop to my knees and fuss Lily, even accepting her vulture-breath kisses, and Austin scratches behind her ears. I like this arrangement—I now get to see Lily any time I want without having had to adopt her myself. Now that I think about it, I have an aunt in Virginia who is dog crazy . . . Maybe I should give her a call and see how she feels about adopting a nice Labrador named Teddy.

"How was your first night with her?" I ask, straightening up as a grumpy Zach approaches with a lawn chair tucked under each arm.

"I rolled over in the middle of the night to give my fiancée a nice kiss on the cheek, only to open my eyes and realize I was kissing a fucking poodle. So, not that great," Zach mutters, and Lily circles his feet, winding the leash around his legs.

My brows lift in surprise. "You let her in the bed?"

"I had no say in the matter."

"She was whimpering," Claire explains, sheepishly batting her eyelashes at Zach.

"If she can play fetch, she might just redeem herself," he says, and as much as he acts like he detests poor Lily, it is clear in the gentle, thoughtful way he untangles her leash from around his legs that he secretly cares for her.

Claire scoops Lily up into her arms and follows Zach over to the beach, and as I set off in their tracks, Austin nudges his elbow into my ribs with a grin and says, "Lily *loves* fetching balls."

It's the perfect day for the beach. Sunday, with clear skies but mild temperatures and a cool breeze, so it's pretty packed. We find a quiet spot further along the golden sand—far, far away from any beachgrass—and set up chairs, a parasol and a cooler full of sodas.

"C'mon then, Zach, throw a ball for Lily," Austin prompts, getting comfortable in a chair and watching in amusement from behind his sunglasses. Half the buttons on his shirt are open, revealing his tanned, trimmed chest, and I fight the urge to salivate. "Look at her. She's dying to play."

I sink down into the warm sand next to Austin's chair, leaning back on my hands and stretching out my bare legs to catch a tan as Claire unclips Lily's leash. Zach grabs a ball, hurls it out of sight down the beach—he was a football quarterback in high school, so still has a mean throw even a decade later—and breaks out into a joyful grin when Lily goes bounding after it. He and Claire cheer as the tiny poodle makes her return, ball in her mouth.

"This was a good idea," I muse, watching Claire throw the ball this time—though not nearly as far—and then suddenly bolt upright. "Oh! Can you pass over my bag?"

Austin reaches for the backpack I filled before we left his house, but doesn't hand it over. He searches inside until he finds a bottle of sunscreen, then holds it up suggestively. "Looking for this?"

"I don't want to burn my nose *again*."

"Then stay still."

He sits forward on the edge of the lawn chair and lathers a small amount of sunscreen in his hands. I whip off my sunglasses and tilt my chin up, my admiring gaze locked on his. Gently, he brushes his fingertips over my cheeks, my forehead, my nose, massaging the sunscreen into my skin. It makes my heart soar.

I don't *need* Austin to look after me, but it means a lot that he *wants* to. My father was always the one who looked after me, and although I'm now twenty-four and independent and apparently a grown-up, sometimes I still crave that feeling of being young and protected.

Austin kisses the tip of my nose. "I won't let you burn. Promise."

The corners of his eyes crease as he smiles and I gaze into the cool blue of his irises. My throat tightens, an ache in my core that's like blazing wildfire, an indescribable feeling that hurts in all the ways I need it to.

You think blue eyes are just blue eyes until you fall in love with someone whose eyes are blue, and then, God, how they become so much more.

"Thank you," I whisper.

"It's just sunscreen," says Austin.

I shake my head, managing a small tinkle of laughter. "You always looked after me when we were kids, and you still look after me now. Holding my hand at the hospital, giving me a place to stay, helping me get my car fixed . . . I haven't felt this safe since I lost my dad."

Austin touches his thumb to my chin. "I can only dream of giving you the same life your father did. He was an incredible man who changed my life. The least I can do now is make sure his daughter is taken care of. Anything you need, I'm on it."

"I think I only need you."

"You already have me in the palm of your hand, Gabby," he says, tucking loose curls behind my ear, "just like you did when we were eight years old."

I stretch up and press my lips to his, a kiss so gentle and endearing that I want to live in it forever.

"Am I interrupting something, Gabs?" I hear Zach ask, and I sheepishly pull back from Austin to find my brother watching us, one eyebrow arched. "Hey, Austin. You mind if I talk to Gabby for a sec?"

"No problem," Austin says coolly. He squeezes my shoulder as he stands from the lawn chair, setting off across the sand toward Claire and Lily, and Zach sinks into the empty chair to replace him.

"What?" I ask hesitantly, glowering at him through suspicious, narrow eyes.

Zach folds his arms across his chest and disapprovingly asks, "Since when do friends kiss at the beach?"

"Did I forget to update you? I'm so sorry, Zachary!" I say with feigned shock. "Austin's a little more than a friend. There. All up to speed. Anything else you want to quiz me on?"

Zach rolls his eyes. "Does Mom know? She'll never allow it. You know she never liked him."

"*Hello?* College dropout, bartender, hellhole apartment, remember? It's pretty clear by now I don't care

229

about disappointing her. Besides, she doesn't care much for Claire, either, and that hasn't stopped *you*."

"That's true," Zach agrees with a laugh. He rubs his jaw thoughtfully as he watches Austin wrestle with Lily. "You definitely aren't on drugs?"

"No!"

"Mom wanted me to ask."

"Of course she did."

"To be fair to her, you *are* acting a bit erratic," Zach says. "You wanted to apologize to Austin, I get it, but now you're suddenly dating the guy? I have no idea how he even trusts you."

"We've worked through things," I say, but I feel my blood boiling at having to justify my relationship with Austin. It's none of Zach's business. "I think it says a lot about his character that he's willing to forgive me. He's a good guy, and he makes me happy. Can we just leave it at that?"

Zach shrugs. "If you say so. But trash is trash, Gabby."

My jaw slackens, taken aback by Zach's cruel words. Now my blood really does burn. "That's a horrible thing to say and you fucking know it."

"He may be doing alright for himself now. May drive the nice car, may wear the suits, but you and him aren't the same. I'm not saying he's a bad guy, but we were raised differently, and it'll never work out with someone who doesn't have the same morals."

"And what morals do *we* have, exactly?" I spit, pushing myself up from the sand and towering over Zach in the lawn chair. "Because I was a raging bitch

230

in high school, and you're being a massive dick right now. So c'mon. What are these great morals of ours you speak of?"

"Jesus, Gabby. Calm down."

But I can't calm down, because I have never seen so much of my mother in Zach before. "Our biggest mistake was not learning from Dad," I mutter through clenched teeth. "He was the only one who ever treated Austin with kindness."

Zach gets up from the lawn chair, chest broad as he stands challengingly in front of me. "What does that mean?"

"Dad never judged him. He was *nice* to him. He wanted the best for him." My eyes travel to Austin further down the beach, and I know I'm not to repeat the secret he shared with me, but I can't sit on it by myself. Maybe if Zach knew just how much Dad cared for Austin, he might cut him some slack. "I'm going to tell you something, but I need you to promise me that you will *not* repeat this to Mom."

"Spit it out."

"*Promise me*," I demand, and Zach nods. "Okay. I don't know how to say this, so I'll say it quick: Dad left some money behind for Austin. It was in a secret trust in the will. Dad was a great judge of character, so shouldn't you trust and value his opinion of Austin?"

Zach's eyes bulge as his features twist with confusion, then bubbling rage. "What the fuck? You mean Dad was handing out charity favors? That money was *ours*, Gabby! How much?"

231

Panic sends my heart racing. This is why I shouldn't make split-second decisions, because I think I may have just pulled the pin on a grenade, and oh, how I wish I could shove that information right back into my mouth.

"I don't know," I choke out as my vision blurs, the beach spinning around me. Austin told me about that secret trust in confidence, and only when he felt he had no other choice. I reach out and lock my hand around Zach's arm. "We are doing just fine. We don't miss whatever amount that was, and it was Dad's wish. It's what he wanted and we have to respect that, Zach."

Out of the corner of my eye, I notice Austin approaching with concern and my chest squeezes so tight, it makes me feel faint.

"Is everything okay?" he asks.

Zach yanks his arm free of my death grip and turns to Austin. "How much was it then?"

"Huh?"

"How much of our father's money did you manage to get your scruffy hands on?" There's a storm raging in his eyes and he bites his lower lip so hard I'm amazed he doesn't shed blood.

Austin glances at me, the betrayal clear as day in those ocean blue eyes. I squeeze mine shut, pressing my hands over my face as the regret twists its way around my chest, my stomach, my heart. I can't bear this.

"Zach, listen. I didn't ask for a handout," Austin starts, his voice displaying only the slightest hint of a tremor that no one else but me would know him enough to even notice. "Your dad was hugely influential to me.

I really looked up to him growing up and I guess I must have left a lasting impression on him. If it means anything, that money was put to good use. I'd never waste it. It was what he wanted, so if you're going to be pissed at anyone, be pissed at him."

And that's too much for Zach, because he swings a fist through the air and clocks Austin square in the jaw.

"Zach!" I scream, stunned.

Austin, who back in high school endured the football team taking shots at him every now and again without ever saying a word to defend himself, throws a punch straight back. My mouth hangs open in disbelief and all hell breaks loose—Zach dives into Austin and the pair of them clatter to the ground, scrapping in the sand, fists flying.

"What's going on?!" Claire screams in horror as she bounds over with Lily bundled protectively in her arms.

"Zach! Stop! *Boys!*" I yell, but my pathetic mediation attempts are unsurprisingly futile. It seems I have no choice but to physically pull them apart, and it's right about now that I regret giving up on the gym after that time I flew off the treadmill.

Sucking in a breath, I force myself in between the pair of them, locking my shoulders as I get rocked around in the fight. I'm on the ground now with them, sand in my mouth as I try to grab hold of either of their arms, but I should have known better than to get involved in a fight between two grown men. I'm no match for either of them, and I'm thrown to the side when Zach accidentally backhands me. The squeak that leaves my mouth halts the fight right there and then.

"Fuck, Gabby," Zach pants, suddenly on his knees by my side as I clutch my cheek in shock. "You know I didn't mean that."

"Let me see," Austin says, breathless as he settles on my other side. He reaches for my hand and gently moves it aside to examine my cheek. It stings like hell. "You're okay. Needs some ice."

"You're a fucking idiot," I snap at Zach, shoving him away from me as I unsteadily get to my feet. I brush off the sand from my body, though I feel my scalp itch and know it's going to take one hell of a shower to wash it all from my hair. "Stupid, stupid idiot."

"You hit her," Austin growls, straightening up next to me and towering over Zach, gearing up for round two. I stretch a rigid arm out in front of his chest to hold him back.

"Leave it, Austin," I warn. "Let's just go."

"It was clearly an accident," Zach mutters, shaking his head furiously as Claire tugs on his shirt, pulling him away from us. As the distance increases, he yells over, "No wonder he forgives you, Gabs. Probably wants his hands on *your* trust fund now."

Austin takes a sharp step forward, but I lock my hand around his bicep and haul him back with all of my might. "*Ignore him,*" I hiss.

In a rage-fueled daze, we gather our stuff and head back to the car before collapsing silently inside. Austin's shirt is torn open and there's a small cut on the bridge of his nose. He stares out over the parking lot, blinking slowly as though he's processing the past five minutes. I sit there and watch him, waiting.

Finally, he looks at me and says, "*This* is why that money was left in a secret trust."

"I know," I say, guiltily dipping my head. "I don't know what I was thinking. I guess I just thought . . . Well, I thought maybe if Zach knew how much Dad respected you, he'd respect you a bit more, too."

"I don't need your brother to respect me, Gabby. What I do need"—he rubs his jaw, massaging away an ache, before the tone of his voice hardens—"is for you to stop breaking my trust over and over again. You just can't help yourself, can you?"

The redirection of his anger at Zach toward me instead should absolutely be expected, yet my stomach still knots. "I'm sorry. I was trying to help, but—"

"But you screwed up. *Again.*"

"Austin," I plead gently, reaching out to touch his arm, but he instantly flinches away from me and the violence of his rejection makes me feel a surge of panic. "Please. Please don't let this ruin all the progress we've made so far."

Austin braces himself hard against his car door, propping an elbow up against the window and resting his head in his hand as he sets his gaze on me. It's like he can't get far enough away from me. "And do you know how difficult it was for me to even let us make any progress in the first place? I gave you a chance when you didn't deserve one, and already . . . *Already* you've fucked it up. I can't just keep forgiving you. Every. Single. Fucking. Time. I need to draw a line somewhere, and I think maybe that line is here."

"What?" I squeak.

Austin swallows hard before confessing, "I think you're going to hurt me in the end, Gabby."

And I burst into tears right there in front of him in this stupid car, because there is no possible way I have blown my one and only chance with Austin already when I was so adamant that I would never again do anything to betray him. And the worst part is that I really, really, really didn't mean to. I feel like the biggest idiot in the whole entire world, and the positive momentum I've been building in my life feels like it's been stopped in its tracks. Where do I even go from here?

"Do you want me to get out of the car?" I manage to splutter despite the panic flooding my nervous system. "Tell me what you want me to do, Austin."

Austin is visibly uncomfortable, his expression distorted, like he's fighting his natural urge to console me. I don't expect him to wipe away my tears this time. "I'm not leaving you here with Zach. I'll take you back to my place, and you can decide what to do from there. Is that okay?"

I nod even though nothing feels okay. I don't want to decide what to do or where to go next. I want to rewind the past fifteen minutes, to the moment Austin kissed the tip of my nose and promised me he wouldn't let me burn in the sun, and when Zach approaches, I'll keep my mouth shut this time around. *Oh, Gabby, why couldn't you have just kept your mouth shut?*

As Austin drives, I bury my head in my hands and smother my sobs, praying with every fiber of my being that there is some way out of the mess I've made.

20

What is wrong with me?

No, seriously.

What is wrong with me?

Why do I keep doing this to Austin? Why do I keep on hurting him over and over again? How difficult is it, really, to be a decent human being and friend?

As I work my way around Austin's bedroom, tossing more of my clothes into my suitcase, I feel deflated and hopeless. The second we got home, he shut himself in his office downstairs and left me to pack my bags. I can't even be angry at him, because he is completely justified in his choice to throw me out of his house. When you've broken someone down so many times before, there's only so many second chances they can give you, and I've wasted all of them. It's all my fault. *Again.* And now I have to crawl back to my quiet, lonely life in Durham and find another way to build myself from the ground up. I can finish my bachelor's degree at Duke, I can find a better apartment, start a career . . . But none of that seems all that fulfilling without my best friend in my life, and I know I need to fight one final time for Austin Pierce's forgiveness. I need to exhaust every apology possible, and if there's one thing we're good at, it's signing contracts.

I ditch the packing for now and make my way downstairs with a newfound surge of adrenaline pumping through my veins. If this doesn't work, then nothing else will.

Outside the office door, I suck in a deep breath and knock gently. "Austin?"

"Not now, Gabby," Austin grumbles, but that will never be enough to stop me.

"Please can I come in for a sec?" I ask, pressing my forehead against the door and waiting out his silence. "Please? There are some things I'd like to say before I leave, because I can't walk out of this house without telling you how sorry I am. Please, Austin. Just hear me out and if you still want me to leave, I will without another word."

A few more beats of silence pass. I hear a chair scoot against the floor, and then the door clicks open. Austin stares down at me with a burned-out expression. At this point in our history, he is tired of it all. Tired of me and my excuses and my apologies.

"Can I borrow some paper?" I ask, and his brows knit together dubiously. "And a pen, too."

"Gabby, what are you—?"

I imitate Teddy the Labrador from the shelter and give Austin the most pleading, adorable puppy-dog eyes I can possibly pull off. "Please?"

Austin sighs as he gives in. He turns back into his office and pulls a small stack of paper out of the printer, grabs a *Pierce Wealth Management* embossed ballpoint pen, then hands them over.

"Come with me," I instruct, gesturing for him to follow me out of his study. I stride over to the kitchen island and slap the paper down on the countertop, then cast a sideways glance at Austin as I hover the pen over the top sheet. "I can promise you a thousand times that I'll do better, that I'll be different . . . But I think you need it in cold, hard ink."

I take my lower lip between my teeth in concentration and write: *Your secrets will always be my secrets too, and I'll never share anything you tell me in confidence.*

I scribble my signature underneath, then flick over to a fresh sheet of paper.

On this one, I write: *I will have your back no matter what, and will defend you in every situation even if you're wrong,* and then sign my name beneath that, too.

I'm so nervous, the tremor in my hands is clear in my chicken-scratch handwriting. I grab another sheet, and another, and another, writing down every single one of my promises:

You will come first every single time, no matter what.
I won't repeat past mistakes.
I'll try my best to always make you happy, and I'll never hurt you on purpose.

I spread out the signed papers across the countertop and step back, practically vibrating from the adrenaline rush of trying to get all of my words out so quickly.

I don't know how else to drill it into Austin's brain that my intentions are genuine, that I want this to work more than anything, that I'm not the cruel Gabrielle he knew when we were teenagers.

He pulls out a chair and slumps down into it, running his hands over the sheets of paper in front of him while I hold my breath. When he doesn't say anything at all, I decide to take a risk.

"Austin," I say clearly, draping my arms around his neck and hugging him from behind. I press my face into the crook of his neck, squeezing my eyes shut. He still smells like the beach. "I was the biggest idiot in the world when we were younger, but I promise . . . *I promise* if ever I am an idiot these days, it is never on purpose. I care about you so much." My words are muffled against the cotton fabric of his shirt, and he remains frozen beneath my grip on him. "Please don't make me leave. I can't bear to lose you after how much progress we've made."

Finally, he reaches up to squeeze one of my hands as he bows his head forward, and my chest relaxes with the tiniest bit of relief. "I don't want you to leave, Gabby," he murmurs, "but the way I feel about you scares the hell out of me."

"The way I feel about *you* scares the hell out of me, too," I whisper, "because I am so terrified of ruining it all. You're my best friend, Austin. You always have been, and I just need you to trust me. Just one more time."

I snuggle even deeper into him, arms wrapped tight around his neck, his hand holding mine. We remain like this for what feels like forever, but I don't even mind. If he still asks me to leave, this will be the last time I ever enjoy his embrace and I want to make it count. I want to drag it out long enough to memorize it.

Eventually, I hear a quiet, "Okay."

I lift my head from his shoulder and my heart straight-up skips three whole beats. "Okay?" I repeat, too scared to believe it.

Austin twists within my arms, angling himself to face me. His hands lower to my waist as he tucks me between his legs, and the way his gaze has softened is enough alone to make me want to scream from the roof-tops. "One more time," he says with a very serious nod, and I mirror him with an even bigger nod of my own. A defeated smile toys at the corner of his mouth, and that's when I finally relax in relief. "Truth is . . . I've missed you the past hour."

"I miss you always," I murmur, cupping his face in my hands and pressing a kiss to the crown of his head. "Oh. There's still sand in your hair."

"Then perhaps a shower is needed," he says with a grin, and a scream rips from my throat as he stands from the chair and tosses me straight over his shoulder, carrying me upstairs.

21

Buck doesn't need me back at the bar on Monday, so I stay in Wilmington for an extra day.

Austin has to work, of course. He leaves a lingering kiss on my forehead as he slips out of bed and I watch him through a sleepy haze as he gets ready for the day. It's incredibly hot watching him buckle his belt, secure his tie, spray some cologne. I love men, and I especially enjoy this one. I was so close to losing him yesterday that waking up with him this morning feels extra joyful.

"You're sure you'll be okay by yourself today?" he asks, straightening out some creases in his shirt. "Call me if you need anything."

I'm on my stomach, face pressed into the pillows as I turn to give him a lazy smile. "I'll be fine. Have a nice day at work, darling."

Austin shrugs on his jacket and adjusts his watch. He smolders his eyes at me across the dim room. "You look so good with your ass in the air like that."

I purse my lips. "You're the boss. Take a sick day and come back to bed."

"If only I could," he says with a groan. He crosses the bedroom, leans down to kiss me once more, then heads off to work to study stock prices on behalf of the wealthy.

I snuggle up in the spot he's vacated and nap for another hour before I drag myself out of bed. I'm not sure *exactly* what I'm supposed to do all day without my best friend, but I start off with consuming a monstrous bowl of cereal in front of the giant TV in the living room, and then I decide to make myself useful. I wrestle fresh sheets onto the bed, throw on a load of laundry, vacuum the carpets. I even, remarkably for the first time in my entire life, *iron*. As I hang up Austin's crease-free shirts in his closet, I stare at my nails.

They are in desperate need of a manicure.

And Sasha Tate requires an apology.

When she showed up at that dive bar a month ago, it was another reminder of the awful way I used to treat people. We were good friends throughout high school, yet the second I left for Duke, I grew too big for my own boots and abandoned my old friends in the dust. The new friends I made at Duke weren't even all that nice, and when you push everyone away, you end up with no one at all.

I turn to the internet once again to help hunt down the ghosts of my past. I found Austin within minutes, and I find Sasha just as fast. Her salon's website is the first result that pops up when I search "Sasha Tate Beautician Wilmington NC."

I call the number and pick anxiously at my cuticles as I listen to the dial tone, before a friendly voice answers with an upbeat hello.

"Sasha? It's Gabby," I say, then clear my throat. "Gabrielle McKinley."

"Gabby! What's up?"

I stormed out of the bar the last time I saw her, thanks to Austin being mean, so I hope she doesn't think I've turned a little bit crazy over the years. "You're probably fully booked, but I don't suppose you could squeeze me in today? My nails need some major TLC."

"Can you make it down here within the next fifteen minutes?"

"I'll leave right now. See you soon!"

I double-check the salon address before hopping in my car and heading downtown. At the worst possible time for distraction as I'm hopelessly attempting to parallel park (not my forte), my mom calls. I haven't seen her since the shelter's adoption event, but I *have* attempted to text her even though our messages are just a thread of agonizing small talk.

I answer the call on speaker. "Hi, Mom. Is everything okay?"

"Zachary came by this morning," she says, and instantly my stomach drops. "His eye is black and blue. Is there anything you'd like to tell me, Gabrielle?"

I put my car in park and squeeze my phone in my hand. My mind races, unaware of just how much Zach has shared with Mom about what went down at the beach yesterday. I'm certainly not going to fall into the trap of telling her myself, so I simply say, "No, I don't think so."

My mother tuts, as she so often does. "You know I'm not fond of that Austin Pierce, and this is exactly why. Fighting with your bother in public . . . That's disgraceful! He seems like a terrible influence and that's not what you need when you're trying to get back on your feet."

"Zach threw the first punch, Mom," I point out, but a trickle of relief works its way through me. If Zach had told Mom the truth about the secret trust Dad left behind for Austin, that would absolutely be the focus of this conversation, and it's not, which means that secret is still safe for now.

"Are you sure, Gabrielle?"

"I witnessed it with my very own eyeballs, so yes, I'm sure."

"Now why would he have done that?" she questions.

"There was a little misunderstanding," I lie. "Austin's allowed to defend himself. Definitely not a bad influence. But look, I've got to go. I'm catching up with an old friend from high school. Don't stress too much, Mom. Bye!"

I cut off the call before she has a chance to respond and head across the street toward the salon. It's in a nice area of downtown, must cost an absolute bomb in commercial rent, and has an Instagram-worthy aesthetic of baby pinks and silvers. Sasha must be doing pretty well for herself, and I feel a twitch of jealousy that, once again, it's clear I've fallen so many steps behind in life compared to my peers.

A bell tinkles as I push open the door.

"Perfect timing!" Sasha says chirpily, bouncing over to greet me. The scent of the most gorgeous perfume follows her. "How are you? Come sit down."

She leads me over to the nail station and I nervously sit down opposite her. We exchange the usual pleasantries as she gets to work on buffing my nails in preparation for a French manicure, and then I take a breath and say, "I'm sorry."

Sasha glances up at me, her soft features frowning with confusion. "For what?"

"I'm sorry for ignoring your attempts to keep in touch after we graduated," I apologize. I drop my gaze to my hands on the table, one held by Sasha as she works. "I was in a Duke bubble and it wasn't right of me to treat the people I grew up with like you were all disposable. We had a lot of fun together back in the day, and I just wanted you to know that you didn't do anything wrong—it was just me being a bitch. That was kind of my thing, I guess. Didn't graduate with a sparkling reputation, did I?"

Sasha's hands pause over mine and I lift my eyes to meet hers. "I appreciate that, Gabby, but honestly? I wasn't much better. God, I lie awake at nights sometimes and cringe when I think of some of the things I said and did."

"If we look back now and regret it, does that mean we've changed?"

Sasha nods with a small, sympathetic smile. "I'd like to think so. Self-reflection and all that, right? These days

247

when I run into people we went to high school with, I make the effort to be friendly. Everyone is pretty cool, you know."

I swallow the lump in my throat. "Like Austin Pierce?"

"Yeah. Like Austin," Sasha agrees, and I swear she bites back a sheepish smile as she returns to working on my nails. "What was all that about in the bar last month?"

"Austin and I were best friends in high school," I say, and that now feels like a smug brag rather than the confession it would have been once upon a time.

"What do you mean?"

"Well, not *in* school," I clarify. "Outside, in private, where no one would know. I thought I'd suffer the same fate as him if I dared defend him . . . so I didn't. He never spoke to me again after senior prom, but can you really blame him after the things I said and did that night? But we're back in touch now, because in case it wasn't obvious, I'm trying to apologize for the old Gabrielle's mistakes."

"If that scene in the bar is anything to go by, it doesn't seem like he's buying your apologies . . ."

I manage a laugh. "It was definitely rough at first, but now we're . . ." My words trail off, because I'm not sure just how honest I should be here. Austin had a previous fling with Sasha, and as much as the old Gabby would fly off the handle into a jealous cat fight, the more mature and improving Gabby knows their history is none of my business. "It's going really well now. This time around, it's more than just a friendship."

I hold my breath as I register Sasha's reaction, but she only lifts her brows in surprise and grins. "Aww! It's like friends to enemies to lovers! That's my favorite trope in romance books. Can you keep me updated on how this progresses? I want to know!"

My smile mirrors hers. "Then how about brunch and mimosas sometime?"

*

Since I'm downtown anyway, I swing by Austin's office with a tray of iced lattes and a box of donuts. Helen on the front desk greets me when I arrive, though her smile is bashful and her eye contact minimal. It's been a while since that afternoon she found Austin and me parading around the office semi-naked, but it's the first time I've seen her again, and clearly there's a lingering embarrassment. Though if anyone should be embarrassed, it's me. And I'm not, because I'm too happy to care.

"Hi, Helen!" I say, sliding the coffees and donuts onto the front desk. "I brought these for you guys. Is Austin with a client right now? I won't hang around."

"Oh, how lovely. Thank you, Gabrielle," Helen says. She plucks one of the coffees from the tray and clicks around on her computer. "He is, but he should be wrapping up soon. You're more than welcome to wait around!"

"Perfect! How's Carly Buck the Cactus doing?" I point over my shoulder at the cactus that sits in the waiting area, and Helen laughs. "She looks a little . . . shriveled. Does she need watered?"

"She definitely needs watered."

While I wait for Austin to finish up in his meeting, I douse Carly Buck the Cactus in water and readjust the spread of finance magazines on the couches, musing with Helen about my upcoming re-enrollment to Duke.

When Austin walks his client out, his eyes find mine the same way they did two months ago when he first encountered me in his office's reception. Except now, I am not an anxious bundle of nerves, and Austin doesn't spiral into rage. His smile is gorgeous and vivacious and I hate that I never made him smile like that in public when we were kids.

"I brought coffee! And donuts," I announce, closing the distance between us and mindlessly reaching for his hand because I crave the feeling of his fingers brushing mine. "I don't know what your associates like to drink, so I just got everyone iced lattes. Though this one is decaf for you."

I pass him a coffee and his gaze shines with appreciation, because I may have forgotten so many of the little things from our childhood, but I'm trying to remember all of the small details now. Like the fact that he drinks decaf and he hates maple syrup and he prefers his showers lukewarm and he wears the green running shoes on Sundays but the white pair every other day. It's easy to memorize someone when you care this deeply for them.

"Thanks, Gabby," he says, pressing a kiss to my temple and setting my skin ablaze. "This is really great of you. What are you doing downtown?"

"I got my nails done," I say, wiggling my fingers in front of his face to show off my manicure. It breaks my heart that by the end of the week, they'll most likely be chipped from working the bar again. "I had a really nice chat with Sasha."

Austin's joyful expression falters with surprise and a touch a panic. "Oh? You caught up with Sasha?"

"Don't look so scared. We aren't going to fight over you," I tease, rolling my eyes. Though if I *had* to, I would. "I wanted to say sorry to her for not staying in touch after high school. We're going to grab brunch sometime. See, now I have *two* friends! Look at me; breaking out of Loserville."

Austin's gorgeous smile returns. "I'm really proud of you."

And there it is again, that flip of my stomach. Those are my favorite words in the entire world, and it makes me want to be the best person I can possibly be just to hear Austin say he's proud of me for the rest of my life.

If we weren't in the office right now, I'd snuggle into his chest, but I don't want to subject Helen to any more PDA, so I keep my hands to myself and blush fiercely instead, like only Gabrielle McKinley can do.

"I'll get going," I say. "I'll make dinner for you getting home later. Though it'll probably be something super simple like mac 'n' cheese, but it'll be made with love."

Austin arches an eyebrow. Helen lifts her head from the front desk. I physically cringe and pray the ground will swallow me whole. Did I really just slip the word *love* into that sentence?

"Okay, I'm leaving now," I say, retreating backward toward the door. "Enjoy the coffee. Enjoy the donuts. Make your clients lots of money. Bye!"

Austin's grin tracks me all the way out the door.

22

"I'm super, super excited to see you in a tux," I muse, glancing into the backseat of the car at the tux inside a dust cover hanging from the clothes hook. "Immensely excited."

"You see me in a suit all the time," Austin points out.

"But not a *tuxedo*, Austin. And you'll be wearing a bow tie too." I flirtatiously whistle and fan my face with my hand. "Hot."

We are two hours into the three-hour drive to Charlotte for the business awards taking place this evening, and I can tell by Austin's demeanor that he's incredibly nervous. He's quieter than usual, lost inside his head. As this weekend drew closer, he became increasingly distracted throughout the week. My jokes and teasing aren't met with the same energy they usually are.

"Hey," I say gently, reaching over to secure my hand over Austin's in his lap. "It's okay. This is an amazing achievement regardless of whether you win or not. To be nominated this soon in your career is incredible, Austin. My dad would be so, so impressed."

Austin releases a long, steady breath. "I don't even know why I'm this nervous. I don't really care if I win or lose, you know?" He yanks his hand out from beneath mine and jerks the steering wheel harshly to one side, saving us from swaying into the opposite lane and getting crushed by a truck.

I chew my lip in concern, because clearly he is too distracted to be in control of my literal life. "Would you like me to drive? You can take this last hour to relax. Maybe close your eyes for a bit?"

Austin flashes me a cynical look. "You? Drive?"

"Excuse *me*. Just because my car is a pile of rust doesn't mean I'm not a good driver. The dent in my bumper? That barrier hit *me*." I smile sweetly and bat my eyelashes, but still Austin's nerves won't let up. I drop my shoulders and turn serious. "I won't crash your car, Austin."

He contemplates the offer for a few moments and then pulls into the next rest stop. As we switch positions, he rattles off some spiel about torque and power to the rear that I completely ignore because I'm too excited by all of the controls in front of me.

"I regret this so much already," Austin mumbles, propping an elbow up against the door and resting his head in his hand. As I merge back onto the highway, I am way too enthusiastic with the gas pedal and the engine growls aggressively as we're thrown back into our seats. "*Gabby*," he warns. "I don't need us getting pulled over. Light foot, please?"

I flash him a pout, my hands gripping the wheel like a race car driver, because that's exactly what I feel like right now and it's so goddamn fun. "But when do I ever get to drive a fast car? Let me play a little."

Austin glares at me through narrowed eyes, but his lips betray him with a smile. He sinks into the passenger seat and folds his arms over his chest as he watches me floor it down the outside lane, making fast progress toward Charlotte. "Hmm," he says after a while.

I glance sideways at him. "What?"

"You look so good driving my car," he murmurs, sitting up. "Too good, actually."

Austin reaches for my right hand on the wheel and moves it to his lips, his kisses brushing my knuckles as he works his way down my arm. By the time he reaches my shoulder, I have goosebumps, and I care less about the thrill of driving a fast car and more about the thrill of his touch. He runs a hand up my bare thigh until his fingers reach the button of my jean shorts.

"*Austin*," I gasp. "I thought you were stressed."

"I can think of a way to distract myself," he mumbles, his lips still trailing over my skin.

"But I'm driving," I say, my heart racing as Austin undoes the button, pulls down the zipper. I make no attempt to push his hand away even though the road ahead blurs, and suddenly his hands are in my panties and he's touching me in all of the ways he absolutely shouldn't be.

I bite my lip hard, blinking manically as I try my damn hardest to focus on the road when all I want to do is embrace the pleasure of his touch. "I may actually crash your car now."

Austin nips my shoulder with his teeth and hisses, "Then crash it."

"Austin, please," I beg, bracing my head against the headrest, fighting the urge to roll my eyes. "I can't . . . I can't focus on the road."

"Concentrate, Gabby. You handle the road, and I'll handle you."

His words alone are enough to weaken me at the knees. I do as I'm told, locking my eyes on the highway in front of me as my breaths grow shallow. I'm convinced Austin has magical powers, because how the hell does he make me come so easily? The moan that escapes me is involuntary and my thighs twitch. I turn to Austin, lips parted, stunned.

"You scare me," I confess as he very kindly buttons up my shorts again. "How do you do that?"

Austin shrugs with a smug smirk. "It's easy when you're that wet for me," he says, then slouches back in the passenger seat again, closes his eyes, and naps the rest of the drive as though he didn't just make me come in less than a minute.

The hotel where the awards are being held tonight is thankfully already plugged into the navigation, so I tour my way through downtown Charlotte and expertly park the car in the hotel parking lot all before Austin's eyes ping open. He seems rather impressed that I got us here in one piece.

It's the kind of hotel you'd expect business awards to be held in. Upscale, luxurious, expensive. Austin carries our bags and his protected tux to our room, pushing open the door to reveal the grand suite he's booked for the night. It's a special occasion, after all, and our first weekend away together. I throw myself onto the huge, plush bed as Austin pops open the bottle of champagne on the dresser. I could get used to this life. The past two months, we have been living in our own little bubble, spending most of our time at Austin's house each weekend, but perhaps it's time we made this relationship more public.

As Austin sits on the edge of the bed next to me and passes me a glass of champagne, I clink my glass against his and say, "Cheers to being a sexy wealth manager with a booming business. You're amazing."

I swear, absolutely positively swear, that the tips of Austin's ears turn red. He takes a swig of the champagne and smiles. "I'm really glad you're here with me, Gabby."

"I'm really glad you invited me," I say, my smile mirroring his. I lean into him and press my lips softly to his, tasting the champagne. "Whatever happens, I'm proud of you."

There are only two hours until the event starts, so we share a couple of glasses of champagne in celebration before I hop into the shower. It's been a long, long time since I've attended an event of any kind, and I've become far too comfortable working behind the bar in sneakers and tank tops. I'm not sure when I last wore a pair of heels. Or a dress, for that matter. But Carly scoured the mall with me before our shift at the bar one morning, offering her opinion on every dress I tried on, until I found the perfect one that is equal parts classy and sexy.

Austin sits up from relaxing on the bed when he notices me pull my hot iron out of my bag. "You're straightening your hair?"

"You don't want me to?"

"I don't mind," he says. "I just haven't seen your hair straight since high school."

And clearly he is invested, because he watches me in the mirror in front of the dresser the entire time I straighten out my curls. It takes forever, since I've embraced my natural curls for years, and my arms ache by the time I'm done. My reflection takes some adjusting to: once upon a time I would never have been caught dead with my curls, but now I miss them already.

Austin disappears into the shower while I do my makeup. I'm not very good at it, mostly because I rarely wear much more than mascara these days, and I nearly have a mental breakdown trying to apply some false eyelashes, because God, why won't those inner corners stay down? I apply red lipstick. Spray some perfume. Slip into my dress. As I'm putting in my earrings, I realize we should really be downstairs by now, enjoying complimentary champagne before the ceremony starts.

"Austin?" I call out, knocking on the bathroom door. "We should really get going."

Austin immediately steps out of the bathroom while securing the cuff links of his shirt, and I widen my eyes at him in awe because I have never in my life seen not only Austin Pierce, but *any* man, look this sexy. I realize right then that my new kink is tuxedos. And bow ties. Definitely bow ties.

"Well, hello, handsome," I purr, smoldering my eyes at him as his cologne fills the room.

Austin doesn't laugh. He stands still, his eyes traveling from my exposed collarbones down to the strappy heels on my feet. "Gabrielle, you look . . . Damn, you look stunning."

I glance down. The red satin shines under the light, the dress's long, conservative length offering a teasing slit in the leg. It has dainty little spaghetti straps and a cowl neckline that makes it extremely delicate and feminine. "You really think so?"

Austin gulps and checks his watch, the silver one that's never off his wrist. "If we didn't have to be downstairs right about now, I'd have that makeup smudged in a thousand different ways. I'm not going to be able to take my eyes off you all night, Gabby." He steps forward, eyes still scanning me, his lip caught between his teeth. His fingers brush over the satin fabric above my hipbone and our eyes lock, an intensity building in the small space between us. "How lucky am I?"

I shuffle up closer, pressing my chest to his. Hooking my hand around the soft, freshly trimmed nape of his neck, I guide his mouth toward mine, but hesitate before I kiss him. Our gazes locked, I smile seductively and dare to whisper, "Can't you just fuck me gently?"

Austin crashes his lips explosively to mine. We should be downstairs, I know, but we can't keep our hands off one another. He backs me up hard against the wall and I swing my leg around his waist, hungrily undoing the button of his pants. He traces a hand up my leg, my skin soft and moisturized, and hikes up the fabric of my dress. Turning me around, he presses me onto the bed. I lean on my arms, refusing to bury my face into the sheets. I didn't have a breakdown applying these eyelashes for nothing.

Austin positions himself behind me, moves my panties to one side, and enters me fully in one solid thrust. Now my eyes do roll back in my head, because it's pure heaven. Quickies are so hot. Nothing but desire and passion and an insatiable hunger. Austin's strokes are fast but careful, and with each thrust forward, a gasped breath leaves my lips.

"Shit, I'm going to come already," Austin groans. "You look so good and you feel even better."

"Don't come on my dress," I warn.

"Then open that pretty mouth."

Austin pulls out and I follow his very clear instruction. Pushing myself up from the bed, I turn around and drop to my knees on the floor in front of him. One hand of his is back on my jaw, the other finishes himself off. I tilt my head back and lock my eyes on his, but he can barely look at me without a moan rising in his throat.

"You and that red lipstick ..." he mutters, and I part those stained red lips of mine, stick out my tongue, and swallow every last drop as he comes. "You're my favorite girl in the world, Gabby."

"I'd like to think so," I say, placing my hands in his as he pulls me to my feet. Just as I wipe away a smudge of red lipstick from his lips, his phone rings from across the room.

Austin dashes over to grab it while buttoning up his pants and tucking his shirt back in, and when I check out my reflection in the mirror, I don't look *too* disheveled at all.

"We're on our way down right now," Austin says into his phone, then hangs up and hastily shoves it into his pocket. He reaches for my hand and tugs me toward the door. "Quick, everyone is seated."

"*Seated?*" I repeat, feeling the color drain from my face. Great. How do I walk into an entire ballroom late without blushing because I was upstairs in the hotel room getting frisky? I grab my clutch as we leave and we hurry down the hallway to the elevator. "Who was that, anyway? One of your associates?"

"No, my mom."

"Your parents are here?" I hiss, because can't a girl get a heads-up when she's about to spend the evening with her boyfriend's parents who hate her?

"Of course they're here," Austin says, repeatedly smashing the button for the hotel lobby as though that'll get us there quicker. "I thought you'd know that? Don't worry. They're under strict orders to be nice."

I don't respond. Between the race to get to the ballroom and this new knowledge of Austin's parents being here, I am now a complete and utter nervous wreck. I quickly touch up my lipstick before we spring out of the elevator. Austin's hand finds mine and he hurries me along in my heels through the lobby. The ballroom doors are closed, and when Austin pushes them open, an entire sea of faces swivels toward us.

Fire. That's what my cheeks feel like right now. A raging, scorching fire.

The crowd is silent as a woman gives a welcome speech up front next to giant digital screens, and I keep my head down low as Austin weaves the way through the circular tables toward ours. Above the floral table centerpiece, there's a sign that says *"Pierce Wealth Management."* We slot into the two empty chairs and when I build the courage to glance up, the very first person I catch eyes with is Austin's mother.

Her mouth is a bold line and she is so very clearly unimpressed. Walking into this ballroom late with her son is doing me no favors when it comes to winning her over, because I'm certain it doesn't take a genius to figure out what we could possibly have been up to. This is confirmed when my gaze shifts to Helen and she flashes me a knowing smile.

Lord, save me.

Austin's hand finds mine beneath the table and he offers it a reassuring squeeze as we focus ahead at the woman hosting the event. I swear I don't hear a single word she says because my ears are ringing so loud. Numbly, I join in the applause when the rest of the ballroom claps, and then the musings of hundreds of voices rises through the room. There will be a meal first before the awards presentation, which means for the next hour or two I am required to make small talk with Austin's parents and his associates.

"You missed the canapés and champagne," Caroline, Austin's mother, says in disapproval. "Where were you two?"

"Time got away from us," Austin says casually, and he reaches for the bottle of champagne in a bucket of ice in the center of the table. He fills my glass, his own, then tops off the rest of the table's glasses. "Let's toast," he says, holding up his flute of champagne. "Thank you all for being here tonight. Mom, Dad, thanks for always pushing me to be the best I can be. Helen, thanks for keeping my diary in check. Alison, Craig, Tyler, thanks for trusting in my vision strongly enough to come on board and be a part of it. Gabrielle," he says, eyes fastening on me with a smile so pure it makes everyone else in this ballroom disappear, "thank you for reminding me that life doesn't have to be so serious all of the time. It can also be about Marvel movie marathons, picking out toys for the shelter dogs, and making pancakes on Sundays."

"Cheers," we all say in unison, clinking glasses.

Austin's parents, however, are still miffed. I get the vibe they weren't given the heads-up about my presence here tonight either, but perhaps this will be a good thing. Maybe they'll see I'm not that bad, that I'm here because I support and care for Austin, and I'd never, ever do anything to hurt him again.

So, I'm on my best behavior.

As we sit through the three-course meal, I dip in and out of conversations with the rest of the table, showing interest and asking questions with Austin's associates and their partners. I don't refill my champagne flute that often, because the last thing I want is to lose all inhibitions. I also don't talk too much, because I have a bad habit of making too many crass jokes that most likely only Austin would find the humor in. Tonight, I am polite, shy, and hopefully forgivable.

By the time the meal wraps up and the awards ceremony gets rolling, Caroline and Mike's icy demeanors seem to have thawed, though I'm pretty sure Mike is just straight-up wasted. Austin, Helen and the other advisors become increasingly nervous as the host works through each award category until she reaches the final award. Pierce Wealth Management is nominated for Best New Business, and as the nominees for the category are read out, I swear all five of them hold their breath.

Now it's my turn to squeeze Austin's hand under the table. "Good luck," I whisper.

The host opens an envelope and leans forward into the mic. "And the Best New Business Award this year goes to . . . Pierce Wealth Management!"

Applause fills the room, but our table is the loudest. Mike thumps the table in celebration, while Caroline jumps to her feet and cheers with pride. Austin slips his hand around my waist as I wrap him in a brief hug with an immense amount of self-restraint not to kiss him. He buttons his tux jacket and exchanges congratulatory handshakes with his associates before they all head toward the stage to collect the award. They each say a few words, then get ushered out of the ballroom to have professional pictures taken.

As the lights dim and music plays through giant speakers, the atmosphere in the ballroom relaxes, yet I am far from relaxed because I feel so vulnerable without Austin here to have my back. I reach for a bottle of champagne to top up my glass in order to keep my hands busy, but Caroline slides over into the empty seat Austin has left beside me.

"More champagne?" I offer with a polite smile despite the tightness in my chest, but Caroline shakes her head no. Her solemn expression is unnerving, so I fill my own glass and take the high road. "How amazing that they won, right? I'm so proud of Austin."

And the decent thing would be to agree with me, to make civil conversation and remain pleasant, but no—Caroline simply says, "I don't think you should be here."

I look at her with indignation. "Excuse me?"

"I don't think you should be here," she repeats. Her eyes dart around the room, perhaps scanning for Austin making his return to the table, and when she doesn't spot him, she scoots in even closer to me. In a low, tortured voice, she says, "You broke him, Gabby."

"Caroline—"

"Listen to me," she cuts in sharply, holding up her hand to silence me. "You think we are holding a grudge against you over some playground games, and maybe that's all it was to you, but you have no idea . . ." She squeezes her eyes shut for a moment and sucks in a breath. "No idea at all what you put him through. We were so happy he'd made a friend when we first moved into your neighborhood, but as the years went on, our lovely, happy boy became a shell of himself. A seventeen-year-old should be enjoying their senior year, attending football games, and getting tipsy on beer for the first time. Instead he'd come home from school with these empty, ghostly eyes and shut himself away in his room all evening. And I know it wasn't just you, Gabby. I know there were a lot of cruel kids at school, but he had such a soft spot for you. You broke so much trust with him. You made him question what he did wrong. You made him ask himself what the point was. He didn't deserve that, Gabrielle, and to let him believe he was taking you to prom . . . It was the height of cruelty, and *you broke him*."

My heart malfunctions, seizing up in my chest. "I know."

"And you show up *now*, all these years later, when he's happy and confident and successful. How can I trust that you won't break him down all over again? How do I accept the girl who once had me holding my teenage son in my arms as he cried his poor little heart out? You have no idea how much it took for Mike and me to pull him out of the hole he was in."

Caroline visibly seethes with contempt, but I reach for her hand in her lap and grip it tight. "Caroline, I know there aren't enough words to convey just how deep my apologies are, but I promise . . . I promise with everything in me that I will *not* hurt him again."

"And how do you expect me to believe that?" she whispers, pulling her hand free of mine.

"Because I'm falling in love with him," I splutter. There is no hesitation when I say it, only frustration. *I'm falling in love with him*, and his parents don't believe me, and they're going to push me away and ruin everything. "I want to support him at award ceremonies whether he wins or loses, I want to wait for him at the finish line of marathons, I want to make terrible jokes around him because it took me far too long to realize his laugh is my favorite sound in the world. *Please,* Caroline," I beg, my eyes wide with desperation. "Please let me make him happy."

Caroline's eyes drift over my shoulder as a flicker of guilt crosses her features. I twist around, and my entire body stiffens when Austin's gaze meets mine.

23

"*Austin,*" I gasp. I haven't said a single incriminating word, yet the heat of humiliation still radiates through my entire body. Did he hear everything I just said?

The expression in Austin's gaze is unreadable. The muscle in his jaw tightens as he looks to Caroline and very sternly asks, "Are you bothering Gabrielle, Mom?"

"Of course not," Caroline stammers, but Austin sees straight through the flustered shaking of her head. "We were just chatting."

Austin reaches for my hand, gently pulling me to my feet and wrapping a secure arm around my waist as Caroline stares up at us both, looking guilty as sin. "Thanks for coming, but I think Gabby and I will continue the celebrations upstairs, where she'll be safe from ambush."

"You're leaving?" Mike asks, staggering over.

"Sorry, Dad, but it seems Mom can't follow my crystal fucking clear instructions."

"*Hey,*" Mike snaps, pointing a finger into Austin's chest, but Austin simply brushes his hand away.

"Goodnight, everyone," he says coolly with a courteous wave to the table.

Hand on my hip, Austin guides me away and I am all too happy to follow. My emotions are so heightened, I have to blink hard to fight the sting of tears that threaten to fall. We make a hasty departure from the ballroom and back into the elevator, though we are accompanied by some guests and their luggage, so Austin and I stand together in silence. As we head down the hall toward our suite, I squeeze his hand and try to pull him to a stop.

"Austin . . ."

"Shh," he says.

"Can I just—?"

"*Shh.*"

Austin releases my hand as he fumbles with the keycard for the room, then holds the door open for me. It's dark out and the lights of downtown Charlotte shine through the large windows, casting an ambient orange glow over the suite. I reach over for the light switch, but Austin steps in front of me, cups my face in both hands, and looks me straight in the eye.

"I'm sorry," he says, and my brows knit together in confusion. "I'm sorry my mom made you uncomfortable. I'm sorry you had to defend yourself again."

And his blue eyes are so beautiful in the dim light that it breaks every single part of me because his mother didn't say a single thing that I didn't already know myself.

My chest heaves and I shatter into sobs, collapsing forward against him, smearing makeup into his pristine white shirt. "But she's right, Austin," I whisper weakly, my voice barely audible. "I *don't* deserve you."

"Oh, Gabby, c'mon," he says into my hair, his lips brushing the crown of my head, "you know that's not true."

I tear myself from his chest and look up at him through wet lashes. "That time you said I'm a loser by choice? You were right. I can claim immaturity, but I knew the entire time growing up that I was a terrible person. When I lost my dad, I thought: this is it. This is my karma. And I *wanted* to suffer. So I quit school, sold my car, moved into the worst apartment I could find and cut off my social circles. I've been punishing myself for years, because I don't deserve . . ." I blow out a breath as my lower lip trembles. "I don't deserve an easy life, Austin. And I definitely don't deserve *you*."

Austin grabs my shoulders and lowers his head to draw his gaze level with mine. "Gabby, you told my mom you want to make me happy," he says, his words entwined with exasperation. "And you do. You make me *so* happy, Gabrielle, you have no idea. I want you, with all your quirks and flaws, because you're the girl I fell in love with when I was a kid, but also not that Gabby at all. You're all of the good parts and none of the bad, and I wish . . ." He shakes his head hard. "Damn it, how I wish you'd see that, too."

The walls feel like they are closing in around me, sucking all of the oxygen out of this hotel suite, and I suddenly feel so claustrophobic that I spiral into panic. I stumble back from Austin, my eyes squeezed shut, my hands in my hair. My breaths are harsh and ragged as I fight to regain control.

"I feel like . . . I can't breathe," I rasp. "I want out of this dress. And these . . . These shoes."

Austin's hands find my waist and he holds me steady until I stop fidgeting. With a delicate touch, he unzips my dress and helps me step out of it, then guides me to sit down on the edge of the bed. He sinks to his knees on the floor and unstraps my heels.

"Is that better?" he asks quietly, looking up at me as he wraps his fingers around mine.

But all I can focus on is my reflection in the mirror behind him, and I hate the straight hair and the heavy makeup. I tear off the strip lashes and claw at the ends of my hair. "I want my curls back. *I want my curls back.*"

Austin thinks for a moment, then rises from the floor and scoops me up off the bed. Naturally, I wrap my legs around his waist and he carries me effortlessly into the bathroom. He sticks an arm into the shower cubicle and turns on the water, and I give in completely as he sets me down and the water cascades over me like a waterfall. I squeeze my eyes shut, collapse back against the wall. The water is steaming hot and incredibly soothing and it's exactly what I need to get a grasp on all of the thoughts racing through my mind.

Austin shrugs off his jacket and rolls the sleeves of his shirt up to his elbows, then reaches for the shower head and rinses my hair for me. He stands at the edge of the shower in his tux, completely unfazed that he's getting wet, too. His hands are so gentle against my scalp as he works them through my hair and I have never felt as safe with someone as I do right now in this moment with Austin. His eyes are soft, his expression tender, and my heart swells painfully in my chest.

"Thank you," I whisper, watching him in admiration from beneath the cascade of water.

His smile is so gorgeous I can hardly bear it. "You've been fighting for my forgiveness this entire time," he murmurs, "but what you really need is to forgive *yourself*, Gabby. Please stop punishing yourself for past mistakes that you've already learned from. You're allowed to be happy. Your father would *want* you to be happy."

He attaches the shower head back onto the wall and steps fully under the water with me. His shirt clings to his chest, highlighting every contour and muscle, and he sinks to the floor and leans back against the wall, his knees pulled to his chest. I mirror his actions, sitting down opposite him as the water flows through the center of us.

After a while, Austin says, "Are you?"

I tilt my head in confusion, watching him through the stream of water. "Am I . . .?"

"Are you really falling in love with me?"

"No," I say, and Austin flinches with disappointment. I stretch forward and reach for his hand, interlocking it with mine. "I'm not falling in love with you, Austin. I *am* in love with you. It makes my stomach hurt. It's this

painful knot that squeezes tighter and tighter, and sometimes I feel it in my chest, too, and—"

"Move in with me," he interrupts, the words spilling
from his mouth as he sits fully upright.

"What?"

"Move in with me," he repeats, slower this time, with
weight. "Don't stay in Durham. I hate only seeing you
on weekends. I want to wake up to you in my bed in the
mornings and I want to come home from work to you
in the evenings, but fuck, I also want you to get that
Duke degree." He runs his free hand down his face in
frustration as beads of water drip from his hair.

"You can't ask me to move in with you after two
months," I point out, shaking my head at him in disbelief as my heart ricochets in my chest, because I so badly
want to say *yes, yes, yes.*

"I can when I'm this in love with you," he counters,
lifting his head to look at me again. He squeezes my hand
harder. "Because I am, Gabby. I'm in love with you, too,
but if I'm being honest with myself, I don't really think
there was ever a time I wasn't. So, it's not two months.
It's sixteen years of knowing you."

"Austin . . ."

"I know, Gabby," he says with a defeated groan.
"I know not yet. But one day?"

"One day," I promise, and then flash him a teasing
grin. "So I think this means you're my boyfriend now.
Or would you like to formally ask me? We can't confess *I love you* in the shower and *not* be together. You're
stuck with me now whether you like it or not. *Forever.*"

Austin's shoulders visibly relax as the sound of his gentle laugh echoes around the bathroom. "There she is," he says. "My goofy Gabby."

"Your goofy Gabby."

We smile at one another through the flowing water for what seems like an eternity, but an eternity I'd be happy to endure. And then he says, in a voice like silk, "I want nothing more than to be stuck with you forever, Gabrielle."

I sit up on my knees, stretch through the water to grab a fistful of his soaked shirt, and pull his lips to mine.

24

There are pancakes available at the breakfast buffet in the morning, so *of course* Austin and I exchange an amused smile before stacking some on our plates. It's Sunday, and we're together, and the rule is that when we're together on Sundays we have to have pancakes. It's literally an official agreement.

"Dad's waving us over to join them," Austin grumbles into my ear, and I follow the direction of his gaze to a table by the window where Caroline and Mike are already tucking into their breakfast.

"Then let's join them."

Austin raises an eyebrow at the suggestion. "Really?"

"Ignoring them at breakfast won't do me any favors," I point out with a shrug, starting forward in his parents' direction. "I have to just keep trying my best to win them over. Since I *am* your girlfriend and all."

We weave our way through the hotel restaurant toward Caroline and Mike, and I greet them with a timid smile. Surprisingly, Caroline seems rather abashed this morning. She nods meekly and then stares into her cup of coffee. Mike, on the other hand, was too drunk last night to have even noticed my chat with Caroline and is none the wiser to the tension. He pulls out chairs and keenly gestures for Austin and me to sit.

"Good morning, Champ!" he says, clapping a hand proudly over Austin's shoulder. "Get any sleep or was the champagne flowing all night? Those glasses went down a little too easy . . . I'm feeling rather tender this morning."

Austin blushes, just a little. We didn't get much sleep last night at all, but it certainly wasn't because we were popping more celebratory champagne.

"It was a great night," is the only response Austin manages. He gives his mother a pointed look. "And how are you this morning, Mom?"

"I think maybe the champagne got to me a little too . . ." she mumbles. Lifting her gaze, she finds mine. "Gabrielle, I'd like to apologize for the things I said last night. Austin can make his own decisions, and I've taken on board what you had to say, and I . . . Well, I believe you."

Mike furrows his brows and glances between Caroline and me with confusion. "What did Gabrielle say?" he questions. "Caroline? What did she say?"

"I'll tell you later," Caroline hisses, shushing him.

Mike rolls his eyes, then points a knife at Austin. "Have you seen the news?"

"No . . .?" Austin answers, narrowing his eyes with curiosity.

"The storm watch was changed to a warning."

"There was a storm watch?"

"Oh, c'mon, get your head out of the stock market and check your local weather reports, for God's sake," Mike says with a disapproving shake of his head. "Winds are starting to pick up on the coast already, and it's looking like the rain will pass over Wilmington in the early hours of tomorrow. We're hitting the road after this to get the house secured and I suggest you do the same."

"Shit, okay."

"And stock up on supplies," Caroline instructs. "Just in case your power gets cut off."

I stare somberly at my plate of pancakes, because although I adore living on the east coast, I do not like our hurricane season. Hurricane Florence was the last major storm to hit the Carolinas six years ago, and coastal homes were submerged as widespread floods wrecked Wilmington. It was the September I started studying at Duke, so I was safe further inland in Durham, glued to the TV news in my dorm while my parents evacuated our home. There was extensive damage to the first floor thanks to the thirty inches of rain that was dumped over the city.

"It's definitely just a tropical storm, though, right?" I ask nervously, glancing up at Mike in hope of some reassurance. I should really get out of my little Austin bubble and pay more attention to the news. "No chance of it being upgraded to a category one?"

"Definitely just a storm," Mike confirms, but is there even such a thing as *just* a storm?

*

Austin and I planned to spend the day in Charlotte, but we check out of the hotel after breakfast, toss our bags in the car, and hit the highway. You wouldn't think there was a storm brewing, given the clear blue skies and blazing sunshine, but the nearer we get to the coast, the more the trees sway in the breeze. Nothing says the first of September like an impending tropical storm.

As we make it back to Wilmington, Austin asks, "Would you like to visit Teddy at the shelter before we swing by the hardware store?"

"I *always* want to visit Teddy," I reply.

Fiona is always thrilled to see us each weekend, and today is no different. She's lugging sandbags out of her van when we pull up, and of course, Austin is quick to take over. He builds a stack of sandbags by the front entrance of the shelter, then moves some outdoor seating inside the building. It's all precautionary, but it does nothing to ease my growing anxiety.

"Will the dogs be okay?" I ask.

"They sure will!" Fiona says, tossing us a leash. "I'll spend the night here to make sure the building stays secure. It'll be one big slumber party."

We make our way down the kennel block, saying hi to the familiar faces and hi to the new ones, and then retrieve Teddy, who seems to be our chosen one to always receive special treatment. We can't help it; we *do* have a soft spot for him, whether or not Austin admits it. Teddy's sign now says he has been here at Saving Paws for nine hundred and eight-two days, and his sweet brown eyes make me crumble.

"Eighteen days," I sniff, following Austin and Teddy outside into the exercise field.

"Eighteen days . . .?" Austin repeats in confusion.

"Eighteen days left to find Teddy a home before he has officially been a shelter dog for one thousand days. *One thousand,* Austin." I fold my arms across my chest and pout my lips at him like it's all his fault. "I can't bear it."

"Look at him! He's happy," Austin says, unclipping Teddy's leash as he dashes off to pee on the fence and kick at the grass.

"He'd be happier on a couch. With blankets, and head scratches, and nibbles of cheese."

"*Everyone* would be happier on a couch with blankets and head scratches and nibbles of cheese."

I sigh and drop to the grass. Strands of curls dance across my face in the breeze as I lean back on my hands, watching Austin play tug over a rope toy with Teddy before he joins me on the grass. It was in this exact spot he first told me he likes it when I blush, and it's the *only* thing I can think about whenever we come out here with the dogs. A core memory.

"Teddy!" Austin calls, patting the grass in the spot between us. Teddy immediately prances over and curls up into a ball, because much like me, he prefers relaxation over exercise. "Gabby is still fighting for you, buddy."

"I am," I say with a steely nod of grit and determination as I scratch behind Teddy's ears. "I'll find you a home, even if it means organizing adoption events monthly and dressing you up in cute outfits."

"Maybe that's something we should look into," says Austin, and when I glance sideways at him, he's gazing pensively across the field. He meets my eyes and adds, "Pierce Wealth Management sponsored adoption events each month. Different venues across the city. Good for business, good for the shelter, good for the dogs. And good for you, of course, because I'd obviously need to hire someone to oversee these events." The corner of his mouth twitches, revealing a smile. "You clearly have a knack for marketing and event organization."

"Oh, Austin," I breathe, a grin stretching across my face, "that sounds amazing. I'd love to help! You wouldn't think I major in economics considering how skilled I am in other areas. Clearly I was born to run events for dog shelters."

Austin laughs and reaches for my hand, drawing it to his lips and brushing a soft kiss over my knuckles. "I'll discuss it with Fiona next week. We'll find Teddy a home, I promise."

"The *best* home."

"The best home," Austin agrees, patting Teddy's head. "C'mon, then. We better get going before the hardware store sells out of plywood."

"And before Walmart runs out of snacks."

"Well, *duh*."

We settle Teddy back into his kennel, bid farewell to the rest of the dogs and Fiona, and hit the stores. We flick between radio stations in the car, trying to catch more of the storm reports, because quite frankly, both of us feel a tiny bit silly for being completely oblivious to the tumultuous forecast until now. This is what I get for only watching Marvel movies and listening to podcasts and ignoring the real world, because now we're fighting over bottled water with strangers in Walmart and ramming plywood into the tiny trunk of Austin's car.

There's still no risk of the storm being upgraded, but after the sheer amount of destruction Florence caused as only a category one hurricane, no one takes any chances these days. *Any* kind of storm warning and people are battening down the hatches, just in case. Austin's house is pretty secure already, but we spend the rest of the afternoon preparing, anyway. We lock our cars up in the garage along with all of the patio furniture from the yard, and I assist Austin by looking cute while holding a tin of nails as he boards up his windows. It's pretty obvious the winds are strengthening as the evening draws closer, because each rumbling gust forces me to dig in my heels to maintain my balance. Just as we finish up and head inside, the clouds turn a threatening shade of gray and the rain arrives.

And I may hate storms, but it turns out I enjoy riding them out with Austin.

We cuddle together on the couch, blankets draped over us as the rain ricochets off the boarded windows and *Spider Man: No Way Home* plays on the giant TV. Every weekend we spend together, I have the exact same thought: that I could live in this bubble forever, just Austin and me, with my head resting on his chest and his heart beating soothingly in my ear. Half the time, I find myself falling asleep like this. His arms feel so safe.

Not only *could* I live in this bubble forever, I *want* to. I need to, in the same way I need oxygen.

I grab the remote and pause the movie. Kicking away the blankets, I swing my leg over Austin and settle into his lap, my hands pressed flat to his chest as I gaze down at his curious, but also confused expression. "What you said last night . . . about me moving in here with you?"

Austin's eyes brighten with hope. "Yes?"

"Obviously, I want my degree."

That sense of hope is instantly replaced with deflation as Austin releases a sigh. "I know, Gabby. I get it," he says softly, allowing his hands to naturally find my hips. "We can come back to the idea once you've finished school. We'll keep visiting each other on weekends until then, and time will pass fast—"

"*I want my degree*," I say again, firmer this time as I press my finger to his lips to shush him, "but I don't care whether or not it's a Duke degree."

Austin parts his lips in surprise beneath my finger and grips my hips tighter for leverage as he sits up. "I like it when you're goofy, but don't be goofy about *this*. It's Duke, Gabby. You can't transfer."

"There's more to this decision than how prestigious the college on my future resume will be," I say, then roll out my shoulders. "Okay, fine. Once upon a time, I cared. I bragged about it to anyone who would listen and I stuck Duke bumper stickers to my car before I'd even attended orientation. Hey, don't laugh." I pinch both his cheeks in one hand, smooshing his lips together and holding him captive like that as I fix him with a stern look. "I love

Duke, but I'm all alone up there, and I'm trying to think of the bigger picture when it comes to what will make me happy. And I'd be happier *here*." I smile. "With you, in our hometown. The UNC campus here is beautiful, and I can look into transferring my credits. I'll help out more at the dog shelter with you, alongside planning my amazing adoption events, and I'll work on my relationship with my mom a little bit because it's rather sad how repressed she is and—*oh my God.*"

"What, Gabby?" Austin asks as I scramble off his lap.

"I'm the worst daughter in the world," I groan, grabbing my phone and scrolling through my contacts until I find my mother's name. I press my phone to my ear and pace the living room in small circles as it rings. "There's a storm kicking off and I haven't even checked in on her. You think Priscilla McKinley knows how to board up windows herself? And she's not answering her phone!"

Austin pushes himself up from the couch. "Try your brother. See if he knows she's safe?"

"I haven't spoken to Zach in weeks. I'm still waiting for him to apologize for throwing his fist into your face," I grumble, but reluctantly call my brother, anyway.

"What?" Zach's angelic voice snaps when he picks up.

"Hi. Just checking everything's good with you guys? You're all safe indoors?"

"Of course," he says, his abrupt tone easing. "At least this storm won't get you up there in Durham."

"Actually . . . I'm here in Wilmington. I'm with Austin." I nervously catch Austin's eye in front of me as he listens in.

285

"Of course you are . . ." Zach sighs, then adds, "Well, stay safe, you two. Have you heard from Mom?"

"That's what I wanted to ask *you*! You normally help her secure the house whenever there's a storm."

"*Normally* she asks me to," he counters in defense. "She didn't this time, so I assume she has it figured out by now. Winds aren't going to be *that* strong, Gabs. She'll be fine. Probably sitting with a glass of wine watching her soap operas right now as we speak."

"But she's not answering her phone."

"Probably just doesn't want to talk to her junkie daughter."

"*Zach,*" I snap, because now is not the time for cracking jokes. When he quits laughing, I say, "I'll keep trying her."

"I'll try, too."

I hang up on Zach and dial Mom again, growing increasingly restless. Zach's rather blasé about the idea of Mom being unreachable during a storm, and I know the winds aren't going to be strong enough or the rain heavy enough to cause any severe damage, but I feel terrible that she didn't cross my mind until *now*. She's alone in that big house, and neither of her children bothered to make sure she was safe and hunkered down. We're the *worst*, and now I need to compensate for it.

"Still no answer?" Austin asks when I lower my phone from my ear with a frustrated groan. "Would you feel better if we went over there to check on her? Make sure the house is secure and she has everything she needs in case the power cuts out?"

"You'd come with me?"

"I followed you into bug-infested lakes when we were kids," he says with a smile, tilting his head to the side. "What makes you believe for even one second that I wouldn't follow you through a tropical storm?"

Yeah, I am *so* transferring schools for this man.

I thank him with a quick kiss and we head upstairs to grab our shoes. This storm wasn't quite in my plans when I packed a bag for this weekend, but Austin has me covered when it comes to a raincoat—he gives me one of his, though it engulfs most of me. It swishes around by my knees as we make our way to the garage and climb into my car, because on the off chance a tree branch falls on us as we drive across town, better it happens to my easily replaced Prius than Austin's Porsche. I let him drive, and he does it with zero complaints for once. He's too focused on squinting through the bucketing rain hitting the windshield.

"Are we idiots?" I ask after five minutes of driving and the realization that we haven't passed any other cars out on the roads. "There's no one else out here."

"Well, you're kind of supposed to stay inside during a storm, but . . ."

"Goddamn Priscilla McKinley," I mutter, and we exchange a grin. My mother really does have a knack for being the center of attention. I swear, if Austin and I are driving through this storm to get to her and this entire time she really has just been drinking wine and watching soaps like Zach believes . . . Oh, she's gonna get it.

We pull into our old neighborhood, the Georgian mansions on the right and the housing projects on the left, and immediately I feel a flood of relief when I spot Mom's car parked in our driveway. Though it lasts only a moment, replaced instead by agitation, because why hasn't she moved her car into the garage? Why aren't any of the windows covered up? Why are her stupid decorative stone bird baths still in the front yard?

"She hasn't done *anything*," I remark in exasperation as Austin parks my car up on the drive behind Mom's. He kills the engine and we meet each other's eyes, the rain thundering against the metal of my car, then nod in perfectly synced agreement—time to get out of the car.

I pull the giant hood of Austin's coat over my head and kick open my door, stepping out into the torrential downpour. After a long summer of scorching sunshine and muggy humidity, the smack of cold rain that blows into my face is a shock to my system. It sends a chill down my spine.

"Run!" Austin yells, and in the seven seconds it takes us to dash to shelter on the front porch, somehow we are both drenched. Austin shakes out his wet hair and raps his fist hard against the front door. "Mrs. McKinley?"

"Mom?" I call out over the rain, following up Austin's knock with more thumps of my own.

We jump back a step when we hear the deadbolt unlock, and the door cracks open a few inches. My mother peeks out, her eyes narrowed warily as she looks Austin and me up and down. When she realizes it's me beneath the hood of this raincoat, she does a double-take. "What are you doing out in this weather?! Come inside right now." She throws the door open wide and ushers us both over the threshold before the wind rips it from her hands and slams it shut again.

"You weren't answering your phone!"

"It's on charge," she says.

"*It's on charge,*" I repeat flatly, then gape at her as I push down my hood and send drops of rainwater flying over her pristine floors. "Why is your car still outside? We have built-in shutters on the windows, Mom. Why are they still open?"

Mom anxiously toys with a loose strand of hair, tucking it behind her ear. "It's fine, Gabrielle. It's not a hurricane."

"The winds are still going to get up to sixty miles an hour out there!" I argue, then press my hands to my temples as I roll my eyes angrily. "You didn't even move the bird baths! That's so dangerous."

"Did you come here to lecture me?"

"No," I say. "I came here to check you were okay."

"Mrs. McKinley," Austin says, clearing his throat and gesturing outside. "If you don't mind, I can help secure things for you. Where are your car keys?"

Mom fastens her attention on Austin, and I wonder if it dawns on her too that this is the first time she has ever let him step foot inside the house. She doesn't hesitate to accept his offer. Grabbing her keys from the hook by the door, she hands them over and tells him, "Thank you, Austin. I'd really appreciate that."

Austin throws up his hood and bows his head, bracing himself to get soaked all over again as he opens the door and dips back outside. It's such an Austin thing to do; helping out my mom during a storm despite the disrespect she's always thrown his way.

"Get out of that wet coat," she instructs, and I immediately shrug it off. "I'll get a pot of coffee going to heat you both up. Austin does drink coffee, right?"

I try not to stare at her too dubiously, for she's being uncharacteristically hospitable. "Only decaf."

"Okay. Pot of decaf coming right up."

She scurries off into the kitchen and I head into the living room to watch Austin from the window. He moves both mine and Mom's cars into the garage, along with all of Mom's yard decorations, and then works his way around the house utilizing all of the shutters. When he gets to the window I'm watching him from, he adorably blows me a kiss before pulling the shutters closed.

Now that the entire house has been plunged into darkness, I turn on some lamps and curl up on the couch with a pillow hugged to my chest just as Mom walks into the room carrying a tray of coffee and cookies. She sets it down on the center table and looks at me awkwardly, unsure how to navigate my unexpected visit.

"You didn't need to come out in this storm to check on me," she says.

"We kind of did. Those bird baths of yours were about to become projectiles."

She purses her lips, almost sheepishly, and settles on the couch opposite me. She doesn't relax, though. She remains perched upright and rigid with her hands interlocked together in her lap. "I'm not very good at these things, Gabrielle. Whenever there were storm warnings, your father . . ."

"Took care of it," I finish, because *I know*. He took care of everything for me, too.

Mom's gaze drops to her hands, and I don't push the subject further. We aren't going to bond over how useless we both are at being independent, functional human beings, but I'm also not going to give her too hard of a time. I'm still learning how to exist in a world without Dad's guidance, too.

"Can you stay?" Mom asks so quietly, I almost second guess the question. I raise an eyebrow at her, seeking clarity. In what universe does my mother *want* me to impinge on her privacy? She explains, "You shouldn't be heading back out across town in this weather. I'd feel more comfortable if you stayed here tonight. And Austin, too."

As if summoned by his name, a gust of wind tears through the house when he returns back inside. He appears in the living room, soaked to the bone with a trail of rain on the floor behind him, hair completely sodden. "All sorted," he announces.

"Here," Mom says, hastily getting to her feet and pouring him a cup of coffee. "This ought to heat you up."

"Oh, thanks, Mrs. McKinley, but I actually only drink decaf—"

"It *is* decaf," she informs him, forcing the cup into his soaking hands. "Gabrielle gave me the heads-up. Now please. Sit down and get out of that wet coat. Would you like a dry shirt? Zachary has lots of spare clothes here. Yes, you can borrow something of his. I'll be right back!" Mom whisks off up the marble staircase, leaving both Austin and me entirely flummoxed.

He collapses onto the couch next to me, his hand rubbing soothingly over my thigh. "What's going on?"

"I'm . . . really not sure. I think she may be—dare I say it—relieved to have you secure the house for her," I say, and my features ache from being so contorted with puzzlement. I break out into an easy smile and turn my head sharply toward Austin. "So hey, what do you think of the house?"

Austin laughs and makes a grand display of looking around, nodding in appreciation at how perfectly maintained everything is while sipping his coffee. "It's exactly how I used to imagine it would be. *Rich people live here* kind of vibes."

"Do you like it?" I press, and Austin eyeballs me with suspicion.

"Yes . . .?"

"Good, because you've been invited for a slumber party!"

"You're kidding."

"Not kidding," Mom says, waltzing back into the room with one of Zach's old T-shirts. As she hands it to Austin, she sternly tells him, "You'll be staying in the guest room, of course."

"Of course," Austin agrees, and I nuzzle my face into the damp sleeve of his shirt to hide my blushes.

It may have taken over a decade, but finally, *finally,* I'm getting that long overdue sleepover with my best friend.

25

Who knew riding out the storm with Mom would not only be tolerable, but kind of fun?

As the storm strengthened and the wind and rain battered the house, conversation became less stilted between the three of us. There wasn't much else to do *but* talk, and Mom was keen to hear the ins and outs of Austin's career so far once I informed her of his big win at the business awards the previous evening. It was nice watching them engage with one another without Mom firing him disdainful glances every time he opened his mouth, and she kept popping back and forth to the kitchen to fetch more snacks.

One thing about Priscilla McKinley is that she has a very fixed nightly routine and sleep schedule. Even in the midst of a storm, that ten-sharp bedtime doesn't budge. So, she retreated off to her room with pleasant *goodnights,* leaving Austin and me alone in the ambient lighting of the living room until long after midnight, snuggled up close as the storm raged outside and talking in hushed tones. We discussed our plans for the immediate future, like who will be responsible for the trash runs when we move in together? (Answer: him. Always him.)

We shared a tender kiss goodnight outside of my bedroom door before separating for the night, because I'm trying my best to be more respectful to my mother and riding Austin like a mechanical bull under her roof doesn't quite align with that plan.

"See? I knew it wouldn't be that bad," Mom muses at breakfast as we listen intently to the weather report on TV. "Only a handful of flash floods and some battered trees."

"Which means I have no excuse not to open the office today," Austin says, disappointedly glancing at his watch. There's a pot of decaf coffee on the go, of course, and he pours himself a second cup and takes a swig as he meets my gaze over the rim. "We'll need to get going soon so I can get suited up."

"And I'm working the bar today, so I need to hit the road," I say. Buck is kind enough not to make me work weekends, so I better not be late getting back to Durham today, *especially* when I need to break the news to him that I won't be around for much longer.

Mom grimaces and says, "The sooner you resume classes and get out of that filthy bar, the better," and I roll my eyes. Last night's pleasantries were a glitch in the matrix—I should have known to expect her usual scathing remarks this morning.

Austin gives me a pointed, suggestive look, for Mom's words are as good an opening as any. I give him a clipped nod and suck in a breath.

"Mom, there's something I need to tell you," I say with the slightest of tremors in my voice. Mom snaps her neck toward me, looking utterly horrified at what's about to come out of my mouth next, so I point a scolding finger at her across the table. "And no, I'm not finally confessing to my drug addiction, *because I don't have one,* so stop looking at me like that."

She makes the conscious effort to relax her features. "What is it, Gabrielle?"

"It's good news. It's exciting news." I reach for Austin's hand on the table and he immediately gives mine a reassuring squeeze, so I don't drag it out any longer. I tell my mother, "I'm moving in with Austin."

And I brace myself for the disapproval, for the argument that it's far too soon to be moving in together, but it never comes. Mom is eerily silent as the gears in her mind process the bomb I've just dropped, and Austin squeezes my hand even tighter.

Finally, she asks, "How are you going to attend your classes? You can't commute to school from *here.*"

Oddly, she is more concerned about my Duke degree than she is about me moving in with Austin Pierce, but I'll take it. I'd rather she slander my education choices than my relationship. "I'm going to look into transferring to UNC . . . the Wilmington campus. I'll go to school here, and I'll be right across town if you ever need me. Being up there in Durham isn't making me happy anymore."

Mom opens her mouth to speak, but she's so flustered, no words are to be found.

"This is good, right? This is what you wanted," I continue with a hopeful smile. "You wanted me to start making positive steps, to have a plan. And this is it, Mom. *This* is the plan. I really hope you can get on board with it, because I'm happy."

"UNC isn't Duke, Gabrielle," Mom mumbles, as though I don't already freakin' know that, and then she drums her manicured fingernails against the table. "But at this point, I'm just relieved you're going back to school at all, no matter where. Have you scheduled an appointment with admissions yet? Are there any clauses for breaking the lease on that terrible apartment of yours? And Austin, you're aware she doesn't tidy up after herself, aren't you?"

"*Mom.*"

Austin laughs and flashes me a dazzling grin as he says, "I guess I'll just have to adjust to Gabrielle McKinley's hair products cluttering my bathroom."

The sound of the front door opening interrupts the conversation, and there's the scratch of paws on the hardwood floor before Lily the poodle bursts into the kitchen with overflowing excitement. She circles us at the table, jumping up on Mom's legs, then Austin's, then mine, unsure of who to greet first.

"Hi, Lily!" I say, sliding off my chair and crouching down to fuss her. "I didn't know you were coming by!"

Zach and Claire enter the kitchen, and before Mom even says hello, she's muttering, "You know I don't like it when you bring that dog over here."

"Oh, relax, Mom," Zach says with a dismissive wave. "She's super clean. Look how excited she is to see you! Be nice to her."

I look up at my brother from my position on the floor. "Woah. Did you just—" I dramatically gasp "—*defend* Lily? Protective-dog-dad mode activated."

"Shut up, Gabster," Zach snarls, and Claire elbows him in the ribs and mouths an apology to me.

"What are you doing here?" Mom asks them, and I still find it so completely bizarre that our family dynamics are so twisted, our own mother is always so mystified when we visit her.

"Making sure you didn't die in that wild, wild storm last night, obviously," Zach says with a sarcastic smirk, then musters up enough maturity to be serious for once as he slides into an empty chair and plucks a croissant off the table. "Gabby was worried about you last night, and we weren't sure if she eventually got in touch with you or not because *someone* never updated us—" he glowers at me "—so here we are. Glad to see everyone is alive and well." He looks across the table at Austin for the first time and asks, "Can I ask why you're wearing my clothes?"

"We spent the night," I tell Zach. "Austin helped secure the house."

Zach bites into his croissant and chews silently for a moment, then rises from the table. "Can we talk outside?" His gaze shifts to Austin. "Both of you."

Austin and I exchange a look. None of us have addressed what happened at the beach and this is the first time the three of us have seen each other since then, so it's not difficult to guess what Zach could possibly wish to talk about. Whether it'll be an apology or further argument, I have no idea.

I kiss the mop of curls on top of Lily's head and straighten up from the floor, following Zach and Austin outside into the backyard while Mom watches the three of us leave with a look of betrayal for being left alone with the soon-to-be daughter-in-law she's not a fan of and the adopted poodle she can't stand.

It's a cool, breezy morning outside as the winds continue to die down and the skies are overcast. The patio furniture is still inside the garage, so Zach leans against the wall of the house instead, crossing his arms over his chest.

"I won't tell Mom about the trust fund," he says, albeit grudgingly, as he fastens his eyes on Austin. "It won't change the fact that that money is already yours, and there's no point sending her into a tailspin, because she's insufferable when she has a meltdown. What she doesn't know can't hurt her."

"Thank you, Zach—" I start, but he holds up a hand to cut me off.

"That doesn't mean I agree with it. I still think you have no right to my father's money, but at least you didn't blow it on something stupid," he grumbles. "I'll learn to live with it, and I'm sorry for hitting you at the beach, I guess."

"I'm also sorry for hitting you at the beach," Austin says, managing a tentative smile to test the waters.

298

Zach rubs his jaw. "You have a pretty solid sucker punch for someone who was on the high school track team. I thought all your strength would be in your legs."

"It is. That's why you're lucky I didn't kick the shit out of you."

Zach's eyes widen in surprise at Austin's confidence and when he looks at me, I laugh and say, "Yeah, not quite the shy kid from across the street anymore."

"Alright, man," Zach says, thumping Austin on the back of his shoulder, almost with a weird sense of appreciation. "Thanks for helping out my mom last night. Maybe you'll win her over one day."

"Here's hoping," Austin says, and Zach saunters off back inside. We don't follow him, because we need a moment to process how surprisingly well things are turning out. I feel like I've entered a parallel universe.

Austin wraps his arms around my shoulders and pulls me in close, our gazes locked. "This weekend has been . . . full of milestones."

"Right?" I say, my head tilted up to look at him as my arms rest around his waist. "Our parents are being reasonable, Zach has apologized, I've accepted your offer of moving in . . . Oh, and I love you." I smile wide as the words ignite a fire inside my body.

"And I love *you*. Always have, Gabby," Austin murmurs, cupping my cheeks in his hands and pressing his lips to my forehead. "Now get your ass up to Durham, quit that job, break your lease, and then come home to me."

26

The two weeks that follow feel like the slowest two weeks of my entire life.

As much as I'd love to move into Austin's house overnight, abandoning the life I've been living in Durham isn't that simple. Before I can make the jump, I need to ensure transferring schools is a viable option for me. I meet with my academic dean at Duke who reassures me I'll be able to transfer just fine, gather my transcripts, then start the application process to UNC Wilmington. If accepted, I'll be able to enroll in classes in January.

I also can't walk out on Buck, not after he gave me a second chance, so I agree to work two more weeks at the bar to allow him enough time to find a suitable replacement, which is no easy task, given I'm obviously the best employee he's ever had. When I wrap up my final shift with Carly, we both get a touch emotional as we say our goodbyes. It took me a while to warm up to her, but we've had some fun times behind the bar together, and

I'll miss the way we communicated our thinning patience with certain boozers via eye rolls and hand signals.

My property manager is less understanding of my sudden desire to move. He won't allow me to terminate my lease early without penalty, so I suck up the fees and dip into my trust fund for the sake of an easy getaway. I pack up my belongings, gag at the cans of tuna on the communal stairs for one last time, then hop into my car and wave Duke University and Buck's Tavern and Durham goodbye.

I drive a little too fast on the highway, because Austin Pierce is waiting for me in Wilmington.

When I pull up outside his house—*our* new home together—he is leaning against the frame of the open front door, looking absolutely delicious in his ocean blue T-shirt that's the same shade as his eyes. He's taken the day off work today, and he's taped balloons to the windows to mark the special occasion. He strides across the yard to meet me on the driveway, impatiently yanking open my car door.

"Welcome home!"

Home. The word feels warm and tingly.

"Hi, you," I say. My grin is so wide, my cheeks ache. I've never felt as happy as I do in the exact moment I step out of the car and into his arms. "Are you ready for a lifetime of pancakes on Sundays?"

"Obviously. We signed a contract."

"Not to be broken."

"*Never* to be broken," he says, planting a kiss on the corner of my mouth.

We unload my car, full of giddy smiles and laughter as we carry all of my boxes and suitcases inside the house, and I can't help but feel like perhaps this is the life I was meant to live all along. When Austin first moved in across the street when we were just eight years old, we were instantly drawn to one another like magnets with a pull that couldn't be fought. My father knew Austin was a good kid, and there's a certain peace that comes with knowing Austin would definitely have gotten his approval if he was still alive. I think I'm finally exactly where I need to be—I just took a very big detour getting here, but it's one that taught me everything I needed to know about myself.

"Don't unpack yet," Austin says, plucking a box out of my arms before I can head upstairs with it. He furrows his eyebrows very seriously. "I have some bad news."

"What?"

"Today is Teddy's nine hundred and ninety-ninth day at the shelter," he informs me, "and I think maybe we should head over there to visit him before they close for the day. We can bring him some new toys to cheer him up."

"Thanks for ruining my day," I say, pouting my lips, though I'm already halfway out the door. "Let's bring him some treats, too."

We hop into Austin's car and head across town to Saving Paws Animal Rescue, stopping by the pet store en route to pick up some gifts for Teddy. He loves plushie toys, so we grab a couple of new ones and also some bully sticks, because although they smell like literal death and make me feel nauseous, they are his favorite treat in the world, and Teddy deserves all of his favorite things today.

As always, Fiona is thrilled to see us when we walk through the door. She's very excited about our plans for monthly adoption events, and we've already started working together to organize September's event taking place at the end of the month.

"Tomorrow will mark a thousand days of Teddy being here, right?" Austin asks, and when Fiona nods glumly, he brandishes the bag of toys and treats we picked out. "We're here to give him lots of love."

"He'll be a happy boy!" she says, then straightens up from the front desk, spinning the keys to the kennel block around her index finger. "He's actually already outside in the exercise pens, so you came at the right time."

We follow Fiona into the kennel block as an eruption of excited barks shrills around us as it so often does whenever we show up to visit, and we give quick pats on heads through the kennel doors as we make our way down the corridor and through the door at the other end. One of the staff members is playing fetch with Teddy, and I'm surprised to see the lazy lump of fur actually participating in exercise for once.

"Teddy!" I call, and his ears instantly perk up in response to his name. He abandons his chase for the ball and barrels across the grass toward us, slamming into my legs at full force and nearly snapping my damn tibias. "Woah, someone's full of energy today! Aww, look at your cute little bandana!"

I drop to my knees in front of Teddy as he slobbers kisses all over my cheeks and I pat my hands over his thick fur. He's wearing a red bandana that makes him look extra handsome, and I grab his collar to hold him steady so I can take a proper look.

"Don't you look so cute—"

My mouth falls open. The bandana says: *Adopted!*

"Wait," I gasp, my eyes flying straight to Fiona as she boasts a cheesy, joyful grin. My pulse suddenly feels out of sync, like it just skipped ten beats at once. "Someone adopted him?"

Austin kneels down next to me, placing his hand over mine on Teddy's collar. When I tear my eyes away from Fiona to gape at him, he smiles and says, "*We* adopted him."

"*What?*"

"I promised you we'd find him a home. The *best* home." Austin scratches Teddy beneath his chin, much to his satisfaction. "I hope you enjoy Marvel movies, buddy."

"Are you . . . Are you kidding?" My legs feel numb as I stand up, turning to Fiona as my head swims with disbelief. "He's screwing with me, isn't he?"

"We finalized the adoption papers first thing this morning," she says cheerfully, and I think there may actually be tears of joy welling in her eyes. "All I need is your signature, too. I'll be right back!"

Fiona dashes inside with the other staff member, both of them ecstatic that Teddy won't hit one thousand days in the shelter after all. He has a home. *Our home.*

Austin is still on the ground, a relaxed, easy smile on his face as he lets Teddy sniff around his ears. "He'll be the Pierce Wealth Management mascot, and he can come to work with me and sleep in the corner of my office during the day when you're attending your classes. Don't people say a house isn't a home without a dog? Well, I'd really like to build a home with you."

My heart absolutely soars. Just when I thought I was at my happiest, somehow there's an entire other level of joy I haven't discovered yet, and it's right here in front of me. I sink back onto the grass next to Austin and Teddy, grinning through the tears that are rolling down my face, because somehow everything has worked out better than I could have ever imagined and I am so, so unbelievably excited for what life has in store going forward with my two boys. *My boys.*

"He's really ours?" I whisper.

"Ours," Austin confirms. He brushes his fingertips over my cheeks, wiping away the tears before tilting my chin up toward him. His blue eyes settle on mine, sparkling with a joy as pure as mine. "If someone ever told me that one day I'd let Gabrielle McKinley talk me into adopting a dog," he murmurs, leaning in close until his mouth delicately skims mine. He smiles against my lips, so perfectly, and whispers, "I wouldn't have doubted them for even a second."

Acknowledgments

I had an absolute blast over the six months I spent writing the first draft of Gabby and Austin's love story, and I'm so lucky to be surrounded by people in my life who cheer me along every step of the way.

Huge thanks as always to the teams at Black & White and Bonnier Books for a whole decade of publishing my stories! Every new project is just as exciting as the last, and I'm so grateful to work with such amazing people who are always so passionate about my work. Alison, thank you for always wanting the best for me. Clem, thanks for being as enthusiastic about my characters and stories as I am. Special thanks also to Kesia Lupo.

The biggest thanks in the world go to Emma Ferrier, Beatriz Matos and Cristina Oliveira for being Gabby and Austin's biggest cheerleaders from day one. You didn't have to read those first-draft chapters I sent over each week, but you did, and your reactions always put a smile on my face. I'm so grateful for all the support you've given me over the years, and for always championing my new projects.

Shoutout as usual to my local Starbucks for being my safe haven, because I pretty much live in the corner of the café during my writing season and may as well be part of the furniture at this point.

Mum, the most amazing best friend I'll ever have, thank you for being there for me through all of the ups and downs in life.

Grandma and Granda, thanks for always being so proud of me.

Anders and Jaxson, my two nephews—you're both so cute and it's so fun watching you grow up.

Heather Allen, Rhea Forman, Bethany Stapley—I love nothing more than enjoying cups of tea and chocolate digestives with you guys as we navigate our twenties together.

Craig, my other half, my rock, and my favorite person in the whole entire world. You inspire me every day to work hard as we chase our goals together in life, and I'd honestly be so lost without you by my side. It's forever and always you.

And finally, lifting a glass to my Granda, George Maskame, who sadly lost his battle with Parkinson's disease in May 2024.

ESTELLE MASKAME published the first book in her international bestselling *Did I Mention I Love You?* series when she was just seventeen. A word-of-mouth sensation, she is also the author of the Mila trilogy (2022), and the "highly addictive" standalone novels *Dare to Fall* and *The Wrong Side of Kai*. Her first adult romance novel *Somewhere in the Sunset* was published in 2024. With over one million copies of her books sold, and rights sold in twenty territories, her fiction attracts countless passionate, loyal fans worldwide. Winner of the Young Scot Arts Award 2016, Estelle has been shortlisted for the Young Adult award at the Romantic Novel of the Year Awards. When she's not catching up with her international fanbase – or travelling to America to research her characters and their lives – Estelle lives in her hometown of Peterhead, Scotland.

𝕏 ⓘ ♪ @estellemaskame
www.estellemaskame.com